D1619935

SUDDEN UNPROVIDED DEATH

By the same author

Filling Spaces

SUDDEN UNPROVIDED DEATH

Stan Hey

Hodder & Stoughton

First published in 1996 by Hodder and Stoughton
A division of Hodder Headline PLC

10 9 8 7 6 5 4 3 2 1

British Library Cataloguing in Publication Data

Hey, Stan
Sudden Unprovided Death
1. English fiction - 20th century
I. Title
823.9'14 [F]

ISBN 0 340 62576 7

Typeset by Avon Dataset Ltd, Bidford-on-Avon, Warks

Printed and bound in Great Britain by
Mackays of Chatham PLC, Chatham, Kent

Hodder and Stoughton
A division of Hodder Headline PLC
338 Euston Road
London NW1 3BH

CHAPTER ONE

Brennan had never known darkness like this before, a darkness so intense that he couldn't even see where land ended and sky began. The night that surrounded him had no stars or moon. He ran a little faster, his bare feet tensed, groping for whatever purchase he could get wherever they landed. He was aware, in the way of a wild animal, of being pursued, but couldn't see what was behind him. Suddenly his right foot found no earth as it came down and he pitched forward into a black void. The adrenalin surge of fear nearly swamped his heart as the fall went on for what seemed like seconds. Then he hit coarse, scree-covered ground, grazing his knees and hands as the stone fragments bit into his flesh. With no time for pain, he scrambled to his feet and, feeling an incline in front of him, began to climb, pulling at tufts of foliage for grip. Despite the chill of the winter night, sweat cascaded down his back, soaking his shirt. He paused for a moment, trying to hear above his own frantic panting whether his pursuer was close. He swallowed a huge gulp of air and held it to try to create a silence. Now the only noise was his heart thumping against his rib-cage. Around him all seemed quiet. But then from above, a snort of hot breath hit his face, and not six feet from him stood a huge antlered creature whose ruby-coloured eyes provided the first light he had seen. Terrified, Brennan relaxed his grip and fell back into the void, sliding, scraping, tumbling . . .

'Frank. Frank, are you all right?'

He opened his eyes. It was Janet, curling back from the bedside lamp.

'Christ, you're drenched. What's the matter with you?'

Brennan could hardly breathe. The banality of words and human touch was overwhelmed by the intensity of his experience.

'Nightmare . . . I had a nightmare.'

Janet pulled back the duvet.

'You've pissed the bed! Come on – get those pyjamas off.'

He sat up as she stripped him of the soaked bedclothes. His pulse was still throbbing like a drumroll. He looked around him. Even something as familiar as his marital bedroom now looked distorted and strange. He felt like a little boy again as Janet pulled off his clinging pyjama bottoms.

'I'll get your dressing-gown.'

Brennan swung his legs off the bed looking for the scratches and abrasions he expected to see on his hands and knees, but there were none. Janet returned with the robe, pulling him to his feet and throwing it around his shoulders.

'Better get the sofa-bed up,' she said as she stripped the duvet and the sheets and tossed them to the floor.

'Sorry about this,' he muttered, catching her eye. 'I'm ashamed to say it, but it was fucking terrifying. I suppose that's why I wet myself.'

'What was it about, then?' she asked as she bundled the soiled sheets and duvet into the laundry basket.

'Dunno. I was being chased. By something. It was so dark I couldn't see. Then I thought I'd escaped. But it was above me. Waiting. Great horns or antlers.'

Janet couldn't help blurting out a laugh.

'What?' Brennan asked.

'Are you worried about your virility, Frank? Anxious about mid-life crisis?'

'Bollocks I am. Why?'

'All that antler and horn stuff. Symbolic of manhood and power. You sure you're not suppressing something about all that?'

'Well, I check my scrote for lumps about once a month, and I practise being able to stop my piss in mid-stream . . .'

'Obviously you're not trying hard enough.'

Brennan glared at her, feeling suddenly vulnerable.

'It's all right between us, isn't it? You know, sex?'

'Sure. I wasn't having a go about that.'

'Not exactly a ringing endorsement.'

'Frank, I'm trying to analyse your dream, see what's behind it.'

'It was a nightmare.'

'Don't be a pedantic git.'

'Well, it was more than a dream, or a nightmare. It felt more real than you and me standing here now. Like a premonition.'

Janet put her arms round him for the first time since he'd awoken, and the warmth of her touch instantly calmed him. She nuzzled his right ear.

'Darkness is the unknown. You thrashing around in it means you think you're losing your way. It's work anxiety, isn't it? Where's the next job coming from, where's the next cheque?'

'Well, if that's the case, it was a pretty extreme reaction to something half the country's going through.'

She smiled at him sympathetically as she pulled away.

'Come on, let's have a pot of hot chocolate.'

She led him down the stairs, looking in on their son Lester on the way. He was sleeping deeply, one leg sticking out from under the duvet. Janet tucked it back in before they resumed their journey to the kitchen. Brennan sat at the pine table, still distracted, while Janet boiled two cups of milk in a saucepan.

'Want an Armagnac to take the taste away?'

'Better not, or I'll be seeing pixies at the bottom of the bed,' he said, shaking his head.

Soon Janet had the cup in front of him, and he was sipping the chocolate, feeling the warmth spread to his toes.

'I suppose it could have been anxiety about work,' he conceded quietly. 'I mean, once the Christmas rush of "that was the shitty year that was" features is over, there's nothing out there for me.'

'It'll turn up. Go and spend a few days in London in the New Year. Do a bit of hustling.'

'That wasn't the point of me moving out west, Janet. To be

another desperate freelance. I wanted to pursue my *own* stories, not just be spoon-fed by all those arse-lickers who edit newspapers these days.'

'That's who it was in the dream, then, your old boss, Stuart Gill. He can look like a moose on a bad day.'

'Don't try to humour me, Janet.'

Brennan finished his drink in silence. In seeking to comfort him, Janet had, perversely, tapped a genuine well of anxiety about his work as a journalist, and his status as a willing deserter of London. But it felt nowhere near as bad as the lingering shiver of fear left by the nightmare. Even when Janet had luxuriously coaxed him into mounting her over the unfolded sofa-bed, he had taken no comfort from the coupling, feeling only a primitive power as he had pushed into her, as if his mind and body had been taken over by a bestial spirit.

The nightmare lingered in the recesses of his mind for several days, like the effects of a dental anaesthesia that wouldn't go away. But gradually the pre-Christmas jollity that Bradford-on-Avon generated among its eight thousand-odd citizens reintroduced a sense of calm and well-being, confirming Brennan's suspicions, held since teenage days, that Christmas had largely been a medieval confection to help dispossessed humanity deal with the bleakness of midwinter.

The town bridge of the Avon was hung with tasteful sprigs of fir and ivy, and lines of pearl-white light-bulbs hung above its two Bath-stone parapets, creating rippling pools of luminescence in the river below. On the two Tuesdays immediately prior to Christmas, the shops stayed open until eight o'clock, serving mulled wine, whisky and hot mince pies to customers, while on the Saturdays a Salvation Army brass band took up position in the town's ancient Shambles and pumped familiar carols into the cold air. With all the pubs and the Swan Hotel decked in fairy-lights, Bradford radiated a spirit of community that even Brennan's cynicism couldn't gainsay. Neighbours and acquaintances stopped on the streets to shake hands, or issue invitations to drinks.

Then, to cap it all, the morning of Christmas Eve had revealed a dazzling white frost across the town and the fields beyond, set against a duck-egg-blue sky. As Janet, Brennan and Lester drove out to the farm in Norton St Philip to collect their organically reared, humanely slaughtered sixteen-pound turkey, the countryside looked as though someone had spun sugar over every inch of it.

'What an astonishing day,' Janet purred as Brennan steered the car down the lanes to the farm, showering frost on to the windscreen as he brushed too close to the hedgerows. He had picked up the car – a five-year-old Renault estate – from a local garage in Bradford, just a few days after he'd got his driving licence back at the end of November. And although he'd safely pottered around Bradford and Trowbridge in it, the year's ban, twinned with his six months in Erlestoke Prison, meant that longer excursions were still a test for his nerves and his eyes. It should also be said that driving stone-cold sober – as he had now vowed to do – was something of a novel experience for him.

As well as the turkey they'd ordered, the Brennans picked up a half-drum of Stilton, a fat bundle of speckle-skinned, home-made sausages and several jars of chutneys and pickles, to complement the shopping that Janet had already done at the frenzied supermarkets, which now littered the outskirts of every town in the area. Just one trip had been enough to repel Brennan – leaving aside the appalling tastelessness of the Amish barn designs, the desperate crowds, with their trolleys loaded like Spanish galleons, had driven him back to the smaller, individual shops of Bradford town centre.

But now the town streets fell quiet in mid-afternoon as the shopping orgy subsided, and as the last light of the day ebbed away before four o'clock it was time for hearth and home. While Lester watched *Ben Hur* on the television in the kitchen, where Janet was preparing for Christmas Day, Brennan sat upstairs in the lounge listening to Art Farmer playing the works of Billy Strayhorn. Farmer's spidery flugelhorn swarmed all over 'Bloodcount', which, with the falling darkness obliterating the landscape outside, created moments of eeriness.

Despite all the trappings of contentment – family, food, festival – Brennan felt the unease deep in his soul. He was a forgotten man as far as London was concerned, with no job, and few prospects of getting one. He knew that the first week of the New Year would bring a tax bill and a snotty letter from the bank. Christmas was all very well, but it would get in the way of whatever it was he could find to do.

'Can I have a word?'

It was Janet, in a flour-covered apron. Brennan crawled across to the CD player and turned the sound right down.

'Look, leave the stuffing and all the vegetables to me. I'll do them first thing tomorrow, promise,' he said, sensing an incoming missile.

Janet smiled. 'The guilty mind. Actually, it's Lester.'

'He wants to open one of his presents now, right?'

She shook her head, and checked the stairs to make sure that Lester wasn't at the bottom of them earwigging. She dropped her voice.

'He wants us to go to church tonight. The midnight service.'

Brennan frowned.

'Where did he get this notion from?'

She shrugged. 'Probably some of his mates at school. I don't know. He just came out with it.'

'He should be in bed well before midnight,' Brennan said tersely.

'Come on, Frank – Christmas Eve. Means we get more of a lie-in tomorrow.'

'Yeah, but – you can't just turn up at these sorts of things. You have to have a season ticket or something. Can't see all the Holy Joes welcoming families who just think "it's a nice thing to do at Christmas".'

'So you agree that it is?'

'Apart from funerals, I haven't been to a church since I was fourteen. Be a bit hypocritical turning up for a Mass. I may even be on the Vatican's list of "banned persons".'

'He wants to go to the C. of E. place, next to the river.'

'Holy Trinity?'

'How come you know the names?'

'Because I spend a lot of time walking round Bradford with my eyes open and my brain switched on. As a result of which my head is full of shite, like the names of the town churches, where

6

you can buy pine nuts, which shop to head for should you find yourself suddenly short of beeswax candles.'

'You're fundamentally a train-spotter, aren't you, Frank?'

'There's a lot to be said for the discipline of detail.'

'So shall we go? Wrap up warm – take a hip-flask for a sly drink?'

Brennan looked at her. He'd spent too much time as a stranger to his family during the mad years in London. If this move to the west was to mean something more than a prettier view from the window, then joining in was an essential part of the agenda.

'If you're going, I'll come with you – how's that?'

'I'll tell him.'

Janet disappeared down the staircase. Brennan turned the sound back up on the stereo – he smiled at the coincidence. Farmer was playing 'Something to Live For'.

The flagstone approach to Holy Trinity Church was glistening with frost, the air, so close to the river, noticeably a few degrees colder. A large crowd of people, chattering loudly, had already gathered by 11.30, an event Brennan linked to closing time in the town's pubs.

But although there was a fair element of drunken boister-ousness in the congregation, the huge, decorated Christmas tree and the thunderous chords of the organ were strong enough reminders of what the occasion signified.

The vicar welcomed them to what he called 'the eve of a very special, historic birthday' before cueing the arrival of the choir, in their red and white robes, leading off with 'Hark the Herald Angels'.

Lester and Janet shared a song sheet and let rip, while Brennan found himself able only to mouth the words, dredged as they were from a childhood ritual and memory in which there was more fear than happiness. He had always found churches intimidating rather than comforting, suggesting a conspicuous failure, in the contemporary jargon, 'to reach out to the customer'. Compelled to worship without knowledge or question, to believe or to fear, he'd taken a subversive route away from the whole business, deploying schoolboy satire and smut, which had often led to a beating by the fathers who ran his school.

But there was no denying the magnetism that the combination of ethereal music and forbidding architecture could still produce. When, partway through the service, a boy treble sang 'Away in a Manger', Brennan's eyes began to prickle with tears, and his mind raced with fragmented images of intense, atmospheric family gatherings, of sensations of smallness in a great void, and, yes, of childish expectation, waking in the middle of the night to search the end of the bed for a pillowslip stuffed with toys.

Janet noticed his tears, but misread them as contemporary symbols of familial emotion. She held his hand discreetly, but found that it was limp and clammy. Brennan took his hand away and ran a finger across his nostril to wipe off a tiny dribble of mucus. He closed the lid on the memories and the tears dried up in an instant.

Later, after the vicar had urged each celebrant to shake hands with his or her neighbour, Janet had kissed Frank to comfort him. Lester had looked almost as pleased as if he'd been given the latest CD of Blur or Oasis. His parents' togetherness was the best present he could have expected. The congregation left the church in high good humour, spilling out into the chill night air feeling full of fellowship and well-being, serenaded on their way by the choir singing:

God rest ye merry gentlemen let nothing you dismay
Remember Christ our Saviour was born on Christmas Day
To save us all from Satan's power
When we were gone astray
Oh – tidings of comfort and joy, comfort and joy
Oh-oh, tidings of comfort and joy!

The stag was snared when it came away from the pool where it had been drinking. The night and the silence had caused it to lose, albeit momentarily, its instinct for fear. But now it was doomed as first one hind leg, then the other were tethered in rough, prickling binds of creeper by what seemed like a dozen hands. There must have been strength of this order to enable them to pull the stag up the slope, especially as its forelegs and antlers thrashed vainly for escape. It took more than five minutes to deliver the beast over the earth ramparts of the hill-fort, and on to the flattened ground of the encampment, where a circle of fires blazed, emitting a thick smell of incense.

Then one of them advanced slowly, almost respectfully, on the terrified animal. From behind his back he produced a long, heavy bone, the thigh of an ox, which he raised with ceremonial intensity and brought crashing down on to the skull of the stag. The beast sagged and exhaled as its senses were stunned, and now other hands grabbed at its antlers and head, pulling them back to expose its neck. The man with the ox-bone moved forward, taking a small, decorated dagger of hammered metal from his robe and pressing its edge on to the great neck of the stag, feeling for its pulse. And then with a swift, slicing stroke the vein was severed and a jet of blood, pressurised by the intensity of the chase, shot high into the air, showering the circle of hunters. The men began to dance around the dying animal, smearing its hot blood on to their faces, watching it slowly exsanguinate on to the hard, frosty earth.

When the blood-letting was completed, two of the men severed the stag's head with a longer, broader blade, while a third gutted the animal, allowing its steaming entrails to spill across the ground. They would all eat well that night, roasting the haunches of flesh over the fires. The gods would be grateful too and spare them the harshest of winters in exchange for this generous gift. No other comfort or consolation could take the tribe through this darkest time of the year, when the pale sun rose then disappeared from the sky in a matter of hours. Certainly not the 'gift' of a baby born of a virgin.

The Brennans exchanged presents at around eleven on Christmas morning, after smoked salmon and scrambled eggs. Frank had bought Janet a hand-knitted cardigan and several pieces of locally made jewellery, a sure-fire indication of how little effort he'd put into Christmas shopping. He gave Lester the latest Arsenal home strip, with Bergkamp's name and number on the back of the shirt. In turn, Lester, having colluded with each parent, had bought a pack of five Romeo y Julieta cigars for his dad, and a basket of ethnically and environmentally correct oils and creams for his mum. Janet's main present to Frank was – and he could hardly believe his eyes – a mobile phone.

He looked at her with a mixture of intense affection and amusement. Janet had always been determined to 'hi-tech' him. When she had worked in his office on the newspaper, she'd constantly badgered him into understanding and then using the Atex computer system rather than his portable typewriter. Now, again, she was dragging him away from his old world, this time of piss-stenched call-boxes on inner city estates and nicotine-stained pay-phones in minicab offices.

'Is this a hint for me to get out of the house more?' Brennan asked, after he'd kissed Janet in thanks.

'It's the key to your future, Frank. Just think what Sherlock Holmes could have done with one of those in his hand. No need to recruit Baker Street irregulars . . .'

'I'm not a detective,' Brennan said, holding his hands up plaintively.

'Everyone at my school thinks you are, Dad.'

He eyed Lester beadily; the red and white Arsenal shirt was already pulled on over his pyjamas.

'Only because *you* go around telling them!'

'Well, it's better than them thinking you're a journalist, Dad. Everybody hates them. Scum-bags, aren't they?'

'Didn't used to be. Not in my day.'

He caught Janet's look of alarm. Every time he touched on the subject of his working past he could sense her tensing, as though the ghosts would come back if he summoned them. These creatures spanned Janet's spectrum of nightmares, from the incapable drunk asleep on the couch, to the no-show husband on special occasions or the zombie too tired, or too bored, to talk to her or the child. Brennan had been all of these monsters at some stage in his previous life, and she feared that there was always a chance that he might fancy a reunion.

'All right – I'm an investigator, then,' he conceded to Lester, with half an eye on soothing Janet. 'But once I've found out whatever it is I'm looking for, I'll write about it rather than go to the police – so that makes me . . . what?'

'A detective *ink*-spector,' Lester suggested, laughing at his ability to make a pun.

'So what do I do now?' Brennan asked Janet, holding the phone out to her.

'Use it. It's all connected up, ready to go.'

'Really? Right, let's have a try!'

He stood up purposefully. Janet waved an instruction booklet at him but he ignored it. Find out as you go along had always been Brennan's method where technology was concerned, as if to say, 'If it's that clever, why should it need instructions?'

'Don't piss about with it, Frank.'

Brennan was staring at the phone's console.

'I'll work it out in a mo' . . .'

Janet made a grab for the phone, but he was determined to get it going for himself, and turned away from her with a smile.

'The on-switch is the red button at the side. Pull the aerial up, dial the number you want with full code, then press the green phone symbol to send the call,' Janet said quickly.

'Ta. You see, I don't need to read instruction booklets when I've got you around, Jan.'

He wandered down the stairs to the front door, still in his pyjamas and dressing-gown, and walked out on to the footpath that ran in front of the terrace of houses on Tory. He padded a short distance up from their house, seeing Bradford below, still bathed in a winter mist. He dialled his parents' number and then pressed the green phone symbol – on the display, the word 'calling' appeared, and then he heard a ringing tone in the earpiece. It was at this moment that he turned to see one of his neighbours, about ten doors further up Tory, performing exactly the same manoeuvre, albeit fully dressed, with his own brand-new mobile phone. They shrugged to each other, wearing huge smiles.

The Christmas bonhomie was, miraculously, sustained over the next few days – Brennan spent Boxing Day afternoon at Wincanton races, and for once finished ahead on his bets; Robert the bookseller and Alice the aromatherapist came round for drinks, bearing gifts of an O. Henry short-story collection for Frank, a variety of scented oils for Janet, and an audio-tape of the dramatisation of Samuel Pepys' *Diaries* from Radio 4; their next-door neighbour, Moira Backhouse, invited them all around for a lunch of boiled ham and cold turkey, and Lester frequently went off into town to see the friends he had acquired over his first term at school.

And then the depression hit him. It wasn't triggered just by the bank statement showing a remarkable consumption of his reserves in December, but also by a belated and curt Christmas card from his former editor, Stuart Gill. There was no personal message, just Gill's signature above a corporate logo for the newspaper group. He'd probably signed off two hundred or so cards in one morning without even looking, leaving the individual touches for those to Cabinet Ministers whose favours he might require, to the chairmen of industries and companies who took advertising space, and to the public relations gurus who fed him his freebies throughout the year. Brennan was definitely off the 'A list', a snub that bothered him less in terms of its social implications than in terms of where he might place any future stories.

His discomfort was compounded by Janet's revelation that, in the New Year, she would be taking up a part-time researcher's job for an independent television production company based in Bristol.

'Why didn't you tell me about it?' he asked by way of congratulations.

'This is a sporting reaction, Frank. You're supposed to be pleased for me. But you're not – and I guessed that much, which is *why* I didn't tell you. It would have ruined our Christmas.'

'I *am* pleased.'

'Then why not let your face in on the secret?'

Brennan smiled, genuinely, and held out his arms to her. Janet paused, measuring the depth of his sincerity. After a few seconds, she stepped into his embrace.

'I didn't want to tell you before because I thought it might depress you. You know, with you struggling for work . . . hurting your pride, your professional ego.'

'I think my ego's pretty intact.'

'It isn't, Frank. Your reaction just now tells me that. And that nightmare you had – that's all connected. You're so anxious you can't even feel it any more.'

Brennan let his head fall onto her shoulder.

'I'll be all right once I've got something . . .'

Once the tribe had stripped the roasted stag carcase of its meat, a process that took three days' feasting, they picked clean its skeleton and laid the bones, alongside its liver and heart, in a shallow pit on the edge of the camp, where other gifts to the gods lay buried – fragments of jewellery hewn from metals, carved bones, tufts of animal hair or tail, even a few crudely hammered coins – returning what the spirits of the woods, of the hill's water springs and its sweet air, had first given to them to enable them to survive.

The winter solstice had passed now, and the feast of Imbolc, when the tribe would light fires to awaken the winter sun from its slumber, could be anticipated within one more cycle of the moon across the sky. But safe and well fed as they were in the camp, they could again hear the noises in the near distance which signalled the movement of their enemy. The rumble of their loaded wagons increased, while the thud of their digging contraptions filled every hour of daylight.

At sunrise, when the tribe went to collect water from the streams at the foot of the hill, dust and debris in the normally dazzling waters signalled the proximity of these hostile forces. And just before sleep, as they lay with their heads to the ground, they thought that they could hear the earth crying out in pain. It was time to resume the attacks on these rapacious strangers, to repel their remorseless advance on sacred territory and to burn or destroy their evil machines.

A pall of quiet depression hung over Bradford after the Christmas and New Year celebrations had been spent. The cold, anti-cyclonic greyness gripped the town in a drab stillness. All the festive lights and trimmings had been stripped down and packed away, and the pubs and shops starved as people cowered in their homes counting the costs of their fortnight of excess.

Brennan managed a few mornings in the Dandy Lion, where even Linda, the irrepressibly cheerful landlady, couldn't lift the gloom. The bar's regular handful of writers and artists swapped tales of penury with him, an attempt at collective help which usually backfired. On two evenings, he played chess in the beamed back room in front of a log fire with other acquaintances that the bar's Bohemian drift had brought his way. But nothing filled the emptiness inside him.

But then, on the first morning of Sandra the cleaner's return to duty, the flow changed abruptly. After her usual half-hour over tea and biscuits nattering about Christmas, and how her bloke Gary had bought her a pair of leather trousers because he liked grabbing her arse in them, she had set cheerfully to work, finding sufficient volume on Radio 1 to smother the noise of the vacuum cleaner.

The boisterous banality of Sandra's presence lifted Brennan's mood. She and her boyfriend – a fifty-one-year-old roadie with a hopeless pub band from Devizes – lived in a one-bedroom council house. They were always in debt, and always being chased by divisions of bailiffs reclaiming televisions they couldn't pay for, or clothes ordered from catalogues under false names and faked credit status.

But, as Sandra never stopped telling Brennan, they shagged like spring rabbits, smoked a little bit of 'wacky baccy' every night, and got pissed out of their brains on cider each Friday. The pressure of bourgeois life had never impinged on their consciousness and, most of the time – certainly when he was feeling sorry for himself – Brennan took heart from Sandra's uncrushable sense of irresponsibility. As he set about tidying up his office, whistling to fend off the sound of her music, he heard a sudden yell from her on the stairs below.

'Frank! Frank! You've got a visitor!'

Brennan guessed that it would be Moira Backhouse with some piddling enquiry about plans for their window-boxes, but when he got to the ground floor, Sandra was standing there alone.

'Who is it?' he asked with a frown.

'I made it wait outside,' Sandra growled, with a look of mixed disgust and accusation, as though Frank had invited her enemy into his home.

'Is it a copper, Sandra?' he guessed, trying to interpret her mood.

'Not human at all, he ain't. Don't know what you're doing having those smelly fuckers round. Specially not when I'm doing me cleaning.'

Brennan crossed to the front door and opened it. Waiting serenely outside was a bearded, tangle-haired youth wearing a rag-bag of clothes in hues of brown and green, with a pair of animal-skin boots tied on to his feet. A leather thong was wrapped around his midriff, and around the upper sections of each arm were bands of reddish animal fur. A stinging waft of body sweat and dried shit accompanied the youth's dishevelled appearance.

Brennan reached into his pocket in reflex for coins – it wasn't unknown for the beggars or homeless of Bath to take 'awaydays' to neighbouring market towns, and exploit the repelled citizens with tales of needing money to get home. The people were usually only too happy to cough up in order to get this human detritus back out of sight.

'I wondered if I could have a word with you, Mr Brennan,' the youth said, in the crisp, perfectly enunciated tones of a public schoolboy. Brennan's hand stayed in his pocket.

'Sorry – who are you . . . what's it about?'

'Well, my name is Lovernios,' the youth announced confidently. 'And I am a member of the Celtic Brotherhood. I think I have information in which you may be interested.'

CHAPTER TWO

Sandra made a melodramatic point of covering the kitchen chair with two layers of newspaper before Lovernios took his seat. She also returned to vacuum around his feet, and once, when she was standing behind him, threatened to spray him with air-freshener, but a glare from Brennan had stopped her just in time. Not that the youth would necessarily have reacted, such was his poise and intense aura of calm.

He would only confirm that his name was Lovernios, seeming innocently baffled by Brennan's need for further embellishment.

'Well, is that your surname or Christian name?' Brennan enquired pedantically, hoping to provoke some irritation.

'Neither term is applicable, actually. One relates to a concept of family, the other to a religion I don't recognise. I have a name that belongs to my culture,' the youth explained assiduously.

'Would you like some tea or coffee?' Brennan asked, seeing the offer produce a first sign of animation.

'They're confections. I drink only water, or the juice of berries.'

Sandra pointedly filled a glass at the kitchen sink and brought it across to the youth, who looked at it disdainfully.

'Lead, chemicals, scores of impurities,' he said, shaking his head.

'I was offering he so you wash in him, not have a drink,' Sandra said with a lipsticked smile of triumph.

Brennan waved for her to put the glass away.

'Could you leave us for a few minutes, please, Sandra? Why don't you have a crack at my office while I'm down here?'

'Right. Don't mind me having a fag in there, do you.' This wasn't framed as a question but as a gleeful expression of habit, Janet having forbidden Sandra from smoking anywhere in the house except in Brennan's already cigar-scented study.

'Off to Nicotine City, then,' she beamed as she rustled across the room in her leather trousers. 'And if it wants a ciggie, don't go sending it up after me,' she warned, nodding across at the youth.

'So what's the Celtic Brotherhood? Van Morrison's new band?'

Lovernios blinked a few times, as though the name were registering somewhere in a deep recess of his brain, but offered no other reaction.

'We are what the name implies. A brethren of Celtic people.'

'Forgive me, but you sound thoroughly Anglo-Saxon.'

As a witticism, it might have passed muster in the bar of the Garrick Club, but Lovernios plainly saw no humour in it.

'In your world, perhaps, but not in mine.'

The youth's serene arrogance was beginning to needle Brennan. He recognised the tone from the days when boy journalists, just out of Harrow with no A-levels but with an uncle on the newspaper's board, would be assigned to his office and would start mapping out their careers for his information.

'Look – from your accent and manner, if not your dress sense, I'd say you had a thoroughly upper-middle-class background, and been educated at public school. So can we stop pretending you're Asterix the Gaul, who's just beamed down from 2000 BC.'

'First century AD, actually, Mr Brennan.'

Brennan took this as the first glimpse of humour in the youth's otherwise absurdly intense façade, but when he laughed, the youth instantly stood up.

'I'm sorry you find my culture a matter for humour. I had hoped that you would be more sympathetic.'

Lovernios headed for the door. Brennan instantly felt cheap.

'Wait a minute . . . wait a minute. Why don't you just tell me what you want and leave the rest to one side? But just acknowledge that I have a world as well – you've seen my name in the papers, heard that I now live in Bradford, looked up my address in the phone-book. Yes?'

The youth sat down again.

'You know the Mendips, I presume, Mr Brennan?'

Brennan resisted the temptation to go for a joke, nodding his head slowly instead.

'Not intimately. But I know where they are – start just the other side of Frome, don't they? Right across Somerset to Weston-super-Mare?'

The youth nodded, with a hint of warmth for the first time.

'Well, I live in the eastern tip of the hills. And they are being destroyed by quarrying.'

A whole card-index of preconceptions flickered through Brennan's mind in an instant – environmental protester, living up in trees, part of a New Age travellers' camp, hippy convoy, public-school drop-out. He had to check himself – instant reactions such as these belonged on the wilder pages of *The Spectator*.

'Right,' he said slowly, masking the torrent of images within. 'And you are protesting against it and think I can help you, is that it?'

'In part, yes.'

'Why? Because I've occasionally campaigned for a good cause, or thrown light on a miscarriage of justice?'

The youth nodded, tacitly acknowledging Brennan's past.

'Well, I'm afraid I don't take sides – not readily anyway.'

'We . . . I . . . didn't expect you to. I wished only that you might look into the destruction these people are wreaking.'

'Hang on, hang on – I believe there's something called planning permission, granted by democratically elected councils, isn't there?'

'We don't recognise their authority. It's granted to them by people who believe in concepts such as tax and private ownership, not common wealth. So the permission they give for the exploitation of our land is unlawful.'

'*Your* land?' Brennan asked, sitting forward. 'You just scoffed at ownership.'

The youth looked at him defiantly.

'Yes. When the Romans invaded Britain, the Celtic people were slaughtered or subjugated throughout most of the mainland.'

'Look, my dad is Irish. Spare me the history lesson, give me the moral logic.'

The youth ran a finger along his lips in thought – Brennan caught a sudden image of him in a private tutorial in some Gothic schoolroom, chewing the philosophical fat with a bow-tied housemaster.

'The Mendips were the habitat of Celtic tribes – Belgae, Dvrotriges, possible the Dvmnonii . . .'

The boy was a scholar, Brennan would give him that.

'But the Roman seizure all but obliterated them. The hills were mined for lead and silver, our religion was suppressed. From worshipping God through nature, through water and fire, Romanised Christianity imposed upon us a man-made religion, and they've caused it to control us ever since. Together with their structures of government and transport. And now it's happening again – these people raping the Mendips of stone so that they can conquer our lands with roads are the New Romans. We have to stop them!'

The youth was clenching and unclenching his fists. Brennan could almost sense the knots in the boy's stomach as they tightened on him. And though the logic was eerily flawed, the passion with which it had been expressed demanded that Brennan choose his next words carefully. If he kicked off with 'yes, but . . .', 'Lovernios' would probably blow a gasket.

'Right – I can see things a little more clearly now,' he said neutrally. 'Would you not, though, accept that what happened was simply a process of civilisation?'

'The Celts had a perfectly acceptable form of it. You mention the word "pagan" to anybody now and they shrivel up in horror because they've been taught that it's evil or maladjusted.'

Brennan walked across the kitchen to switch on the kettle, partly because he needed coffee, partly because it bought him time to decide what to do about the mad – no, make that 'preoccupied' – youth. He had the same glazed intensity as any doorstep Mormon, but there was no denying his fevered intelligence.

'Where do you live exactly?' Brennan asked.

'In a camp.'

'What, a tented village, travellers' vans – that sort of thing?'

The youth looked at him accusingly.

'They've even shaped your opinions, haven't they? You saw my clothes and my hair and you thought, "Just another crusty".'

'No, I didn't,' Brennan insisted. 'If I'd thought that, would I have let you through the door?'

'So you admit it – had I *been* a "crusty", you wouldn't have allowed me into your house.'

Brennan ran a hand through his hair, scratching his scalp. Trying to keep up with the youth's switches of logic and language was beginning to hurt his brain.

'Can we stick to one issue. Which is more important to you, the quarrying, the demise of Celtic civilisation or my prejudices and how they were received?'

For once, the youth looked chastened.

'They are expanding the quarry without permission.'

'A permission that you don't think is valid anyway?'

'They have secret trains taking the stone out in the night. They have gouged so deep into the earth that sacred springs are drying up.'

'Look – do you have documentary evidence that this quarry operation is exceeding its legal constraints – and I mean contemporary law, not as it was two thousand years ago?'

'We see what goes on. Night and day.'

Brennan turned away ill-temperedly. He should have stopped worrying about his liberal credibility and just told the kid to fuck off when he'd opened the door.

'I'm sorry – but for better or worse, my life involves writing stories for newspapers or magazines. That means I have to abide, to a certain extent, by their requirements for truthful and accurate reporting. I mean, that's why you came to me, wasn't it?'

Lovernios shrugged with indifference.

'So unless I find – or you lead me to – evidence which convinces the people who trust me, you might as well go to the *Sunday Sport* and tell them that spacecraft from Mars are digging up your precious Mendips for a house-building programme back home.'

'You can see them from the moon, you know.'

'What?'

'The biggest quarries in the Mendips are actually visible from the surface of the moon.'

'Impressive image, but bullshit. Are you really trying to tell me that Neil Armstrong made a special point of picking out Frome and said, "Look at those big holes down there" to Buzz Aldrin?'

The youth stood up again and glared at him.

'You have no feeling for this planet, have you? For its history. For its place in our lives. Your mind is built around work, money, consumerism, gratification.'

'Hey, look – if it's a choice between a vintage bottle of claret and not growing grapes, I'm right there with Julius Caesar.'

'The Celts were making wine long before the Romans. And it was Claudius who ordered the invasion of Britain.'

The youth headed for the door and opened it, turning only to offer a polite apology for intruding. He then closed the door gently behind him. Brennan exhaled. He felt like an utter shit, but he'd been hijacked so many times in the past by fringe groups or deranged individuals that there was a point where self-protection was called for.

Sandra appeared on the stairs, ostentatiously blasting her sickly potpourri air-freshening spray at the ceiling.

'He'd got a niff on him, and no mistake, eh?'

Brennan wafted his hand at the cascade of scented droplets, and hurried to the door to let real air into the room. He stepped out on to Tory's footpath. The youth was sitting on Moira Backhouse's garden wall, eating an apple. Brennan imagined that Moira would have already summoned the Wiltshire Police's helicopter, complete with trained marksmen to 'take out' this disgraceful intruder on her wall.

'Do you want a lift back?' Brennan asked as a gesture of conciliation.

'In a car? Rather defeats the purpose of our objections, doesn't it? Besides, I walk everywhere.'

'You mean you came from Frome on foot?'

The youth nodded.

'Surprised you didn't get picked up by the police.'

'I came across land, Mr Brennan. It's much shorter than walking the roads. Not that . . .'

'... you would use them anyway?'

'Of course not. You should try walking the fields and hills, Mr Brennan. I find mushrooms, wild garlic, berries, deer and partridge ...'

'What happened to that stance on "gratification" just now?'

'There's a difference between what is given and what is bought.'

The youth swallowed the last piece of apple, core and all, and slid off the wall.

'Say I decide to have a look at this quarry. Where do I contact you?'

'At the camp ... Tedbury.'

'Which is ...?'

'Have a look at a map. It's been there for over two thousand years.'

'Just ask for Lovernios, eh?'

'That's correct. Goodbye, Mr Brennan.'

With that, he turned and walked up the path, away from the route down into Bradford. Five minutes later, Brennan had him square in the lenses of his racing binoculars as he tracked him along the grassy banks of the River Avon. Then Lovernios turned south and headed up into one of the woods that overlooked the river, and was gone.

That evening, after Janet and Lester had detailed their first days of the new year at work and school respectively – 'really good,' according to Janet, 'boring,' according to Lester – Brennan told them about the visit from the strange youth, and then afterwards Janet went up to the lounge and brought down an Ordnance Survey map for the area embracing Frome in the north and Yeovil in the south. She opened it up and spread it across the kitchen table to begin her search.

'What did you say this camp's name was?'

'Tetbury, I think.'

'Dad, that's where Prince Charles lives.'

'Well, it wouldn't be a complete surprise to find my chap and Charlie together, actually, hugging trees.'

'There's a dozen or so quarries marked here,' Janet muttered as her eyes scanned the map. 'Look – all along this line here.' Her finger traced a path across a section of the map where the contours were swirls of dense loops.

'What does it mean when the contour lines are close together, Lester?' Brennan asked his son as a test.

'That's easy – did it last year.'

'Yeah, but say I've forgotten. Tell me.'

'The closer the lines are, the steeper the ground must be,' Lester announced wearily, as if he were discarding surplus knowledge.

'Here it is!' Janet exclaimed, jabbing her finger down on the map. 'Tedbury Camp – it's printed in an odd typeface.'

Brennan peered at the green rectangle marked on the map. He sucked in air through his teeth, as if suddenly old.

'Looks like Gothic three-point to me.'

'Is that scum-bag biz, Mum?'

' 'Fraid so – the papers used to have all kinds of typefaces – the style of the letters – in your father's day. All cut into metal on Linotype machines . . . not a computer in sight.'

'Are you even older than you look, Dad?' Lester asked with a wide grin.

'That's only twenty or so years ago Mum's talking about. There weren't even many computers till the mid-eighties when friend Murdoch took over.'

In the meantime, Janet had folded the map over to check the symbols, hoping to find the significance of the lettering.

'Here we go – that typeface is used for non-Roman antiquities.'

'That's what he said it was – *pre*-Roman, to be precise.'

'And he *lives* there?'

'With his Celtic Brotherhood, whoever they are.'

'Must be pretty precarious,' Janet murmured, still decoding the map. 'There's a cliff on the western edge of the camp here. And on the southern side, down the bottom, there's a railway line . . . freight . . . which runs through to a quarry.'

'Okay – so he wasn't making it up. Doesn't mean the rest of his story's true, does it?' Brennan said, defensively. Having aroused Janet's curiosity, he knew he'd have a hard job talking himself out of any commitment to follow up the youth's allegations.

'I can't tell, Frank. I didn't meet him. You know what he said, so follow your instinct.'

'My instinct is that it was an attempt to con me into taking a partial view, to oppose the quarry's expansion.'

'You're surely not in favour of it?' Janet asked.

'Look – quarries are somewhere up there with dressage and yachting as interests in my life. If their development is correctly policed then I don't see a story.'

'There's a place called Murder Comb near where they live, Dad. Should be interesting,' Lester interjected with relish. Brennan ignored him.

'What if I decide to follow up on it? How would you feel about that?' Janet asked pointedly.

Brennan's eyes narrowed theatrically, as if a pantomime villain had just arrived on stage.

'You mean for your new employers? But you're ... a researcher,' Brennan said, omitting the 'just' in speech, if not in tone.

'Well, they made it plain to me today that if I have any ideas for documentaries I can put them up. They have an output deal with one of the local broadcasters for half-hour programmes.'

'But they've done all that by-pass protest stuff to death, they're not going to be interested in another group of loonies dancing around the countryside.'

'You're trying to put me off now, aren't you? Reclaiming it as your own territory,' Janet said with a knowing smile. Brennan played the innocent.

'Tell you what I'll do. I'll pop over there some time next week and have a look at this camp. Maybe get some background on the quarry. If it seems promising, I'll have a go at it.'

'And if it doesn't, you'll dump it on to me. You cheeky sod, Frank.'

'Ah, but I saw him first, Jan.'

No work offers, no letters of enquiry, nor any telephone calls requesting his services disturbed the remainder of Brennan's first week of January. With Lester and Janet out of the house for large sections of the day, he found himself re-enacting the mental routines of his time in prison. The establishment of the day's objectives in chronological order – getting hold of a paper early; a long and contemplative ablution accompanied by reading of said paper; personal hygiene matters; thinking about lunch; lunch; then deciding what to do afterwards.

By the Friday of this inauspicious start to the year, he had resolved to visit the camp of the Celtic Brotherhood, in order to eliminate it from his thinking. A possibility of a story was usually worse than no story itself, because it condemned the journalist to a lingering death of false expectations, redundant research, time-wasting travel and dubious expenses.

This latter item may not have been an issue in Brennan's heyday of the 1980s – nuclear paranoia, right-wing plots, corporate and local government corruption, the crushing of the unions, had generated enough work for him to be granted virtually a blank cheque by his bosses. But now that he was out on his own – coinciding with the public's more muted appetite for the big themes – he needed to watch every penny, and to cost every hour.

So he had allotted just the one afternoon to establish the potential of this story brought to him by the strange youth. He'd arranged for Janet to be home in time to receive Lester from school, and had done twenty minutes of guesswork shopping – milk, bread, oven chips, pizza, soap, toilet roll – in Bradford's only supermarket so that Janet couldn't moan about not having the use of the car.

Then, after a sandwich and a glass of milk at home, he drove south out of Bradford and soon crossed the border into Somerset. He avoided the A36 trunk route, cutting across the northern edge of Frome, before finding the narrow country road that ran closest to Tedbury Camp. The landscape around him began to rise and swell as the first fringes of the Mendips appeared, and although the fields in view were still agricultural in nature, their billowing profiles, ancient oaks and elms, and their unkempt hedgerows suggested that the tendency towards manicured countryside, which had grown during the past century, had passed this corner of England by.

This impression was confirmed to him as he turned his car off at Great Elm and manoeuvred it nervously down into a tree-lined hollow, where a small stream bubbled into a picturesque duck pond. Despite the surrounding half dozen houses, the hollow seemed quiet and deserted as he parked his car by the stile to a footpath, leading out to Tedbury Camp.

It was yet another still, grey afternoon with the bare winter trees utterly motionless. Brennan gratefully left the car, checked his map, and climbed the stile and set off down the path that ran alongside the stream. A few hundred yards ahead he could see a closed, iron-barred gate and warning signs where the railway line ran. But although this short distance took less than a minute to navigate, there was a palpable change in the atmosphere. He could feel a sudden sense of isolation, of being cut off from the everyday traffic of life. To his left, the single railway line disappeared into a dank tunnel cut into the hill above, and its bare rock-face loomed above him. To the right, the freight line ran down the ravine created by the rock-face on one side, and by the rising ground of the hill-fort on the other.

Brennan listened again. He thought he heard an echoing metallic sound ripple down the ravine – a train moving, a digger at the quarry? But then there was silence again. He looked around and noticed a thin grey layer of dust on the wooden gateposts, and as he bent down, he could also see it on the wild grasses and ivies that grew alongside the track.

On the other side of the path, there was a narrow iron footbridge over the stream. He edged across it, able to see the sudden risen ground of the hill-fort for the first time. It was protected by a tangle of dull, brown brackens and shiny green ivies, and a slalom course of trees. The course of the public footpath veered off to the left, around the base of the hill, but there were sufficient trails of well-trodden undergrowth to suggest human traffic up and down the slopes.

Brennan could see little of the hill's summit, a hundred or so feet above, just the creeper-covered ramparts of earth, and a further line of thin, misshapen trees beyond. It would probably need little effort to take the fort with modern warfare, or indeed police tactics, but he'd guessed that an assault two thousand years earlier would have been a more demanding, and life-threatening business.

He sniffed – there was wood smoke in the air. And not the sour, gagging taste of the leaf or rubbish pyre. This was almost scented. He looked at the wall of undergrowth rising in front of him and took a cautious few steps off the footpath. He paused to listen again. He knew that he would be prone to the urbanite's paranoia when in the countryside, but even allowing for that he sensed he was being watched from within, or beyond, the hill's protective trees.

But his speculation was cut short by a growing roar behind him. A train was coming through the tunnel. Brennan scrambled back across the bridge and up to the gate just as a huge locomotive, with a gleaming corrugated-steel body, burst out of the tunnel, pulling behind it a column of empty hopper-wagons, each marked with the Roadstone International logo.

The great diesel's wheels screamed and scraped along the rails as the empty wagons clattered slowly along behind, juddering with the strain of movement. Brennan began to count the wagons as they lumbered past, but gave up once he'd got into the high thirties. The train's progress, slowed naturally by the twisting course of the ravine, probably exaggerated the length of the convoy, but he calculated that it took a good seven minutes or so before it was all past him, and a further two for the silence of this eerie little site to return.

He turned away from the gate and saw the youth – what did he call himself again, Lovernios? – standing on the bridge, watching him earnestly.

'Our enemy is mighty, is he not, Mr Brennan?'

'The driver looked a bit on the old side, I thought. And the wagons make a bit of a racket, but . . .'

'You should see and hear them when they're fully loaded. Two thousand tonnes of limestone on each train. Five or six trains a night. Taking our land away from us, eating the heart out of it.'

Brennan nodded up at the hill.

'Can I come up and see the camp?'

'Not now,' Lovernios said evenly. 'The tribe is sleeping, ready for tonight.'

'You're all taking the dirty washing over to your mums', right?'

'Please don't mock, Mr Brennan. It's so easy to do that.

28

Understanding what we say is harder, but ultimately more rewarding.'

'Well, I'll be the judge of that,' Brennan said sharply. 'What about a look at the quarry, then? Go in along the railway line, do you?'

'Sometimes. They have guards patrolling down there, protecting the railhead. We know other ways in. But it will have to wait until after nightfall.'

Brennan looked at his watch – ten past three. The grey sky was already darkening.

'What time do you suggest?' he asked Lovernios.

'We no longer live by formal time, Mr Brennan. Our days are book-ended by light and darkness, with gathering, hunting and feeding in between.'

'You're not allowed to have a pint, I suppose?'

'We brew our own,' Lovernios said with a rare smile.

'I don't suppose the local pubs take too kindly to you turning up?'

'I've never tried, but I would think not. There's an old inn at Mells – the Talbot. I can meet you outside. There's a courtyard.'

'Do you want to borrow my watch?' Brennan asked, thrusting his wrist at the youth.

'One of the things we find with our life, Mr Brennan, is that we know the rhythm of time. It's the same as the heartbeat, but we don't have to count.'

'My seven o'clock, your sun over the yard arm, or whatever. Okay?'

'I'll be there,' Lovernios said, before turning and climbing back up the hill. Brennan watched his nimble progress – pulling on branches for support, getting a toehold on rocks studded into the sides of the fort – before the trees and the undergrowth claimed him. Seconds later, he appeared on the ramparts and then dropped out of sight.

Brennan took out his new mobile phone, a bizarre token of the modern age in the context of the camp. He switched it on, seeing the display panel light up. The battery-level indicator showed full strength, but the message display on the screen was 'No Signal'. So much for technology.

He drove into Frome to kill time, instantly taking to its gentle hills, its stone buildings and its market-town bustle. He found a large car park adjacent to an arts complex in what looked like a converted bakery. The courtyard here had the usual *faux*-rural crafts – pottery, baskets – albeit more individualistic than the stuff you'd pick up in a trendy home furnishing store, and there was a lavishly twee gift shop inside. Opposite this was, predictably, a wholefood coffee shop, featuring a jumble of white-wood tables – all from sustainable sources, he was sure – and a wide fireplace in which a pile of neatly cut logs sizzled and burnt in an iron grate.

The cafe was less than half full, and Brennan managed to install himself at a table near the fire so that he could feel the full benefit of its warmth. While eating his carob slice and sipping his sugar-free cappuccino, he made notes on what Lavernois had said to him that afternoon. Writing up an instant account was a chore, but not as burdensome as trying to do it several days later when memory had faded, or had been challenged by later details. In any case, writing allowed Brennan to avoid the possibility of finding himself accidentally staring at any of the women who dominated the café. They were mostly of a type – arty-but-homespun, feminist-but-married – who would enjoy taking loud exception to any incidental eye contact from a married, white male.

He survived safely until five o'clock when the fire was dying and the tables were being wiped down, and then passed an enjoyable few minutes looking at the cards on the noticeboard in the corridor outside. It was the A–Z of contemporary therapies – acupuncture to zen theory.

Walking out on to the main street, Brennan found the shops closing and the town rapidly emptying, but he did make a prize find – a corner shop dedicated to cigarettes, pipes and cigars. He slipped in just as the middle-aged lady assistant was approaching to run up the 'closed' sign. She kindly allowed him a quick look at the cigar cabinets – one on the counter, one free-standing against a wall – and he rewarded her good citizenship by claiming two Romeo y Julieta Churchills at ten pounds each.

He returned to his car. The streets were even emptier now. It was, so far, the one major irritation of moving to the country, the way shop shutters came down at 5.30, killing a town centre until the pubs and the takeaways geared up for their night's business. A lot of the bars didn't even open until seven, such were the ingrained habits of those who went straight home from work for their early dinner.

It didn't matter too much to Brennan tonight because he wouldn't allow himself to drink more than a pint anyway, now he had the car back. And the sudden transition from the street-lit town to the pitch-dark countryside required particular alertness in a driver reared on the sodium overkill of the big city.

He shamelessly whacked on the full beam of his headlights as soon as he could, giving himself at least a hundred yards' notice of creatures crawling across the road, or staring out of the hedgerows with glassy green eyes. For he dreaded the thought of flattening a hedgehog, or embedding a badger in his radiator – he even empathised with their terror, finding himself startled and discomforted by any oncoming lights.

With some relief he found Mells, and parked beside a long wall outside what was plainly an old coaching inn. The Talbot even had its original cobbled courtyard, stacked with logs for the lounge's fire. The old stables looked as if they'd been turned into not-so-new lavatories.

The lounge at the back of the yard seemed to contain a rather smart restaurant – lit candles were on the tables, a blackboard shone with the night's menu – so Brennan opted for the public bar, a small room with a bare wooden floor, and barrels of guest ales lurking on a trestle table. He glimpsed a cribbage board and puce-faced locals as he crossed the short distance to the counter. It was no place to be seen smoking a ten-quid cigar.

He took a half of Butcombe bitter and decided to stay at the bar rather than sit at one of the small tables, like a sad git who still lived with his mum. Although there was no obvious hostility, he'd plainly been clocked as a new face, a passer-by at best, a weekender from London at worst. He exchanged a little small-talk with the barman about the beer, and Somerset cricket (a biography of Viv Richards was on one of the shelves behind the bar). Despite the presence of a man in Roadstone International overalls, there was no easy way to bring up the subject of quarries. But that didn't stop him listening.

After some impenetrable overtime references, and a verbal going-over for a site manager, Brennan then overheard that two lurcher dogs had been found dead on the floor of the quarry that morning, together with the rabbit they'd foolishly chased under the fence that guarded the edge of the quarry. Brennan's relish for his imminent visit lessened somewhat at the thought of the dogs suddenly finding themselves thrashing nothing but air as they hurtled to a bone-shattering death.

'Pity it wasn't one o' them long-haired weirdos from the hill,' the quarry worker's companion offered with a jovial laugh.

'Could always be arranged,' cackled the worker. Probably no harm in it, Brennan thought. Six thirty on a Friday night – the average wine bar in the City of London would have dozens of vile threats and curses being uttered. But there was genuine hostility when one of the cribbage players noticed Lovernios lurking in the shadows of the courtyard, trying to see through the window of the bar.

'There's that mad smelly bastard – get he out here!' The handful of other drinkers turned and swore at Lovernios as he huddled back into the shadows. Brennan felt a sudden surge of pity for him.

'Take a shotgun to creatures like him, I would . . .' wafted across the room. Brennan sensed the lad might be in physical danger if he hovered around too long. He ordered another half and brazenly announced his intentions to the room.

'I'll see him off . . .'

He mustered as much swagger and menace as he could as he went out of the door. Lovernios stepped forward a little from his hiding-place.

'Get the fuck out of here, you toe-rag.'

He mimicked angry gestures, but his left eye, out of sight of the bar, was offering a wink of reassurance which he hoped Lovernios would register.

'Go on – bugger off back to your hole.'

He shooed the youth out of the courtyard, back towards the road. Once clear of the bar's windows he tossed Lovernios the car keys and whispered loudly, 'The green Renault estate. I'll be out in three minutes.'

Lovernios looked at the keys as if they were instruments of the devil, but nodded his understanding. Brennan rejoined the locals in the bar, preening for their benefit.

'Can't drop out of society *and* still expect to be allowed in pubs, that's what I say.'

This drew a few murmurs of agreement. He allowed for a pause, and sipped his new half, before turning to the quarry worker.

'Who is he anyway – one of them travellers?'

'Worse 'an that – whole gang of 'em living up on Tedbury Camp, making a nuisance of themselves in the quarry.'

'Nuisance?'

'Oh, aye – they climb in at night, put sugar in the petrol tanks of the diggers, or super-glue the locks on the dumper trucks. They'll even have a go at the trains if they've taken enough drugs to give 'em the bollocks to try.'

'Surprised they haven't been cleared. Can move 'em all on without an excuse now with the Criminal Justice whatsit,' Brennan offered, unsure that he was making a convincing impersonation of a bar-room bigot.

'Coppers are too spooked to go up there,' the quarry worker said with contempt. 'One of these nights, some of the lads and the drivers'll go up with dogs and baseball bats an' sort 'em out. Black magic or no black magic.'

Brennan felt a sudden chill on his neck. A flicker of his nightmare came and went – antlers and hot breath. He finished his drink in four gulps, and clapped the quarry worker on the shoulder, wishing him good luck.

Outside, Lovernios was hovering by the car.

'Get in,' Brennan commanded, taking the keys back.

'I don't think that's too good an idea, actually, Mr Brennan.'

'This is no time for an environmental stance, mate. There's guys back in there who'll rip my head off if they see me talking to you. Now get in.'

With great reluctance, Lovernios installed himself in the passenger seat. Brennan started the engine, backed out on to the road, and made the youth bend down in his seat as they passed in front of the pub.

He drove through the village and headed out on the road that he hoped, according to his reading of the map, would lead to the quarry.

'From what I heard in there, sounds like your idea of protest is more than just writing a letter to *The Times*.'

'What do you mean?'

'Chap said you sabotaged machinery, damaged the trucks. Even tried to fuck up the trains.'

'We're at war, Mr Brennan. Anything goes.'

Brennan made a right at a junction. He could already see the bizarre orange glow in the sky given off by the quarry's night lights.

'You'd better park up somewhere along here. They have security patrols around the perimeter roads. Any cars will usually get towed away.'

Brennan found a lay-by and parked. They got out.

'Now what?' he asked.

'We walk,' Lovernios said, pointing across the field on the opposite side of the road.

Brennan took out one of his Churchill cigars, cut it, and lit it with relish. Lovernios looked at him in bemusement.

'I'll need something to light my way,' Brennan said, sucking on the cigar to produce a deep red glow.

CHAPTER THREE

Nothing in his expectations had prepared Brennan for the sight of the quarry as he finally looked out over it. A huge crater, perhaps two hundred feet deep, spread out as far as he could see. In the light of the eerie yellow arc-lamps it looked like a devil's cauldron. At the quarry's base was a complex of buildings, and beyond that a tangle of conveyors and overhead chutes, which squatted over the railway tracks and a line of empty rail wagons. Massive forty-foot-high dumper trucks, with wheels like dinosaurs' haunches, their tyres meshed with chains, were parked inside a cavernous hangar. From the tallest of the buildings came a demonic, grinding cacophony.

'That's the primary crushing house,' Lovernios said. 'They break up the stone in there after it's been dumped down that chute by the trucks.' His finger drew a line across the moonscape for Brennan's benefit. 'The stones are graded according to size and then either stockpiled or loaded on to the conveyors.'

Brennan's eyes panned around the quarry. He could make out the sheer stone walls and the lorry paths gouged out below them. At the lowest level, a greenish lake rippled in the lights.

'They've got water coming up,' Brennan said, a tad too knowledgeably.

'No, no – that's just the run-off from the pumping system. If that wasn't working, the whole quarry would be three-quarters full. The water table's only about fifty feet below the surface level, you see. They're completely destroying the flow of water through the hills. The hot springs in Bath are threatened now – the very facility which brought the Romans there in the first place.'

' "Aquae Sulis" – that's what they called it, wasn't it?'

Lovernios nodded.

'We'd better keep moving. They have cameras as well as patrols.'

Brennan took a last peek over the wire fence in front of him, seeing the sheer drop to the bare rocks below. He shivered at the thought of those dogs falling to their deaths. He followed Lovernios, and they skirted around the perimeter fence, where a small amount of landscaping had been done to hide the quarry from view. In the lights he could see the beautifully subtle grain of the latest limestone rock-face to have been exposed by the blasting. And he thought, with a sudden tingle of awe, that it must be many millions of years old.

'It's about three and a half miles going round the edge, and a mile or more across at the widest point. Be nearer two when they expand,' Lovernios added solemnly. 'They're vandalising history.'

Brennan paused to relight his cigar.

'They've got permission, though, you say?'

'Parish council, district council, county council have all fallen under their sway. The jobs argument wins all the time. The quarry employs about four hundred people as workers or in administration, and there are about five hundred trucks a day passing through and loading up. It isn't part of the local economy, it *is* the local economy!'

'So what would the Celtic Brotherhood offer the people as an alternative?' Brennan asked pointedly.

'The alternative to exploitation is non-exploitation,' Lovernios said, obliquely.

'I can't see cutting the grass as a viable option,' Brennan countered. 'You can't win the economic argument, can you? That's why you resort to your own form of vandalism, isn't it?'

'There are plenty of people around here who support us, Mr Brennan. Who can see the link between this monstrosity here and our land being swamped with roads and motorways.'

'You can't stop progress,' Brennan said blithely.

Lovernios rounded on him.

36

'You call this progress? The Romans were raping these hills two thousand years ago. It's history repeating itself. The people being subjugated by a tyranny of profiteers under the name of civilisation. That's why we must beat them.'

A new noise disturbed the night air, as an overhead conveyor began to pass over the railway wagons, showering stone into each one with a torrential rattle.

'Five or six trains a day,' muttered Lovernios. 'One million tonnes of stone for every five miles of motorway. It is madness on a huge scale.'

There was violent anger in his voice now. Brennan suspected that if he argued back he might well be physically attacked by this strange, intense youth.

'Why "Lovernios"? What does it mean?'

'It's the fox,' the youth said, touching the red fur armbands.

'You kill for fur?' Brennan said provocatively.

'We take the fur only from those already dead.'

Brennan's eyes were suddenly distracted by a light emerging from trees ahead of them, followed by two figures in day-glo jackets and yellow hard-hats.

'Security!' he hissed at Lovernios.

Lovernios turned in an instant and began to run. Brennan followed.

'We'll have you fuckers!' shouted one of the guards as they now gave chase.

Lovernios angled his run up the bank towards the perimeter fence over which they had climbed. Brennan followed, already panting, his shoes sliding on the dew-soaked grass. The guards were closing. Lovernios let out a rippling yell and charged at the guards, throwing himself into a flying kick that knocked the first one right off his feet, throwing him several yards backwards.

Brennan watched in horror as the second guard produced a truncheon and advanced on Lovernios.

'Watch out!'

But the youth took the blow smack on the side of the head and went down. The first guard got to his feet and buried a kick into Lovernios's side. Brennan ran towards them.

'You bastards are well out of order!'

They both turned to look at him.

'New recruit, eh? You'll have to get rid of the designer walking clothes if you want to live with this bunch of sheep-shaggers.'

'You hit him again and I'll have you up on assault charges, cunt!' Brennan spluttered. 'He may not have a name, but I do.'

The first guard paused with his next kick, and nodded to his colleague. The second guard now took a small black object from the bellows pocket of his nylon jacket. Brennan's heart flipped over – for a second, he thought it must be a handgun. But then a sharp white light issued from the top of the machine, and the guard trained it on Brennan. It was a bloody camcorder!

'Smile, cunt, 'cos now you've been framed!'

Brennan tried to shield his eyes and his face from the stabbing light. And then an instinct made him relent, and he stared full-face at the camera.

'Get a load of it, then,' he said defiantly. 'You'll be seeing a lot of me in court!'

The threat worked. The guard lowered the camera, while his colleague dragged the groaning Lovernios to his feet and flung him back in Brennan's direction. Lovernios staggered and Brennan took hold of his arm and steadied him.

'You okay?'

He nodded.

'We're going,' Brennan said as he backed himself and Lovernios up the slope.

'Next time,' said the guard with the truncheon, smirking.

They watched Brennan and Lovernios all the way back to the fence, retreating only when they had climbed over it and returned to public property.

'God knows where the car is,' Brennan panted as they slithered down to the road.

'Back this way,' Lovernios mumbled as he led Brennan into the darkness.

'Do they always react so violently?' Brennan asked as they walked along the edge of the road, keeping a watch for oncoming headlights.

'It's become a part of their routine with us. They're not employed directly by Roadstone International – they're brought in on contract. That way the company can keep its distance if the guards overdo the strong-arm stuff. Which they do, because they know that we have no legal recourse, and we know that they'd just move on elsewhere if we ever complained.'

'How's the head?'

'Throbbing a bit.'

'Do you want me to run you to hospital?'

'We have a doctor in the camp.'

'Oh, yes, private or NHS?' Brennan asked acidly.

'He's not that sort of medic. He's a herbalist. A potion-maker. A spiritual healer. A leader. All in one. You'd call him a Druid.'

'What's *his* name?'

'Cernunnos.'

'Sounds more like a breakfast cereal to me.'

'You need to brush up on your Celtic mythology, Mr Brennan. It will help you.'

Brennan found the stub of his cigar and paused to relight it. In the glow of the match, he could see a large bruise swelling on the side of Lovernios's head, and a patch of discoloured skin.

'I have to admire your dedication,' he admitted, 'if not your cause. Sleeping rough on a Friday night with a sore head isn't my idea of fun. Mind you, it was, not so long ago,' he added ruefully. 'The piss-artist formerly known as Frank Brennan.'

The joke went straight by Lovernios.

'The Celts were skilled survivors, Mr Brennan. The members of the tribe supported each other. There were warriors and strategists and moral leaders.'

'And which one are you?'

'I'm Lovernios – the fox. An advance soldier used to lure the enemy into an area of ambush.'

'Didn't work tonight,' Brennan said as they reached the car.

'We win more than we lose, Mr Brennan. After all, they're only doing it for money. We're not.'

'Get in – you're in no fit state to slog across fields.'

For once there was no argument from Lovernios. Brennan checked the car over – no flat tyres, no smashed windows. He'd been lucky. He drove back towards Tedbury Camp, seeing Lovernios fall asleep in an instant as the adrenalin surge of the fight drained him. Out in front the car's headlights rippled up off the road and starkly illuminated the dead winter hedges and bare trees, making them look like highwaymen in waiting. God only knows what life must be like in that camp, Brennan thought. At least in the sixties there was sex, drugs and music to compensate the drop-out. Now it was all about spiritual matters and being at one with nature.

He turned off at Great Elm, descending the narrow road past warmly lit cottages which glowed with familial security and good cheer, before swinging right past the duck pond and on to the fringes of the wood. A parked car up ahead was suddenly caught in his headlights, revealing a pair of heads and naked shoulders writhing on the back seat. Brennan killed his lights and parked tactfully on the opposite side of the road. He got out and walked round to the passenger door, opening it before gently shaking Lovernios awake.

'Are you sure you want to go back up there?' he asked.

'I must.'

Brennan held the door open and kept it so, allowing the car's courtesy lights to illuminate the stile and the path to the camp beyond it. He walked as far as the stile.

'Do you want me to make sure you manage the climb?'

'My brothers will be down to help me. Thanks.'

'I'll go and see Roadstone International first thing Monday,' Brennan offered as a token reward. 'If there's anything for me to write about, I will.'

'I understand, Mr Brennan. Thank you for making the effort. Goodbye.'

'Take care,' Brennan said, fatuously, he had to admit.

Lovernios was soon swallowed up by the darkness. Brennan slid over the stile in curiosity. He had a niggling, mischievous thought – based on his prolonged observations of ex-public schoolboys who had claimed to be 'roughing it' – that Lovernios might have a luxury Winnebago tucked away in the trees where he could go to take off his first-century make-up before bombing home to his weekend country manor outside Bath.

But as he advanced into the gloom he suddenly saw three or four burning torches weaving their way down from the hill – an escort for the warrior who'd come home. He glimpsed Lovernios in their light, together with three heavily-built male figures in a similar patchwork of clothing. Brennan began to back away. But now the largest of the pack, maybe six feet five, with a full reddish-brown beard and a cascade of hair, advanced towards him, torch aloft. What had looked like shadows falling across his face was in fact, Brennan could now see, a lattice of elaborate tattoos. More alarming, though, was the ornate dagger, with a carved handle and a flat, pewter-coloured blade at least ten inches long, which was tucked into the man's leather belt.

Brennan decided to stand his ground – after all, tonight he had been 'one of them'. The big man stopped about six yards short and stared at him intensely.

'I brought Lovernios back,' Brennan said by way of conversation. 'He got smacked around by the guards. He needs looking after. They filmed us on a camcorder too. Though, come to think of it, I don't suppose you had them in the first century . . . did you?'

His voice tailed off – it was obvious that he was talking to himself. The big man turned and walked away.

'Are you Cernunnos, then?' Brennan shouted.

The big man paused for a moment then resumed his stride. Brennan followed the path of his flaming torch as it rose through the undergrowth and trees and up to the ramparts. And then all was darkness again. He turned and hurried for the comfort of home.

When they had safely returned Lovernios to the camp and laid him out close to the fire on a sheepskin, the tribe set about treating the wounds to his head. Cernunnos mixed a potion of mistletoe and comfrey which he applied to the bruising and swelling on the side of Lovernios's head, while another member of the tribe brewed up a batch of betony tea, a soothing drink which Cernunnos prescribed for the prevention of frightful or monstrous visions in dreams

Once Lovernios was asleep, Cernunnos called up three of his brothers to prepare an attack to avenge this assault. From his store of herbs and grasses, he took a handful of dried wormwood and tossed it into the fire. The pungent, aromatic smoke that arose engulfed both Cernunnos and his chosen warriors. As they inhaled the smoke, their pulses began to race and a sense of excitement gripped them. Cernunnos drew his dagger and let rip a bellowing roar. The warriors collected their swords and followed him down the hillside.

Once at the foot of the ravine, they lay in wait in the undergrowth, alongside the track where the stone trains travelled. Soon they heard the first noises, as the metal rails began to sing of a train's movement. Moments later, the single cyclopic light of the diesel pierced the thin night mist, as it dragged its haul behind it.

The warriors waited until the diesel had passed and then mounted the platforms at the rear of four of the wagons, and began to hack away at the cables and couplings that joined one wagon to another. Sparks flew as their swords beat against the metal couplings, but the brake tubings were sundered, spilling fluid that looked to the warriors like dragon's blood. The train was pulling towards the tunnel now, escaping the tribe's territory. Their work done, Cernunnos signalled for them to leap down. He waited for the last wagon and dragged off its red warning lamp. With due ceremony he raised his dagger high and then jabbed it into the glowing red eye, plunging it instantly into darkness.

Lester was already in bed when Brennan returned, which enabled him to launch straight into his account of the night's events. Janet listened as she cooked and then, satisfied that Brennan had been sufficiently hooked by the conflict between the protesters and the quarry company, she took a file of printed sheets from her briefcase.

'What's this?' he asked suspiciously.

'Background on Roadstone International, the public enquiry over the quarry, and the campaign by Friends of the Earth.' She looked pleased with herself – the researcher feeding her investigative journalist, priming him with enough stimulus for battle, arming him with the right information, was still part of the professional pride she had developed when she had worked in Brennan's office. The fact that their relationship had spilled over into sex, marriage and parenthood didn't diminish the frisson of excitement she felt when she could help even before he'd asked.

'Where did you get this?'

'This company's got quite a good library of local cuttings. They're also on the Internet.'

Brennan growled at this mention.

'I know you shrivel up when new technology is ever mentioned, Frank, but compiling this lot took me less than my one-hour lunch break.'

'All right, so it's efficient. But where's the fun of blagging your way into places? Of bunging an employee for information? Or of getting someone pissed enough to talk candidly? Human contact, I'm talking about – I can tell when somebody's lying when I'm face to face with them. I can't do it just by looking at a computer print-out.'

'I'm waiting for the magic word, Frank.' Janet smiled.

'What, do you mean "invoice"?'

'A simple "thank you" will do,' she said. Brennan was up on his feet in an instant, pulling her towards him, kissing her neck, running his hands up and down her back.

'Don't you want to sample the research first?' she giggled.

'Nutshell it for me,' he panted theatrically, sliding his hands up inside her top in pursuit of the fastening on her bra.

'Basically, the quarry company can do what it wants. It's had an Interim Development Order since 1948, when it was part of the postwar reconstruction, with no limit on depth, none on output either. So it actually doesn't need planning permission – it only needs consent. Are you listening, Frank?'

Brennan had his face buried between her breasts, where his hands now followed.

'You could have told me you were wearing a front-loader!'

He unhooked the bra, allowing the two black lace cups to slide away. His mouth pounced on Janet's left nipple. She was battling now, between passion and professionalism.

'The county of Somerset is obliged by statute to provide twelve million tonnes of stone every year. That's shared between about seven quarries in the East Mendips – so if one closes, the others have to expand. How many tonnes did I say, Frank?'

'Twelve million,' Brennan panted. 'Do I pass "Go"?'

'Can't this wait till after supper?' she asked wryly.

Brennan took her hand and kissed it.

'I'm sorry, love. I just . . . I just got excited.'

'About the story, not me.'

'About both, actually. You know what I'm like when I suddenly get that buzz.'

'Sorry – are we talking about sex or journalism?' she asked teasingly.

'The two are inextricably linked,' he said with an air of mysticism.

'Ah, but which gives you the bigger hard-on?'

'Jan . . . give me a break. You know what a miserable bastard I am to live with when I'm not working.'

'Can you sign a statement to that effect?'

'And you also know how alive I am when I think I'm on to something. It transforms me. I feel like a man again.'

'Well, I'm sorry to douse your ardour, lover, but I'd think twice about this story. The quarry people are doing what they're allowed to do – and eco-warriors are a bit old hat, aren't they, unless there's a new angle.'

'There is! This lot, the Celtic Brotherhood, are a hundred per cent proof nutters. They really believe they live in the past.'

'But that's just offbeat feature material, Frank. Lynda Lee Potter could write about them. It's not the cutting edge of investigative journalism.'

Brennan's mouth tightened – he hated it when he was contradicted, especially when he knew he was wrong.

'But it might be. These two forces – the quarry on one side, the tribe on the other – are immovable.'

'If you read the research I've prepared, you'll find that the quarry people are anything but immovable. They've made all *sorts* of concessions to local opinion.'

'But they're not going to stop digging, are they?'

'That's a fatuous point, Frank. You can't uninvent the wheel. This is just about managing progress. You admit these protesters are nutters, so you can't even claim a rational case on their behalf.'

'But they're sincere nutters.'

'Have you gone native or something?'

'Oh, yeah, sure – I just love spending my winters camping out in the fog, with no access to hot water and only a hole in the ground to shit in!'

'So why the admiration?'

'Because it takes a lot of balls to do that stuff.'

'Let me play devil's advocate here, Frank – pretend I'm Stuart Gill, and you've just pitched me this story. His face is all wrinkled up because he hates offences against personal hygiene, and he just knows these people smell. He also thinks they're a bunch of layabout wankers who are probably signing on for all kinds of state benefits, and conducting this campaign in lieu of anything useful they might do. So, unless Joanna Lumley suddenly joins them and starts living in a yurt, all he's going to ask you to do is dish the dirt on them. Isn't he?'

'All right, so I've got work to do.'

'No – you have to think whether it's *worth* doing any more work, that's what you've got to do.'

Janet refastened her bra, and returned to the stove. Brennan poured himself another slug of red wine and sat down at the kitchen table. He took a brief look at the notes and papers that she had brought home, and then pushed them to one side.

'Do you want to take it over, then?' he asked cautiously.

Janet half turned to give him a frown.

'The story. For your documentary company.'

'This isn't about territory, Frank. I'm not trying to subvert you – just stop you wasting your time.'

'So it wouldn't interest your people?'

'It might. I haven't put it to them yet. As I said, I think they've had enough road protests.'

'I'm planning to go in on Monday to see Roadstone International, and if I draw a blank I'll let the story go. How's that?'

'You don't need my advice. You know when you're itching to do something or not. Trust your instincts.'

'I'm not sure I can any more. I'm on a different beat now, aren't I? Odd people drop me letters, or call at my house – it's a world away from secret briefings in Whitehall, or illicit tapes, or stolen documents.'

'You sound nostalgic.'

'Not really – I just remember it still. The former life. Which means I can't fully understand this one yet.'

'Must be a boon not to have MI5 dickheads tapping your phone or following you around.'

'Who says they have?'

'Dream on, Frank. All that stuff died with Mark. They got him, you didn't get them. It's over – you're not a "player" any more.'

Brennan reflected sadly on the unfinished business of the strange death of his Home Office 'mole', Mark Fraser-Williams. The acute frustration of not being able to find or expose his killers had ebbed away now to become just an occasional spasm of guilt, but the spasms were becoming more and more infrequent. Maybe time did heal the hidden wounds as well as those on the surface. But in the private corners of his heart, he did miss the idea of the security services having to pay him attention. He was definitely Endsleigh League material now, not Carling Premiership, the only remaining doubt being in which division he was actually placed.

The footballing metaphor lingered long enough for Brennan to suggest to Lester the following morning that they should go to a game. Lester expertly sprung the trap.

'Arsenal are at Villa today, Dad. It's only an hour and a half or so on the train from Bristol to Birmingham.'

'I was thinking more of a local game – Swindon or Bristol Rovers.'

Lester clapped his hands to his face in melodramatic fashion.

'Somebody from school might see me.'

'You're a local lad now, so support a local team.'

'Only the "sads" go and watch them, Dad. Everybody else supports Spurs, or Manchester United or Liverpool.'

Brennan could sense his son's anguish, vaguely remembering one of his own teenage tantrums when he'd been denied the ultimate Mod icon, a pink Ben Sherman with button-down collar, by his parents.

'All right – Villa Park, provided they're not sold out.'

Fortunately, the allure of Arsenal – even with Dennis

Bergkamp and David Platt – was still not convincing the nation, and Brennan was able to secure a credit-card booking for two good tickets in the visitors' section at Villa Park that afternoon. Lester had whooped with joy at the news, a pleasure that dissolved all parental worries about expense or travel. He quickly changed into his new Arsenal shirt, though the effect was somewhat muted by Janet's insistence on him wearing his padded winter jacket over it.

The journey up to Birmingham went smoothly enough, but the match was no great shakes, despite Lester's enthusiasm for every touch Bergkamp made. Brennan wondered, silently, whether English football might be becoming a substitute for empire, replacing the lost colonies by way of the acquisition of foreign talent. The notion didn't last much longer than the first drink on the return train, and Brennan dumped an idea to sell a piece on his theory to the *New Statesman*.

Lester was already yawning as he and Brennan made their way back up the hill to Tory from Bradford's station. They were back on time as promised, but the instant Brennan saw Janet's face, he knew something was wrong.

'Go and have your bath right away, Lester,' she commanded. Lester, sensing her mood, didn't argue, but gave Brennan a sympathetic look as he disappeared upstairs to his room.

'Let me guess – you suddenly found yourself asking why you were at home preparing dinner while Lester and I were out enjoying ourselves? And then, having established an ongoing New Man conspiracy involving us making all the right noises about sharing the work, but then doing nothing about it, you decided to get angry.'

'The police have been round looking for you, Frank. They want to interview you regarding an incident of "aggravated trespass" on last night's excursion into the quarry.'

'How – all we did was climb over a fence?'

'That's what this copper said. Wants you to report to Bradford police station Monday morning at eleven – otherwise they'll issue an arrest warrant.'

'Did they say how they'd got my name?'

Janet shrugged angrily.

'What am I? The National Council for Civil Liberties?'

'Those bloody security guards have got a cheek, considering what they did to that lad. If they want to start playing court games, I'll have them in for GBH. See how they like that!'

'Oddly enough, the police seemed to think that your mate would be charged with assault if they can get hold of him.'

Brennan registered the arch and agitated tone in her voice.

'Hey, come on, Jan, you've had worse than this – local coppers wittering on. It's not so long ago we had MI5 freelances swarming all over the house. Things *are* improving.'

'I still don't like them coming to our house, Frank. I respect your work, and I love you as a man, but this part of the job just does my head in, you know. Turning up on the doorstep just as it's gone dark, eyes turning over every corner of the room.'

'Janet – it's a very minor charge. It's a frightener from the quarry company, that's all. The security guards probably get a bonus for every name they come up with.'

'Your name will end up in the papers – for the *wrong* reasons.'

'Oh, come on, calm down. I was being charged with murder last year after Mark's death, and half the town knows I did time for contempt of court. Aggravated trespass isn't much of a stain on my character, even if they make it stick.'

'Maybe not – but in the context of a small town, it marks you down as, what, a loony, a troublemaker.'

'I'd prefer the word "dissident", but even that's exaggerating the issue here, for God's sake.'

'I just worry about Lester – what they might think of things like this at his school.'

'He told me that all his mates were seriously envious of having a father who'd been to gaol.'

'I meant the *teachers* – what they might think of you, and of him by association.'

'They can think what they like, frankly. Their job's to teach children, whatever their parents do for a living. Nobody said anything to you at the parents' evening last term, did they?'

'No – but I could tell that a few of them had us down as media ponces.'

'It's more likely to be simple curiosity – trying to balance all their lurid preconceptions about us against what turns out to be our overwhelming ordinariness.'

'You don't think we're ordinary, do you?'

'Damn right I don't,' Brennan said with a smile. 'How many teachers get arrested for aggravated trespass on a Friday night?'

Roadstone International's Head of Public Affairs was already waiting in the lobby for Brennan when he arrived at their regional offices outside Frome first thing Monday morning. Brennan had asked at the reception counter if he could speak to somebody in public relations, but it just happened that Mr Len Trilling was right there.

'We phoned your home, Mr Brennan. Your wife told us you were on your way over to see us. Understandably so in the circumstances.'

'I just wanted to . . .'

Trilling struck a sudden, forced pose of hospitality, gesturing Brennan towards the lift doors as if he were a visiting dignitary.

'If you'd be so kind. We can talk in my office.'

Brennan hadn't expected a charm offensive – if that's what this was going to be – and was consequently unnerved for a few moments. The self-righteous momentum he'd been building since breakfast suddenly had nowhere to go in the face of this bland welcome. As the lift doors opened on the third, and uppermost, floor, the first thing he saw was a large Technicolour photo, taken from a plane or, more likely, a helicopter, of the quarry site, and the fields and lanes that surrounded it. The photo had been framed, but not glazed, and hung on the wall of the main corridor. So much for corporate art.

Nevertheless, Trilling stood before the photo as if it were a Constable landscape, oozing pride at its presence.

'I don't imagine you managed to see too much on Friday night, Mr Brennan.'

'You'd be surprised,' Brennan said acidly, but to no effect.

'That's roughly where you were. Down here's the offices, then these are . . .'

'The primary crushing sheds,' Brennan interrupted, before placing his own finger on the photograph. He traced a line across

49

the left-hand edge of the quarry, circling a farmhouse and a narrow lane alongside it.

'And that's your proposed expansion area, isn't it?'

'Subject to Department of Environment approval, yes.'

'Come, come, Mr Trilling – you know you'll get it, don't you? Your parent company donated two hundred thousand pounds to Conservative Party funds in the year 1994–95. I've seen the accounts.'

'The DOE is not the government, Mr Brennan. Look, my office is right here. Why don't we have a coffee and a talk.'

Brennan looked at his watch theatrically.

'I'm due to see the Wiltshire Police in Bradford in an hour or so.'

'You'll find the charges have been dropped, actually, Mr Brennan. Do come in.'

Brennan had no choice but to accept Trilling's invitation. The pleasant reception and the waiving of criminal charges had outflanked him completely. Trilling may have been Head of Public Affairs for the company in this region, but all the evidence suggested some late spin from Head Office.

As Trilling poured coffee in his office, Brennan guessed out loud what the small chain of reaction might have been over the weekend.

'The guards report the trespass, selectively, and show the video to their superiors; my name is somehow extracted, probably from a patrol spotting my car parked close to the quarry, and then the police are informed; regional office faxes London expecting a Blue Peter badge; Head Office faxes back saying you've got a bolshie journo in the net, drop him out.'

Trilling brought the coffee to him in his chair, offering him a small tray of cream, sugar and fancy biscuits.

'You're not far out, Mr Brennan. I'm afraid it was a case of our security people getting a little too excited.'

'In terms of what – trying to put the frighteners on me?'

'The quarry is a very dangerous place, Mr Brennan. We accept that intruders and protesters will get in from time to time, but we cannot be held responsible for their safety. That's what really frightens us – the possibility of a horrendous accident. Sometimes it pays to scare people for their own good.'

Brennan looked at Trilling – he was about the same age, wire-framed glasses, greying hair – checking for the possibility of a coded warning, the equivalent of the old East End 'We wouldn't want anyone to get hurt' mantra. But there was no edge or additional tone in his voice.

'I accept your reassurances,' Brennan said blandly, 'but from what I saw on Friday, your security people have an emphatic way of dealing with people.'

'You were most unfortunate in your choice of company, Mr Brennan. We've suffered multiple incursions and massive vandalism from these Celtic Brotherhood people. The guards have been threatened and terrorised several times.'

'To be frank, they looked to me as though they could handle themselves.'

'You don't understand. It's been not so much physical as mental. These people, the tribe, have put curses on the guards. They leave dead animals in their cars, or smear the windscreens with blood. Bones have been left in strange configurations.'

Brennan sucked in air in a gesture of mock horror.

'Wow – and I thought hitting people over the head with truncheons was bad.'

Trilling crossed to a glass-fronted wall cabinet and took down a tape from a stack of about a dozen or more. He crossed to the television and video unit on a stand by the door and inserted the tape.

'We filmed this about a month or so ago.'

He switched on the television and soon shaky, obviously hand-held footage appeared on the screen. A loaded quarry train was trundling out from the railhead under the road bridge outside the quarry and on into a cutting beyond. From the slopes, shadowy figures now emerged, clambering on to the wagons waving what looked like sticks. Whoever the cameraman was, he had now broken into a jog, trying to get closer to the attackers. They numbered about eight from what Brennan could see, and among them he recognised the forms of Lovernios and Cernunnos. Trilling froze the tape for a moment.

'This one's their leader apparently.' His finger rested on the eerily preserved image of Cernunnos.

'We think that's probably some kind of sword in his hand. If I roll the tape on . . . you can see that he's making hacking motions. And what he's actually trying to do is sever the brake cables which link each wagon to the diesel power-train.'

Brennan peered at the images. Trilling's interpretation seemed undeniable. He could now see Lovernios standing in the centre of one wagon, throwing great handfuls of stone out on to the track, even directing one at the cameraman.

'I understand from the interviews our security people undertook with the guards that this one' – Trilling instantly fingered Lovernios on the screen – 'was your companion. And that he committed the first assault by drop-kicking one of the guards. True or false?'

'Technically true – but I'd say it was a case of him getting his retaliation in first. He knew what was coming.'

'You don't know that, Mr Brennan. You also don't know that later on Friday night, well into Saturday morning in fact, one of our trains was the subject of another attack. They managed to sever the brakes on four wagons, and worse still, to remove the red warning light on the last truck. It takes upwards of a mile to stop these trains at the best of times, Mr Brennan. But with faulty brakes and no warning lights, you have the recipe for a major rail disaster.'

'Look – I am not an apologist for these protesters. I went along to hear their argument, to see their evidence.'

'Of what? We're completely open about our business. We sell roadstone, seventy per cent of it to construction companies in the south-east for road maintenance work. We are demand-led. We don't blast for the fun of it. If the orders are there, we fulfil them. If not we have to cut back on production and stockpile material.'

'Business must be booming if you're planning an expansion?'

'One doesn't follow the other – there are cuts in road spending now. But we must plan for the future. To go wider, rather than deeper. It's all been heard at the public inquiries.'

'It's just a job, then?'

'Several hundred jobs, actually. Thousands if you count the lorry drivers, the train crews, the distribution staff, the . . .'

'Please. You've made your point. I understand it even. But

what I don't get from you is any sense of history, or spirituality. And for better or worse *they* have it.'

Brennan pointed at the screen, where the train was now leaving its rag-taggle attackers behind, waving and gesticulating triumphantly.

'I'm not sure where either of those come into it. It's a hole in the ground, that's all.'

'To them, it's sacred.'

'I think that's sentimental tosh, to be frank. Sorry, no pun intended.'

Brennan smiled wearily. He'd heard it hundreds of times.

'Well, I'd say that as long as you don't understand them, you'll never defeat them. Technically perhaps, but not emotionally.'

'Oh, we'll beat them all right. At the right time and in the right place. We've bent over backwards to tolerate them, for fear of inflaming emotions. And every time we give in to them, they keep taking liberties. But it'll end soon.'

'What do you mean?'

'I can't give out operational details. All I can say is that we will continue to operate within the law. I hope you'll put that in your newspaper story.'

'I'm not writing one. Yet.'

Trilling rose to indicate that Brennan's time was up. Brennan drained his coffee cup and stood up.

'One last question – how did you trace me? I used to have a photo above my column in the old days, but I wouldn't have thought your security boys were typical readers.'

'Well, there must have been a bright one on duty that night.'

'If you're getting access to police computers for private addresses, that's an offence. I may also exercise my rights under the Data Protection Act to see the file you have on me.'

'There isn't one, Mr Brennan. And we'll destroy your rather offensive little declaration to our video camera. That could damage your image if it fell into the wrong hands. You didn't trespass. We didn't press charges. You and I have never met. How's that?'

'A little melodramatic, if I may say so. Thanks for the coffee.'

He made his way out of the office, and Trilling escorted him to the lifts. But while he was waiting for the lift to come up to the third floor, the phone on Trilling's desk began to ring.

'I bet there's a few of them stacked up while we've been talking,' Trilling said self-pityingly. He shook Brennan's hand and dived back into his office, closing the door behind him. The lift arrived. Brennan took one last look as the aerial photograph of the quarry and went into the lift.

'No, no – he's just left this instant,' Trilling said to his phone caller. 'He wasn't too bad, actually. No pushover, but not the screaming Trot one might have suspected. Anyway, his visit's timed and logged now. You can release the news as soon as you like. Quietly, and with great regret, of course. Indeed, the word "tragic" *does* spring to mind.'

Chapter Four

They had found the body at around 7.30 that morning at one of the depots in West London where the roadstone was transferred from rail to lorry for, as Trilling had said, 'onward distribution to customers'. It had been mere chance that the driver of this particular lorry had been watching the flurry of 'scalpings', the smallest calibre of stones, tumble off the conveyor belt into the back of his truck. His eye, unused to anything other than the grey shower of dust and stones had instantly registered the larger object which had tumbled off the chute. It had taken him a minute or so to get the belt stopped, so by that time the body had been reburied under the load in the back of the truck.

The depot manager had been sceptical at first, but the driver had pointed out that he wouldn't move until he'd had his load checked. He wasn't about to deliver to the site of a new by-pass in Kent, only to find he was tipping a body into the path of the bulldozers and steam-rollers.

'Are you sure it was a human?' the depot manager had asked. 'We sometimes get dogs or even farm animals who've slipped down sidings and into the rail wagons.'

'Well, I could swear it had arms and legs, so that makes it human in my book.'

The depot manager reluctantly gave the order for the lorry's load to be tipped out on to open ground. At first, as the lorry bucked and stuttered its load out, nothing could be seen. Then suddenly, the lower section of an arm poked up through the stones.

'Stop, stop!' the depot manager had yelled.

The lorry driver had jumped down from his cab and come round to see that he had been proved right after all.

'See, told you. Want me to dig him out?'

'You stay right there. The police can sort this.'

The depot manager had then crossed to his little administration hut and called his local police station. He'd also called the main Roadstone International office in London to warn them of the finding. Len Trilling's colleague, Steve McMichael, Director of Communications, had shouted 'Bloody fuck!' down the phone in reaction to the news, but had then agreed, as he calmed down, that the police should make the running. He drove over to the depot immediately, ringing around the company's directors, including Trilling, from his car phone to alert them to the news.

By the time he'd got to the depot, two police constables were already at the scene. They were reluctant to disinter the body until a forensic scientist and a police photographer arrived. Instead, they took notes and statements. From the lorry driver, and the depot manager, about how the body had been discovered, and at what time.

The train that had carried it had been one of four that had travelled through the night from the railhead at the Roadstone International quarry in the East Mendips. The train driver, a British Rail employee, had by now signed off and gone for a late breakfast at one of the local caffs. He was due back at eleven to take the empty train back up to Somerset.

So the lorry driver and the depot manager repeated their stories for the police, while Steve McMichael listened in, and every so often wandered off with his mobile phone clutched to his ear, whispering tensely into it.

The depot manager had been obliged to suspend unloading operations while the initial enquiries were made, and there was soon a noisy jam of lorries demanding access to their loads, body or no body. One of the policemen had had to break off to let these drivers know that nobody would be going anywhere until the body had been examined and taken away, so they could just shut it and sit in their cabs until they were told.

Eventually, the police photographer and the forensic scientist had arrived, donned their white nylon boiler suits, bootees and gloves and set about their work. The photographer took some stills of the arm projecting from the stone, and then the scientist clambered up the slope of stones and began to scrape them away by hand to reveal more of the body, taking care not to discard any unusual items.

By now a detective had arrived to supervise the enquiry. Chain-smoking, paunchy, polystyrene cup permanently in his hand, he'd urged the forensic man to get a move on. But this only encouraged the scientist to go even more slowly. Gradually, though, the shoulder and chest of the body were revealed, clothed in a tattered mixture of green, hand-knitted top and a cloak or jacket of other material, probably canvas. And now, on the upper arm, there was a band of reddish fur. The forensic scientist paused while more photographs were taken and then cleared more stones off the body. Both arms were now free – the other was decorated with a fur band too – and so he called up one of the constables to help him lift the body by pulling on both arms.

The little clutch of people gathered around, whose day had suddenly turned unnatural, watched as the policeman and the scientist tugged gently on the arms. Slowly the body rose from the stones, but it was clear as soon as it was pulled into an upright position, that whoever it had been had suffered a violent decapitation, for only the stump of the neck, with flaps of raw bloodied skin dangling and the point of spinal cord protruding like a fish-bone, remained.

'Fucking hell,' the detective had moaned, not in horror, because he'd seen much worse in his time, but because he knew that the remaining twenty tonnes of stone which had passed from wagon to lorry, and perhaps the whole trainload, would now have to be searched in order to find the head.

'I fucking hate torsos,' he snapped before lighting another cigarette. 'Fucking hate them.'

Within half an hour, the body had been removed to the morgue of the nearest hospital and more policemen in blue boiler suits had been brought in to sift through the lorry's load.

Meanwhile the train driver had returned from his fry-up to find a maelstrom of questions flying at him. 'Had he seen any "jumpers" from bridges? Had he seen anybody climbing on the wagons?'

And when he said, 'Only the usual lot, outside the quarry, protesting,' both Steve McMichael of Roadstone International and the police detective had smiled simultaneously in relief, because they knew that the case was no longer 'on their patch'.

Indeed, after a fruitless search for the missing head, and a decision by the detective to free the train's load for distribution – 'Tell all your fucking navvies to keep their eyes out for big lumps in the tarmac, eh?' he had told the lorry drivers – the photographer and the forensic scientist and the policemen and the corporate spin doctor went off to resume their working days, while the depot returned to its daily drudgery of shifting stones around South-East England.

The first Brennan heard of the death was later that evening, on the regional television news. Janet hurtled down from the living-room, shouting anxiously.

'Frank, Frank – get up here!'

By the time he'd climbed the stairs to the first floor, the news report was halfway through. Janet simply pointed at the screen. Brennan looked. A reporter in his mid-thirties was standing outside the main gate of Roadstone International saying: '. . . although identification has yet to take place, it is believed that the body may be that of one of a regular group of protesters against the quarry's expansion scheme. Drivers of the quarry trains have reported frequent incidents of the protesters climbing aboard the wagons. With me is Roadstone International's Director of Public Affairs, Len Trilling . . .'

The camera now panned left to reveal Trilling standing alongside the reporter, wearing a blue hard-hat.

'It's a tragic event,' Trilling was saying, as if in a trance. 'But some of these protesters have taken their campaign to the very limit of safety, both their own and that of our staff.'

'Did they give any descriptions?' Brennan asked Janet quickly.

'No – just male, that's all.'

'Will you be stepping up security in the light of this accident?' the television reporter asked Trilling.

'Well, we wouldn't wish to prejudge the outcome of any inquest, but obviously we have to look at our operational methods in a new light,' Trilling said.

'Bastard!' shouted Brennan.

The report ended. He punched at the off-switch.

'No wonder Trilling was so keen to sweetheart me this morning. He must have known about this already.'

'Wouldn't he have wanted you well out of the way?'

'They were about to press charges against me when somebody at Head Office must have twigged my name, and they suddenly realise they have a shit-stirrer on their hands.'

'So? I'd still want you at arm's length in that case.'

Brennan's face suddenly whitened.

'Christ, it's Lovernios.'

'What?'

'The kid I was with on Friday night – it must have been him who got killed. That's why they were so keen to accommodate me. Better to have me pacified than storming in there demanding to know what had happened.'

He moved quickly to the stairs.

'I'm going to the camp.'

'Is that wise?'

'Fuck wisdom, Janet. I saw two guards beat the shit out of this kid on Friday night, and now he'd dead.'

'Wasn't your fault, Frank.'

'No, but it may not have been bad luck, either. Can you tape any other news reports for me?'

He turned back to collect his mobile phone.

'I'll call you later.'

'Frank – for God's sake take care!'

But he was already at the foot of the stairs, ripping his coat off the wall rack.

He drove across to Frome in a turmoil. Deaths still got to him despite years of covering murders and vile killings. It wasn't just the fact of death which disturbed him, but the implications it created. Silencing witnesses, hot-blooded revenge, sexual jealousy, corporate intrigue were all motives he'd come across before, revealing a side of human nature he preferred not to think about. And although a death elevated his investigations to the status of urgent, he knew the journalistic frustrations it also created, because half of the story had usually died with the victim.

Soon he was turning his car down the hill towards the duck pond at Great Elm, and approaching the footpath that led to the camp. A car was parked up alongside the wooden stile, and as his headlights illuminated it, he could see the day-glo orange strip on its flanks. The uniformed constable was out of his car as soon as Brennan approached, flashing his torch into his face.

'It's all right, Officer. I'm here for the same reason you are.'

He held up his yellow, laminated press card, carefully keeping his thumb over the expiry date of 1994.

'Sorry, sir. Who are you with?'

'I'm a local freelance. One of the nationals asked me to come down and find out what was going on.'

The constable put his body between Brennan and the stile.

'Sorry, sir. There's a press conference tomorrow morning at ten a.m. in Frome.'

'They want something from me before then,' Brennan blustered, putting on his 'isn't life a bitch?' expression which had served him well enough in the past.

'Sorry, sir – I can't let you go through there. They'll be mounting a search at first light.'

'A search? What for?'

'Whoever it was didn't have his head on when he was found. They reckon it may be along the railway line somewhere.'

Brennan reeled at the horror of the image.

'Who does – Roadstone International?'

'Well, London – they've handed it over to us.'

'Look – I think I know who it might have been.'

'How's that, sir?' asked the constable, taking a step closer.

'Long story – but if I'm right, your male body's no more than twenty years old. About five ten, with his head that is. Dressed in rags. Fox-fur armbands on each arm. Am I close?'

'How did you know him?' the constable said, inadvertently confirming Brennan's suspicions that Lovernios was indeed the victim.

'Well – I'd been preparing a piece on the protest about the

quarry. I talked to this kid. He took me in there on Friday night. Showed me around.'

The notebook came out instantly. A keen sort, Brennan guessed, probably sees himself as CID material.

'Do you have a name?'

'No – only what he called himself. Lovernios.'

'What?'

'It's a Celtic name – something to do with a fox. He belonged to something called the Celtic Brotherhood. They seem to live up there – it's the site of an old Celtic hill-fort.'

The policeman's pencil sped across the page.

'I think you'd better talk to one of our detectives.'

'Sure. Anybody been up there to talk to them yet?'

'We're waiting on the coroner. There's a preliminary inquest tomorrow morning. That'll be adjourned while further enquiries are made.'

'I know the procedures, Constable. Done plenty of these in my time.'

'These?'

'Suspicious deaths.'

The constable blurted out an ironic laugh.

'Not much suspicion about it from what I hear. Stupid bastards have been climbing aboard moving trains. Only a matter of time before one of them got himself killed.'

Brennan checked his urge to argue. That would have to wait for the inquest.

'Any other papers been around?' he asked, with an edge of furtiveness that suggested it was just another enquiry. The policeman smiled in weary recognition – the desperate hack, trying to keep one step ahead of the opposition.

'Not down here. Local TV's been up to the quarry getting statements.'

'I saw the report.'

'That's all there is so far.'

Brennan hunched up his shoulders into his coat.

'Thought I'd given up ambulance-chasing years ago. Oh, well. Suppose I'd better get off and file some bullshit to keep them happy. You on all night?'

61

'Just till eleven. Got some other poor bastard coming on till morning.'

Brennan cursed himself – he should have brought his hip-flask. There was nothing like a nip of brandy to get a cold, resentful, bored copper on your side.

'Want me to pop up to the pub and get you a drink or anything?'

'Thanks – but I've got a flask of coffee in the car.'

'Good thinking. I'll be off, then. Have a quiet night.'

He turned to go.

'One thing . . .'

'Yeah?'

'Your name and address, sir?'

Brennan gave his details and returned to the car, giving a fraternal toot on the horn as he turned it and steered back past the duck pond up into the village. Once he'd reached the row of cottages, however, he parked up, fished out his torch, and made his way back down the hill on foot. The policeman was back in his car. The map-reading light was on, and he was pouring himself coffee from a flask. Brennan hugged the edge of the road, where the night was darkest, and skipped into the undergrowth out of sight. He couldn't put the torch on yet, so he paused and listened for the bubbling of the stream, and then moved closer to it. Soon he was upon it, and moved out along its bank, parallel to the footpath, and began to climb the hill towards the camp.

He switched on his torch, grateful for the instant companionship its light delivered. He advanced up through the bracken, dodging around the bare branches which tugged at his jacket. The night was a cold one and his breath steamed out in front of him, looking ghostly in the torchlight.

As he reached the upper levels of the hill, he became aware of scented smoke and, after switching off his torch, could see the glow of a bonfire among the trees at the top of the hill. He crouched low and advanced cautiously. And then, as he reached the hill's overgrown earth ramparts, he could, for the first time, see the broad plateau that was the hill's summit.

A large wood fire was burning at the heart of a clearing in the trees about forty yards away, sending out billows of richly perfumed smoke. And around the fire, sitting cross-legged, were six or seven figures in the familiar ragged garb of the Celtic Brotherhood. Brennan couldn't be certain whether Lovernios was one of them or not, such was the camouflaged unity of their clothes. But standing in front of them on the other side of the fire was Cernunnos, although Brennan had to guess this from his size, for his body was draped in an ashen-coloured Druidical robe while over his face was a carved metallic mask. It was almost featureless, literally faceless with only three slits to represent eyes and mouth, and it was so long that it also concealed the man's beard. Brennan could now hear a low rhythmic chanting, a response to the noises and gestures made by Cernunnos.

Brennan had been a reluctant door-stepper at the best of times, preferring research and oblique contact to out-and-out confrontation, and this certainly didn't seem the moment to approach the tribe for a considered opinion about the death of one of its members. More potently, he felt a genuine apprehension at the strangeness of this ritual, even though its tone was one of lament rather than threat. He slid noiselessly back down the hill, alert to pursuers from above, or indeed police from below. By the time he'd got back to his car, his pulse was racing, his skin felt clammy with sweat and his throat was parched from the smoke. There was also a perceptible sense of giddiness, an effect he put down to whatever incense had been added to the fire.

Against his better judgment, Brennan found himself driving towards the quarry in a spasm of curiosity. As he hit the perimeter road, he immediately saw two security guards patrolling inside the boundary fence, and at both main gates there were another four helmeted guards, conspicuously flashing their torches at passing cars in a show of bravado and intimidation. He hoped that they had spotted his car's number-plate again, because any further comeback would give him conclusive proof that the security guards, or the company that supplied them, had illicit access to the vehicle licensing computer in Swansea. A security company jeep, with an orange light flashing self-importantly on the roof of its cab, began to loom in his driving mirror. He accelerated away, spinning his rear tyres. The guards would love that.

Once clear of the quarry, he drove home more steadily, becoming aware that his senses had been distorted. Car chases were not his scene. Nor was parading in front of his opponents. It felt as though he'd been induced into a show of aggression. As though he'd had several shots of brandy – but he knew that he hadn't. The scented incense of the bonfire plainly boasted more than just pretty smells.

He opened his window, grateful for the burst of cold air, and gradually a sense of calm and relief came over him as the effects of the incense wore off. The road into Bradford, with its warmly lit pubs like beacons in the night, comforted him with its familiarity, and for the time being at least his glimpse into another world faded.

Brennan was up, breakfasted and out, dressed like an ordinary commuter, the following morning, dropping Lester off at school before heading for the police station at Frome. The intense overnight frost had iced almost every surface, whether man-made or natural, and the stretches of road between towns and villages remained treacherous, adding to his pulse rate as he tried to keep control of the car while de-icing the inside of the windscreen with the back of his glove.

Gradually the car warmed up, and the welcome crunch of grit under the wheels – he didn't care whether it came from shore or quarry as long as it saved lives – removed one level of agitation. But he knew that, unlike his millions of fellow commuters, he was using the weather as a distraction from his real thoughts.

He was going back where he started – police rooms, cautious briefings from officers with every understanding of crime but no grasp of the English language, planted hints about what they thought they couldn't say officially. He must have been through the routine a hundred times or more, from small-town killings to big-city corruption cases, but this particular morning felt like it was the first day of his career all over again. And it certainly didn't help his equilibrium that, when he was escorted down to the briefing-room by a WPC, the other four journalists in there looked half his age. He recognised the local TV reporter from the previous evening's broadcast and nodded at him in recognition, although the gesture wasn't returned.

'Frank Brennan,' he announced tamely, but the other three journalists looked at him blankly – the name meant nothing to this new generation of truth-hunters. He mooched around the room. A desk and two chairs had been laid out at the back, in front of a wooden replica of the badge of Avon & Somerset Police.

'They not letting your camera crew in?' he asked the TV reporter chattily.

His observation drew a first sign of fraternity from the TV reporter.

'I bet the Chief's been on to them. Get them to damp it all down. They hate it when a case touches on a public issue. The anti-quarry mob will try to turn this daft sod into a martyr now.'

Brennan felt a sudden stab of anger at hearing Lovernios talked about in such functional terms, but allowed himself a moment before responding.

'He *had* a name,' he said curtly.

'They haven't released it yet, have they?' said the TV reporter, completely missing the tone in Brennan's voice. The boy obviously had a great future sticking a microphone up the noses of the bereaved and asking, 'How does it feel . . . ?'

'No,' said Brennan. 'Nobody knows who he was.'

The door to the room swung open and a suited detective and a uniformed sergeant marched in.

'Morning, lads,' burred the detective. 'Surprised you ain't down on the A303 waiting for pile-ups in the ice.'

The detective sat behind the desk, taking the name-tag of his lapel – DI Gary Blackwell – and then putting it on to the Formica surface in front of him. The four journalists promptly placed tape recorders on to the desk. Brennan winced – he'd been in too much of a rush to remember. He folded his notebook open and scraped the barnacles off his shorthand as the press pack seated itself.

'This is Sergeant Dean Harris,' Blackwell said, emphasising all three syllables for the journalists' benefit. 'He will be acting as the coroner's officer in the lead-up to the inquest, making any enquiries the coroner deans . . . *deems.*' He thumbed his front teeth in mock retribution.

'How come the inquest's down here?' asked the TV reporter.

'West London don't want it. They take the view that although the body was found there, it emanated – is that the right word? – from here. Also, obviously, any potential witnesses will be mainly local. So the East Somerset Coroner has accepted jurisdiction. He has formally opened and adjourned the inquest just now, to allow Dean to get on. And I can confirm that the coroner will be conducting the inquest before a jury.'

Brennan raised a hand.

'A new face . . .' Blackwell smiled. 'But been around, by the look of it.'

'Frank Brennan. I . . .'

'Of?'

'I'm freelance.'

Sergeant Harris leant across and whispered in Blackwell's ear before Blackwell nodded at Brennan to proceed with his question.

'Any progress towards identification of the body yet?'

'Not much. The corpse is being transported up here this morning for a post-mortem. Still no sign of the head, so there won't be no photographs for you lot to go on.'

There was a rustle of grim laughter among the journalists.

'You any nearer knowing how he died?' asked one of the cub reporters.

'That's what the inquest's for, son. We just help gather evidence for now.'

'What about interviewing the other members of the tribe?' Brennan asked earnestly.

Blackwell and Harris laughed openly.

'They ain't no "tribe" as far as I know. Just the usual New Age travellers an' such,' Blackwell said, with a look to the other journalists which said, 'Who *is* this berk?'

'With respect, Detective Inspector,' Brennan said, retaliating politely, 'I think you'll find they are a bit more organised and purposeful than New Age travellers.'

'I'll be talking to them as soon as possible,' Sergeant Harris interjected, catching Brennan with his look.

'Can I just offer a word or two of advice on this, fellers,' Blackwell cajoled. 'This quarry has been the scene of a lot of protests over the years, some more extreme than others. So I'd request that you be careful about inflaming old wounds. We don't want mass demos or nothing down here because of what this kid managed to do to himself.'

'Did to himself? You're prejudging the inquest a little, aren't you?'

Blackwell glared at Brennan, sensing a 'smart-arse' for the first time.

'No, that's what I'm trying to stop any of you lot doing – I wouldn't want anything too lurid. So I'd ask yourselves a few questions about the effect of what you might say or write before you starts mentioning missing heads an' such. We'll have all the ghouls from miles around out otherwise.'

Blackwell stood to bring the conference to an end. The journalists and the TV reporter collected their tape recorders and muttered their thanks.

'Mr Brennan,' Blackwell called out, with a smirk playing right across his chubby face. 'Sergeant Harris needs to talk to you, I gather. So, no time like the present, eh?'

He ushered Harris and Brennan out of the room before turning to answer the inevitable question on the other journalists' lips.

'He ain't getting no favours or nothing, fellers. Just that he was with the deceased the other night, so he might have something for us.'

'Pity the bastard wouldn't share it with us,' growled the TV reporter as he pressed the rewind button on his cassette recorder.

Sergeant Harris brought Brennan a mug of tea and a Kit-Kat and then sat down opposite him in the cramped interview room. He sipped his own mug of tea and nibbled a biscuit before opening up his large red notebook.

'I expect you've done one of these before, man of your experience, Mr Brennan?'

'Not from this angle, Sergeant. I'm usually out there asking you questions.'

'How did you manage your time in Erlestoke?'

Brennan could see the top sheet of a photocopied file under Harris's ledger.

'Fine – I dried out, lost weight, got fit. I can recommend it. But my being in there has no relevance to your enquiries.'

'Coroner wouldn't like it if he knew I'd been taking an ex-con's word as gospel.'

'What is it – got a journalist with attitude on your hands, not that bunch of yes-kids outside? Is that what's eating you?'

'Just be careful with your smart-arse London stuff, Mr Brennan, that's all I'm saying. Can get people's backs up round here.'

'I *live* here. I'm not visiting.'

'Right. We know from what Roadstone International told us that you were trespassing on the quarry site last Friday.'

'I was looking around, not trespassing. They dropped the charges, remember?'

'For now they have. You told one of our constables at the travellers' camp . . .'

'They're *not* travellers. They've been living up on that fort for a while. They're trying to re-create a Celtic camp. As part of their protest against the quarry.'

Harris sipped his tea, waiting for Brennan to finish his point.

'You told our constable that you thought you might know the identity of the deceased.'

'Only in terms of the name he used in the camp.'

'This business about the fox-fur armbands . . .'

'That's what he wore. Lovernios means "the fox".'

'But some of the others might be wearing the same gear?'

'It's possible.'

'If the bloke you spoke to is our body, what can you tell us about him?'

'I gave age details to the constable. I presume they fit?'

The sergeant nodded.

'He seemed very well spoken. Educated. Probably public school. Intense kid – but likeable in his way.'

'Opinions are for the expert witnesses, Mr Brennan. Did he tell you about attacking the trains?'

'More or less. He didn't go into specifics.'

'But you formed the impression that part and parcel of living at this camp was attempting to stop the stone being taken out of the quarry?'

'Kind of you to put words into my mouth – if anything I think the protest came first followed by the camp. I think I remember him saying he was "at war".'

'With the quarry, it's guards?'

'Both, I expect. Certainly seemed that way when the guards beat him up on Friday night. You will be talking to *them*, I hope?'

'I'm sure. What happened?'

'It was obviously a common enough skirmish. He recognised them, they recognised him. He, Lovernios, had a go first, then one of them whacked him on the head with a truncheon. You can probably still see the wounds.'

'If we ever find the head.'

Brennan mentally noted the convenience of its disappearance in this instance.

'Did it surprise you to find that this . . . man should die?'

'It shocked me. If I'm truthful, I can't say it was a surprise. There was something doomed about him. He was passionately committed to fighting what he believed was a crime against nature. That kind of passion always gets you into trouble, in my experience. Sometimes gets you killed.'

'You wouldn't be trying to put words into *my* mouth now, would you?'

'I don't think this death is as simple as it looks. I know you want it to be a relatively straightforward accident. A protest too far. Something to discourage all the others from acting up. You wish people like him would go away and let you lead a normal life catching thieves and rapists and con-men. Real crime.'

Harris made no attempt to make notes of what Brennan was saying at this point.

'You'll be summoned as a material witness for the inquest, Mr Brennan. Save it for then.'

'When's the likely date?'

'They're usually Thursday's in Frome. Doesn't clash with the market that way. Probably be a week this Thursday.'

'Clashes with Wincanton races,' Brennan said with a pained smile. 'In the meantime, you'll try and find out who he is?'

'My job's to provide evidence on the cause of death to the coroner. Identifying a body is a secondary priority for now.'

'But somebody out there will know who he was. He must have

had a family. A mother and father, worried about where he is?'

'If your kids ran off to one of these hippy camps, Mr Brennan, I think you'd feel you'd lost him already, wouldn't you?'

Brennan wondered briefly what problems lay in store for him with Lester.

'One last thing, Mr Brennan.'

'Yes?'

'Can you tell me what you were doing on Sunday night and the early hours of Monday morning?'

'Why?'

'The body was on a trainload which left the quarry's railhead at three forty a.m. Just checking you weren't up there walking around or anything?'

'I was at home in bed. With my wife. I hope you'll ask the same questions of those security guards?'

'I'm sure I'll get around to it. Thanks for coming in, Mr Brennan.'

'I was *already* here.'

He left the police station seething. He could sense the way they would try to discredit him as a witness, implicate him even, all in the interests of a quiet life, when whoever the kid Lovernios was had suffered anything but a quiet death.

The morning frost and its veil of mist had lifted from the camp. The cooking fire had been kept burning, even through the coldest depths of the night, and now a freshly slaughtered young pig had been gutted and slotted on to a wooden spit. Cernunnos basted the pig with fat collected in a pewter cup as it frothed off the cooking flesh. Around him, he gathered his remaining warriors, preparing for this feast of renewal.

'Fear not for Lovernios, friends, he has found the sanctuary of Otherworld now. He is at one with the springs and the trees and the hills. He is one of the gods. He will look down with great anger at our enemies. But he will also regard them with contempt. For while they see our diminishing numbers as an advance towards victory, he will know, as we do, that the seeds of their destruction have now been planted.'

Cernunnos thrust his huge bear-paw of a hand into the hot

ashes on the fringe of the fire. Scrunching up the grey flakes in his palm, he proceeded to circle his warriors and to mark their faces with streaks of ash, so that their fighting spirit would be renewed.

'We must watch for strangers now. We must be as elusive as the fox now. Our enemies will claim the pursuit of justice, but we do not recognise their codes, nor their right to bear judgment upon us.'

Cernunnos produced a bronze-handled dagger from his belt and brandished it above his head.

'This is our land, our earth!' he bellowed.

'Our Land! Our Earth!' shouted the warriors in acclaim of their chieftain. They would fight to the death for him. And their shouts rippled out down the hill, shattering the dead silence of the winter's day.

CHAPTER FIVE

Brennan twitched and bickered throughout the run-up to the inquest. It wasn't nervousness at the thought of being called as a witness, but more the sense of impotence which frustrated him, as due legal process took its stolid course. He knew that he couldn't attempt to talk to Cernunnos or any of the other members of the Celtic Brotherhood. He couldn't call Trilling at Roadstone International, or find out the name of the train driver and talk to him. Had he tried to do so, he would probably have been slapped down with another contempt of court charge, or even an accusation of attempting to pervert the course of justice. An inquest completely stymied the investigative reporter because it assumed all inquisitorial powers for itself.

He still put in a daily call to DI Blackwell to see if the head had been found, or if the body's identity had been confirmed, each time receiving a brusque 'no' to each question. He also spent a few hours on a couple of evenings at the pubs that bordered the quarry. There were four that fell into this category, so he had to be careful how much he drank, as well as being cautious in what he said. None of the pubs were unfriendly or outwardly hostile, but there was a thin crust of civility between their regulars and those who were only visiting, which could easily be broken if someone who was not a local started asking too many questions, or mouthing off his opinions. Brennan contented himself with apparently idle gambits – 'funny about that bloke getting himself killed', that sort of thing – and then monitored any echoes. But he was also aware, in the comments he garnered – most of them being in the 'served him right' vein – that the *vox populi* wasn't necessarily represented by blokes drinking in a pub.

For this reason, he also spent time frequenting the haunts of the dispossessed, which were often less obvious in the country-side than they would be in the cities. Sure, there were the usual handfuls of youths and girls – noses and ears pierced and studded, a can of Special Brew seemingly welded to their lips – who loitered around the shopping areas of Frome to beg for money, or collect the bin-bound scraps left by the market stalls or bread counters. But his acceptance here was no easier either. He was an enemy, or at least a stranger, to both sides of the divide.

He also found that his assumption that a huge network existed among the rootless and abandoned youngsters of 1990s Britain was a false one. The last things they wanted to know of each other were their formal names and backgrounds, when they had been rendered anonymous by the state. None of those he talked to would admit knowledge of anyone fitting Lovernios's description.

Even when he found a New Age travellers' caravan of old vans, coaches and buses circled around a lay-by off the A361 one morning, none of this particular tribe had ever heard of the Celtic Brotherhood. The probability seemed to increase that Lovernios, for all his apparent education, had been a 'runner', from both family and modern society.

When Brennan phoned DI Blackwell to suggest that he check the national computer database on missing persons, he was told to piss off and mind his own business. He took the hint, but had in any case decided that further enquiries prior to the inquest would now be fruitless.

He thought about contacting his former editor, Stuart Gill, to run the story by him, but even as he considered this its premise was transformed in his mind into 'Gill-speak' – 'loon loses his head in crackpot protest' – and was thus soon dismantled.

So he brooded over his course of action, out loud over dinner when Janet could bear it, which was more often than she deserved.

'You don't think it was any more than a tragic accident, though, do you, Frank?'

'The evidence suggests that's all it is. I just wonder what was in the kid's mind. Whether he felt anger, or that he had to prove himself to the tribe somehow. And then overreached himself. The other night, I could have sworn they were burning some kind of dope in the fire. The scent of it was very heady.'

'Maybe they needed to get toked up before taking on a train? The Celtic equivalent of Dutch courage. It may show up in the post-mortem.'

Brennan went across to the dresser and made a note on the pad next to the telephone.

'I must remember to ask that.'

'I thought only the coroner could ask questions?'

'I think what they define as "any interested party" can get involved. And if they haven't discovered Lovernios's true identity by the time of the inquest then presumably there'll be no family there to represent him.'

'Maybe the Brotherhood will turn up?'

'I doubt it somehow. Not exactly on the electoral register, are they? Probably all got names like Lovernios and Cernunnos – addresses: the first century BC.'

Janet smiled. She preferred him when he was able to make jokes about the cases he was on. And with two glasses of red having gone down, this seemed as good a moment as any to approach him.

'I found something in Lester's bedside drawer this morning,' she said as she crossed to the dresser.

'Not a Durex already?'

She shook her head.

'Not a pack of E pills or something?'

'Potentially more addictive.'

She took out a book, bound in black leatherette, its pages tinged with gold.

'A Bible?'

'He's written his name inside it too. Must have bought it for himself.'

She handed the Bible to Brennan who checked the inside cover, where Lester had neatly printed his name and address in ballpoint pen. And then, as he flicked through it casually, he could see that passages had been marked with a yellow high-lighter pen.

'Probably religious studies.' He shrugged.

'He dropped that when he was still in London.'

'Well, maybe he's taken it up again. They didn't say anything about it at that parents' meeting as I remember. It's not compulsory at his age, is it? I thought it was just morning assembly, a hymn and a prayer?'

'He might be doing it after school,' Janet guessed. 'I'll ask him tomorrow morning. See what's behind it. Quite a few of the masters at the school are God Squadders – evangelicals.'

'Wrote the music for *Chariots of Fire*, didn't he?' Brennan said, deadpan. Janet kissed his forehead. Her new work had been going reasonably well. She felt occupied and rewarded, even if it was largely desk-bound, and the sense of well-being in the house when Brennan felt similarly motivated was almost tangible.

'What'll you do if they decide it was misadventure?'

He poured himself an inch of Calvados.

'I'll just have to see what comes out in the court. See how much of a gap there is between my instincts and the jury's judgment.'

'Your instincts being entirely unaffected by the need to earn some dosh?'

He wagged a finger at her good-humouredly.

'I'll listen to my conscience on that one, thanks.'

The good humour of the evening did not survive till the morning. Lester had a screaming tantrum about Janet 'searching' his bedside table once she had shown him the Bible. Brennan tried to play the role of honest broker, but Lester rounded on him too.

'Don't try that old routine, Dad. I've seen it on the telly – the soft cop and the hard cop. This is my business!'

'We're just interested, that's all – is this for work at school, or is it more personal?'

'Mind your own business!' Lester shouted.

'It is our business until you're sixteen, Lester,' Janet chided him.

'All right, then. I enjoy reading it – how's that?'

'So did I when I was a kid, but I believed it on the same level as I believed in Superman, or in the Justice League of America,' Brennan said soothingly.

'My form teacher, Mr Parker, asked if I was interested last term, that's all. I was. I am. We do twenty minutes or so after school every Wednesday.'

'We being?'

'About six of us.'

'Lester – are you getting God?' Janet asked a touch too succinctly, provoking another stomping tantrum, but this time more tearful and genuine.

'What if I am? I don't have to be embarrassed about it. Or to apologise to you. You decided not to give me any religious beliefs, now I've decided I want to try.'

'But why now, son?' Brennan asked.

'I don't know. I just lie in bed at nights and I can't get to sleep. I haven't got a brother or a sister to talk to' – he accompanied this with an accusatory look at both Brennan and Janet – 'so who do I ask about what's going to happen? One day, you two will be dead and I'll be on my own. I've got to think about that, haven't I? Especially if it happens soon. I can feel something out there, that's all – something comforting when I get afraid. Something light when it gets dark.'

There were tears of frustration and emotion swilling down Lester's burning cheeks, and Janet too was close to blubbing. Only Brennan remained seemingly unmoved – but then he'd been rendered dumb by the realisation that his son and Lovernios were perhaps only three or four years apart in age, and that their sense of spirituality, or vague mysticism to be precise, was even more closely shared than that.

The Coroner's Court in Frome was a rather drab, one-storey 1950s building – all red brick and white wood – adjacent to the police station. And it promised little majesty or ceremony as the witnesses, jurors and journalists gathered outside in the grey chill of a mid-January Thursday. A robed clerk opened the door and asked the jurors – there were nine of them, two more than the minimum – to come inside, and then moments later, the witnesses were admitted.

Brennan included himself among these, further compromising his status with his young journalist colleagues, who were left to wait. He laser-scanned the faces around him – the shiny, scrubbed, just-shaved pathologist in his pinstripe suit and two-tone shirt; the lined, jaundiced-by-cigarettes profile of the train driver, with his trade union lapel badge in place; and Len Trilling, skin stretched taut over a jutting jawline as he whispered in the ear of a smartly dressed, discreetly made-up woman in her late thirties, who Brennan guessed would be Roadstone's solicitor. There was no obvious sign of family, and certainly no attendance by the Celtic Brotherhood.

Sergeant Harris was checking the names of the jurors against a wad of summonses on his clipboard, and when he had completed that he asked the witnesses to sit down. The journalists were then allowed to take their places in the two rows behind the witnesses, and finally a half-dozen members of the public were ushered through to the benches at the back of the room.

Harris nodded to the clerk that all was in order and moments later the coroner, a tall, gaunt man in his early fifties, emerged from a side room, wearing a midnight-blue robe with black trim. Sergeant Harris commanded all to rise while the coroner took his place on the bench, and arranged his case notes and writing pads.

'You may sit down,' he said quietly, and the people in the room shuffled into their allotted places, clearing their throats and coughing in anticipation of an enforced silence.

The coroner assumed an air of intense gravitas as he peered around the room, before launching into his formal opening of the inquest.

'All manner of persons who have anything to do at this court before the Queen's Coroner for this county, touching the death of this person yet to be identified, draw near and give your attendance. And if anyone can give evidence, on behalf of our Sovereign Lady the Queen, when, how and by what means this person came to his death, let him come forth.'

The coroner's gaze now fell upon the jurors, ranged to one side.

'And you good men and women of this county summoned to appear here this day, to enquire for our sovereign when, how and by what means this person came to his death, answer to your names as you shall be called, each at the first call, upon the pains and perils thereon.'

'Not exactly *Have I Got News for You*, is it?' Brennan whispered out of the side of his mouth to Trilling's lady solicitor, prompting a controlled smile. The jurors were named and then sworn in by the coroner and, satisfied that all those who had been summoned had arrived, he embarked on his opening remarks.

'Ladies and gentlemen, let me just say at the outset that a coroner's court is one of enquiry, not of accusation. We are here solely to ascertain the circumstances of this person's death. You will hear both witnesses of fact and observation, and professional experts who may give their opinion. You must decide after hearing their submissions whether you have a clear picture of how the deceased met his death in order to reach your verdict. I will lead the questioning of witnesses, but the jury may ask for clarification through my officer, and witnesses may also put questions, at my discretion.'

Brennan thought about asking the whereabouts of the security guards who had assaulted Lovernios that Friday night, but made a mental note for his own testimony.

'Now we have an unusual aspect to this case, in that the deceased has yet to be identified. Despite publicity attached to the death – some of it too extreme for my taste,' the coroner said, glancing at the press benches, 'his family either are not aware of his death, or are not prepared to come forward. If any of you have *any* evidence, no matter how small, which may help identification, then please bring it to my attention. The Avon & Somerset Police are meanwhile continuing their enquiries.'

He then read the sworn statement made by the depot manager in West London who had first seen evidence of the body. It gave details of time, the source of the train, the ownership of the roadstone, the procedures undertaken to call the police, and the removal of the body from the scene.

And now the coroner summoned the first expert witness, the pathologist, Dr Frederick Scott, of Wells and District Hospital. There was an exchange of polite smiles between the two men – they must meet like this all the time, Brennan thought, cynically – before Dr Scott was invited to give his evidence.

'The deceased is male, in the age range of seventeen to twenty-four, he is around five feet ten inches in height, although this cannot be categorically stated due to decapitation.'

The tone was cold, clinical. Brennan bet himself that the pathologist would probably have shown more passion for a steak and kidney pudding than a human being.

The coroner leant in the jury's direction to ask them if they were aware what decapitation meant. They all nodded and muttered, 'Yes, sir.'

'The decapitation was the cause of death, or was it subsequent to death, Dr Scott?' asked the coroner.

'Oh, unquestionably the cause. This was a traumatic decapitation, severing just above the level of the acromio-clavicular joint.' Dr Scott didn't wait to be asked for clarification. He drew a line with his index finger across his collarbone.

'Roughly, from here – to here. There were some remnants of the first and second thoracic vertebrae,' he said, indicating their location in the throat, 'and a section, about seven centimetres in length, of the cervical vertebrae.' He turned to the jury and prodded his finger into his neck muscles for their benefit. 'Death would have been sudden, if not instantaneous.'

'In the absence of the head, can you determine likely causes of decapitation, Dr Scott?' asked the coroner.

'Yes – it would have needed an impact of tremendous force. From a moving and heavy object.'

'You say "impact" rather than perhaps "blow"?'

'Well, yes – there being no evidence of surgical or martial equipment. This young man's head was literally torn off.'

'Were there any other wounds on the body?'

'A few scratches and bruises on the chest, consistent with the weight of the roadstone in which the body was buried. There were also some small scars on the forearms. I don't count his tattoos in that category.'

Brennan scribbled a note, remembering the intricate tattoos across Cernunnos's face. Lovernios having them seemed like further evidence of brotherhood.

'Now, time of death. We know the body was discovered in the rail wagon, just after seven a.m. on Monday the eighth of January.

And I don't wish to compromise his statement, but the train driver will say that he left the quarry at two forty a.m., some four and a half hours earlier.'

'Death occurred somewhere between, say, eleven thirty p.m. the previous evening and three, maybe four a.m. that morning. The intense frost may throw the timings out a little.'

'Finally, for the moment, may I ask your considered opinion about the means of death?'

'Well, I discovered some tiny metallic fragments, no more than shavings, embedded in the loose flesh left on the remains of the neck. I can only speculate – a cable, the edge of a vehicle, the wheel of a train. That sort of thing.'

'Thank you, Dr Scott.'

Brennan slipped himself an extra-strong mint, his mouth having dried considerably during the pathologist's evidence, and offered one to Trilling's solicitor. She took it without looking at him.

The coroner called up the train driver, who confirmed the start and finish times of his journey – verified by a log-book and a Railtrack print-out – and then went on to describe the occasions on which he and his train had suffered attacks in the night by protesters.

He told of one night when one of them – a large man with a beard – had managed to mount the front platform of the diesel power-train, and had shattered a window in the driver's cab. The driver referred to what he called 'his nightmare' of seeing one of these young men falling under the train as they came down the hill to attack it in the narrow ravine, about a mile from the quarry.

'You travel at no great speed at this stage, do you?' asked the coroner.

'No, sir – ten miles an hour, maybe fifteen. We don't pick up speed until we reach the main line at Westbury. That's what they take advantage of – so they can climb on. These protesters.'

Brennan checked his notes so far. The pathologist had just referred to 'an impact of tremendous force, from a moving or heavy object' – Brennan wrote 'Is a 10 mph train fast enough to do damage?'

The driver's statement – which concluded that although he had seen no direct attacks on the train early on the Monday morning, there were 'figures by the trackside in the ravine' – was now consolidated by Trilling's evidence, which confirmed the frequency of what he called 'the vandalism of these protesters.' Indeed, he'd even arranged to show to the jury more of his videos, shot by the security people, showing what looked like Celtic Brotherhood members, swarming all over moving trains.

By the time of the lunch interval, there seemed little doubt that a verdict of accidental death would be returned, although what had happened at the precise moment of Lovernios's death had yet to be explained. If he'd fallen under a train wheel how the hell had his body ended up in a truck full of stone, Brennan noted to himself as he left the court, passing the TV reporter preparing to do his bulletin for the lunchtime news.

'Like an England Test innings, this – all over by tea,' Brennan offered cheerily.

'If you're holding something back on me, I'll have you, mister,' the reporter hissed.

'Now, now,' Brennan cooed, 'you're getting paranoid. You boys are supposed to be the future of modern news journalism. *I'm* the dinosaur.'

He crossed the main road outside the police station to a pub, and took a half of bitter and two cheese and pickle sandwiches for lunch. While he was there, Trilling and his lady solicitor came in, but made sure they occupied a distinctly separate area of the lounge.

Only when she came to the bar to order a drink was Brennan able to speak to her.

'I'm Frank Brennan . . .'

'Save the introductions – we have a file on you.'

'I know. You'd have been prosecuting me if they hadn't dropped their charges.'

'I think I'd have enjoyed that,' she smiled.

'Don't I get a name?' he asked through a mouthful of cheese.

'Lydia Pearson, Legal Affairs, and yes, I've heard all the jokes.'

Pearson collected her drinks and returned to sit with Trilling. Brennan wondered idly if Trilling was giving her one, or if, in these politically correct days, it was her who was doing the giving.

He finished his sandwiches and took a stroll around Frome for half an hour, buying a small Havana cigar at the Pipe Shop. Then he checked himself – he was in danger of enjoying himself here, of getting off on the thrill of being back on the grubbiest beat in town. But this was Frome, not Chicago – who was he kidding? How dare he use his incidental acquaintance with Lovernios as the springboard for a story? He was hearse-chasing now.

He skulked back up the hill to the court, taking the Golgotha route up through the main church and its yard, and past the coroner's offices. But as he approached the court, he saw a young girl of no more than sixteen prowling around the entrance. She was dressed in green leggings, with a drab cotton coat and scarf wrapped around her for warmth. Her hair was plaited haphazardly into a kind of dreadlock perm, and she wore several gold earrings and a nose-stud.

'Can I help you, love, you look lost?' he offered.

'Are you a policeman?' she asked.

'No – but I can get you one if you want.'

'Are you something to do with this inquest?'

'Well, I'm a journalist . . . and a witness, yes. Why?'

'I know who the dead body is.'

Brennan stiffened. He half expected the eager young TV reporter to rugby-tackle him out of the way, but he'd filed his report and gone to lunch.

'Right – so who is it?'

'His name was Humphrey Castleton . . . but I called him Lovernios.'

'So did I. Look, love . . .'

'Epona . . . they used to call me that.'

'They?'

'The Celtic Brotherhood. Humphrey's friends . . .'

'You'd better come with me. You'll have to tell the Coroner's Officer what you know about Humphrey.'

'Main thing I know is I'm expecting his baby in the summer.'

The coroner adjourned the inquest once DI Blackwell and Sergeant Harris had confirmed with Castleton's parents that their son had indeed left home nearly a year ago. They had not reported him missing because he had left the family home of his own free will, after a prolonged argument. This had not been the usual stuff of teenage rebellion, or even drug-taking. Humphrey had just felt unable to live with a father who, as the Liberal Democrat chairman of the district council, had voted through approval of Roadstone International's quarry expansion.

Brennan was briefed on these details by Sergeant Harris, in the company of the other journalists, who had immediately set off for the Castleton home on the outskirts of Wells. But Brennan needed to still his spinning head. A suspicious death, a quarry, a teenage pregnancy and now a local politician with connections to all three – he was dangerously close to calling Stuart Gill about doing a little story.

CHAPTER SIX

Giles Castleton formally identified the body of his son Humphrey in the morgue at Wells District Hospital later that evening, just seventeen and a half years after the boy had been born at the same hospital. Not that any such irony impinged upon Castleton's mind as he heard that X-rays had indeed confirmed the repairs to the right ankle, a legacy of a rugby injury at Downside Abbey School. He felt a loss, certainly, but nothing as disturbing as those moments a year ago when Humphrey had verbally assailed him, before packing a few belongings and leaving, vowing never to return.

He had, emotionally, said goodbye to his son then. He'd been dismayed that Humphrey, blessed with a large family home, a private education, and social access to some of the best families in Somerset, had squandered such opportunities. And Humphrey's constant opposition to the policies that Castleton had endorsed on the district council had seemed both puerile and spiteful. So, no, Castleton would not mourn his first-born son – he now had other children by a second marriage – but he would, at least, deliver him back to the Catholicism that Humphrey had spurned so tetchily throughout his teenage years. It would now be God's gift to wash away such iniquity and to cleanse such sin.

The mortuary attendant and the pathologist, Dr Scott, stood in silent respect before Castleton nodded his readiness to leave and the attendant filed Humphrey back into his cabinet of the dead.

'You needn't attend the inquest when it's resumed, Giles,' Dr

Scott offered his brother-in-law by way of consolation. 'I can confirm evidence of identification, and your acceptance of it.'

'Thank you, Fred. I must say I don't see much point in my turning up. It seems to me it would only spur the news hounds on to greater acts of trespass. They just drove up to my front door this afternoon – less than an hour after I'd heard the news about the likelihood of Humphrey being this body. Grief is no longer private.'

'I shall certainly make the coroner aware of this. But I think you're right. There's nothing to be achieved by your presence. The quicker we can lay Humphrey to rest, the better.'

'Did he suffer, do you think?' Castleton asked suddenly.

'No. His death would have been instantaneous. You can also console yourself with the thought that, misguided as he was, he died for something he believed in.'

'I can think of no greater waste than that, Fred. I'm sorry.'

This wasn't the time, and definitely not the place, for a debate about the most meaningful way to live one's life. So Dr Scott restrained himself, put an arm around Castleton's shoulder, and led him upstairs to his office, where he gave him a large whisky to numb the emptiness inside. Though, in truth, from Scott's knowledge of Castleton – through his marriage to his younger sister, and the Rotary Club dinners, charity balls, local hunt meetings which were the Castleton family's social beat – he guessed that the emptiness had been there from the day the man was born.

Brennan used the three-day break before the resumption of the inquest to catch up on his notes. Although the cause of Humphrey Castleton's death – and how much better and nobler a name Lovernios now seemed – pointed at an accident whilst attempting to vandalise one of the quarry trains, Brennan had noticed the absence of a security man to offer testimony to the jury. He wondered also whether to bring up with the pathologist the question of whether Lovernios had been under the influence of any stimulant in the hours leading up to his death. Nobody had mentioned a blood test, which would usually have been carried out had the incident involved a car or a motor-bike. But if it had showed up positive, it would presumably only load further evidence in favour of Lovernios's own recklessness as the key factor in his violent end.

He also kept all the cuttings on Giles Castleton, landowner, gentleman farmer and district councillor, an upstanding man except when it came to relating to his son. The statement he had issued to the rampaging press pack on the afternoon of the girl's identification had been a masterpiece of English restraint and understatement, of the sort usually found in *Daily Telegraph* obituaries. 'Regret' was expressed, but there were also the coded references to 'family difficulties' and 'unfulfilled promise'. Indeed, the strongest theme of the statement was that the Castleton family should be left to grieve in peace.

Most interestingly, however, there was no reference in any of the newspaper articles to the girl – named as Brigit Parry, of Frome – being pregnant with Humphrey Castleton's baby. Brennan found it hard to believe that the hacks would have held back on that element given the other details of the story, which suggested that she had told Brennan, and Brennan alone, of this sad tail-piece to Humphrey Castleton's short life. He would have to find out why this was the case after the inquest had finally been completed. Janet meanwhile suggested that she should talk to the girl, in case she needed any advice on benefits, housing or – and it had to be considered – an abortion.

So Janet accompanied Brennan to the Coroner's Court on the day of the inquest's resumption, taking care to arrive separately and to sit well away in the public benches.

The coroner apologised to the jury for the interruption but explained that identifying a victim was one of the functions of an inquest. Brigit Parry's evidence would supply details to confirm that, and she had been pressed into appearing as a witness.

But first, Dr Scott testified to the process of identification, producing Humphrey Castleton's medical records, and the X-ray photographs of his ankle, to confirm him as the headless body. It was at this point that Brennan caught the coroner's attention and asked him if the pathologist had conducted a blood test.

The coroner looked gravely at him, as if he had questioned the seating plans for a superior dinner party.

'Could you explain the relevance of this question, Mr Brennan?'

'Well, yes – I simply wanted to know if Lovernios – Castleton – had been under the influence of any drinks or drugs at the time of his demise.'

The coroner passed the question on to Dr Scott with a simple raising of an eyebrow.

'Of course I conducted a blood test, sir,' Scott announced tetchily, 'and it was completely normal. No traces of anything unusual.'

The coroner noted the answer without asking why this hadn't been mentioned before. He then called Brigit Parry to the bench for her evidence.

'Miss Parry, may I ask first of all why you didn't make yourself known to my officer before the inquest started?'

'Didn't know that's what I was supposed to do,' she said in a quiet, nervous voice. 'Besides, I'd only heard about the death that morning.'

'By what means?' asked the coroner.

'Local news on the breakfast TV. Moment I heard I knew it must be him. Humphrey.'

'How so?'

'Because I'd always told him that he'd get himself killed one day.'

'By attempting to board and disable a quarry train?'

'Well, by keeping up the protests. I knew they'd get him in the end.'

Seeing Lydia Pearson rise to her feet, the coroner gestured for her to sit down. They were both thinking the same thing.

'Miss Parry, this is a court of investigation, not of speculation or accusation. Were you with Mr Castleton on the evening he died?'

'No – but I did live at the camp with him for a few months.'

'This is the so-called Celtic Brotherhood who occupied the site at Tedbury Camp?'

'Yes.'

'And during your time with him, did Mr Castleton ever embark on an attempt to vandalise or disable one of the quarry trains?'

'To stop them, yes. Many times.'

'Did you take part in any of these attacks?'

'No. Women weren't allowed to. But I heard what they planned, and what they did.'

The coroner turned to Sergeant Harris.

'Sergeant Harris, you say in your report that you have made several visits to the Tedbury site?'

'Yes, sir – three in all.'

'Were you able to establish contact with any members of this self-styled tribe?'

'No, sir. The camp was plainly lived in, there were cooking fires burning, shelters, food stores, clothing – but no sign of any people.'

'So you were unable to obtain any statements from them?'

'That's correct, sir. They were either hiding, or they may have moved on. I should say that the police force has no means of knowing who they are anyway. These are people who have dropped off any electoral register, if they were ever on one.'

'And despite the vandalism, no attempt has been made to interview or arrest them?'

'Well – we'd have to have a complaint first, sir.'

Lydia Pearson rose again.

'Sir, I should say that Roadstone International's policy has been only to press charges when we have caught people in the act of sabotage. You will be aware of feelings running high over the expansion of the quarry. Our view is that in order to lower the temperature of the argument, we only act in the most conclusive of cases. We have no wish to create martyrs for the anti-quarry lobby by pursuing a policy of mass arrests.'

The coroner frowned at her, and made an irritable scribble on his yellow legal pad.

'I think I may have to return to this point in my summing-up, Miss Pearson,' he said darkly.

His mood wasn't improved by the reappearance of Brennan's raised arm.

'Yes, Mr Brennan – do you have a point to put to Miss Parry?'

'To Miss Pearson, actually.'

'You may notice that she is not a witness, Mr Brennan.'

'She's just given testimony, sir, so I thought . . .'

'She was making a point of order.'

'Well can I make one back?'

'Be very brief, Mr Brennan.'

'I want to know why none of Roadstone International's army of security guards has been called.'

'I don't see the relevance of this, Mr Brennan.'

'They have eye-witness accounts of what Castleton and his fellow tribe-members have been up to.'

'I think that issue was covered quite sufficiently by Mr Trilling and his security videos.'

'With respect, sir – there was a climate of deep hostility between the protesters and the security guards.'

'Of that I have no doubt, but I don't see its relevance. Can we move on?'

This wasn't a question anticipating the answer 'no'. The coroner asked Brigit Parry if Castleton had ever shown an awareness that what he was doing was dangerous, and once she had said 'yes' he thanked her for coming and asked her to stand down.

Brennan caught Janet's look from the back of the courtroom, urging him to press on. His chance was now upon him as the coroner called him warily to the bench, and he took a – non-religious – oath, before settling to answer the questions the coroner would put to him.

'I understand from your statement to my officer that you were with the deceased two nights before his death, Mr Brennan?'

'That's correct.'

'In what circumstances?'

'Briefly, he wanted to show me the quarry operation because he believed that they were exceeding their agreed quotas. And he wanted me to write an article about it – if that proved to be the case.'

'Do you mean he hired you?'

'No, no – I hope, no I *think*, that I can claim to be an independent writer. I didn't go there with any preconceptions, merely an investigative mind.'

'So you broke into the quarry?'

'Climbed a wire fence, actually. At about seven thirty p.m. We walked around the perimeter, and he pointed out the quarry's features, its depth. His view was that it was an offence against nature.'

'Did he talk to you about the manner of his protest?'

'He did. I remember he used the phrase "we're at war" – meaning with Roadstone International.'

'Did he invite you to join him in any sabotage that night? Or offer to put on a display for you?'

'No. There was no sense of him showing off or anything. He seemed to be a very serious, passionate young man.'

'Please restrict your observations to facts, Mr Brennan, not opinions,' said the coroner, idly checking his watch.

'Certainly – may I talk about the fact of the attack on Humphrey Castleton by two of Roadstone's security guards?'

Brennan could see Lydia Pearson instantly on alert, whispering into Trilling's ear.

'Do you think it relevant?'

'In the context of a violent death, yes.'

Lydia Pearson now stood up.

'Miss Pearson?'

'Forgive me, but before Mr Brennan embarks on his story, I would just like to point out that the two guards who intercepted Mr Brennan and Mr Castleton on their trespass have sworn statements that they were assaulted – to be precise, that Castleton fly-kicked one of them to the ground.'

'She's right – he did,' Brennan confirmed. 'And then the one who was left standing beat him over the head with a truncheon.'

Pearson was back on her feet again.

'Both guards deny using such force.'

The coroner held up his hand to stop the argument.

'I think we're straying from our brief here.'

'No we're not,' Brennan insisted. 'All that's being presented to this court is the implication that Humphrey Castleton was the architect of his own death. I suggest that the violence shown to him the night I was with him raises another possibility – that he was killed by another hand.'

There was a loud murmuring throughout the court. The coroner glared at him.

'Please stand down, Mr Brennan. Your contribution isn't helpful in the slightest.'

'These guards threatened that they'd get him next time . . . I heard them!'

'Enough, Mr Brennan!'

'Why aren't they in court?'

'Mr Brennan, I am minded to find you in contempt of this court.'

'I'll happily plead guilty to that.'

The coroner gestured to Sergeant Harris who approached Brennan quickly and grabbed his arm.

'Out. Now,' growled the sergeant.

He pulled Brennan by the arm, though he offered little resistance. He'd made his point, and if his colleagues in the local press were men not boys, they now had a chance to make some trouble. Harris led Brennan out into the corridor.

'You stupid twat,' he sneered.

'You stupid twat, *sir*.'

'Kid gets killed and you try to stir it up for your own benefit.'

'Just trying to find out the truth, Sergeant, for *your* benefit. I mean, who set your agenda for this inquest – the three wise monkeys?'

'You're going the right way to making yourself really unpopular around here.'

'Good. Thanks for the compliment. Now tell me why you didn't go and interview any of the security people?'

'Not my brief. There's two company honchos in there who can do any talking for Roadstone.'

'And what happened with the Celtic Brotherhood – I bet you didn't even go up there, did you? Too scared!'

'Listen, Brennan – this isn't London. You can't hide out with all your fancy left-wing friends. You're on your own down here.'

'Go on. Say it. "We know where you live." Well, I don't think you'd even have the guts to make the climb to my front door, Sergeant Harris.'

Harris left Brennan alone and returned to his official duties in the courtroom.

Brennan paced the corridor for several minutes, wishing he had a cigar to calm him down. Now Janet eased her way out to attempt the same process.

'You okay?'

'Just about. Sorry – couldn't help it. I just blew a gasket.'

'You'd better get back in. He's about to sum up.'

She slipped back into the courtroom, sliding in through the barely open door. Brennan thought about making a more dramatic return, something along the lines of impersonating Ethel Merman singing 'There's No Business Like Showbusiness' perhaps. He took several deep breaths, holding them for as long as he could before exhaling, and then composed himself for his entrance.

The coroner was asking Len Trilling whether it was possible that Castleton's accident could have happened inside the quarry itself, since that was the likeliest source of heavy machinery, conveyor belts and such.

Trilling shook his head emphatically.

'There would have been nothing working at that time of night. The crushers were off. The trains would have been loaded up. No lorry movements. It's our quietest time of the week.'

The coroner nodded his thanks. Brennan knew that the question had been a fairly blatant attempt to demolish his theory before any of the journalists could get carried away with it – not that any of them looked as though they would.

The coroner asked if there were any points the jury wished to be clarified, but they shook their heads. He outlined the verdicts available to them, based on the evidence they had heard. Natural causes was plainly out. But they might consider 'Suicide'. Then there was 'Accidental Death', or 'Misadventure', though they were both the same terms in the eyes of the court. And, last of all – he paused theatrically – 'Unlawful Killing'. With that he discharged them to their room to consider their verdict.

As the inquest witnesses waited, Brennan watched the elements that had contributed to the show – the corporate spin doctors, trying to have it all ways; the humdrum pathologist, eager to confirm his professional status; the bemused young girl with her baby, a living victim for whom there would be no inquest; a train driver who'd just have to live with the fear of who might be lurking in the dark next time he pulled out of the quarry; and finally himself, a pushy, self-employed journalist, always ready to take the converse view, especially if there was a story in it. What a shabby bunch, not just in terms of the machinery of justice, but also as a cortège for an idealistic young man who had never even reached voting age.

Brennan's self-administered depression was compounded when the jury, having presumably picked up tips on brevity from the O. J. Simpson trial, returned to the courtroom inside ten minutes. Everyone took their places for the formality of stating the obvious, although they did add a last little twist of the knife with their insistence that the verdict be 'Misadventure', and not 'Accidental Death', suggesting that Humphrey Castleton had had only himself to blame.

But then the coroner himself, metaphorically speaking, began jumping on to his own set of peculiar wagons. He wanted the outside world to take heed that protests which involved damage to property and risks to human life were unacceptable. He admonished the dead youth for taking self-indulgence to its ultimate extreme; and he attacked both the police and the security operation at the quarry for their failure to 'nip in the bud' this apparently reckless group of protesters who, in his opinion, bore almost as much responsibility for Castleton's death as the lad himself. In an act of pedantic triumphalism, he announced that since the presumption was that the death had occurred on the railway, he would be obliged to forward details of the case to the Secretary of State for Transport. The final, pathetic act was the formality of releasing the body of the deceased for burial.

Sergeant Harris called the courtroom to its feet as the coroner himself stood and glanced from jury to witnesses to press.

'All manner of persons who have had anything to do at this court before the Queen's Coroner for this county touching the death of Humphrey Castleton, having discharged your duty, and you good men and women of the jury having returned your verdict, may depart hence and take your ease.'

The coroner left, leaving Harris and the court clerk to supervise the clearing of the room. The journalists and the TV reporter made an instant beeline for Trilling and Pearson, presumably because they had been cleared of direct responsibility for the accident, but also indicted as circumstantial contributors to its creation. Lydia Pearson smiled calmly and suggested that they all went outside where Trilling would give one interview to television which could be used by all.

Janet sidled up to Brennan.

'Shouldn't you be in there with them?'

'Can't take the pace these days.'

He watched as little Brigit Parry slipped away almost unnoticed.

'You don't fancy following the girl for me, do you?'

Janet smiled her instant acceptance, kissed Brennan's forehead and purposefully slung her bag over her shoulder.

'I'll meet you in the tea-rooms by the car park!' Brennan shouted as she left, acknowledging the rendezvous with a wave. Meanwhile, the small media pack brushed past him, with all bar Pearson too preoccupied to give him a look.

'Nice try, Mr Brennan,' she said with an acid smile. 'I didn't know you were branching out into fiction.'

Brennan wrestled for something dashing and witty as a rejoinder but all he could manage was: 'Piss off.'

Reluctantly, he wandered out after the reporters and hovered around the edge of their circus as Trilling tried to find the right level of solemnity for his interview, furrowing his brow in apparent pain as soon as the television lights went on.

Janet did think of calling out to Brigit as they walked back down the hill into the centre of Frome, separated by about twenty yards of pavement. It seemed a ridiculous subterfuge when all she was proposing to do was enquire if the girl needed any advice. But Brennan had specified 'follow', and she knew from the past that he must have had his reasons for her keeping a distance.

In the end, the pursuit didn't take up much time at all. Brigit trudged halfway down the hill and turned left just after the old-fashioned, sawdust-on-the-floor, carcase-in-the-window butchers, with its pre-war tiles and tiny wooden kiosk for settling accounts. But the shop proved to be only the gatepost for entry into a timewarp as Janet now followed Brigit along an eighteenth-century terrace of small houses and antique shops. The bustle of the road through the town had died in an instant. Here there was no traffic, just a slope of immaculately relaid cobbles, flanked by a raised flagstone walkway with a wrought-iron rail.

It reminded Janet of pre-gentrification Docklands, with its lingering shiver of Victorian menace. The air was tinged with the smell of coal fires, and she glimpsed ancient passageways and a forbidding Baptist chapel as she now climbed another cobbled hill. Although the town centre was no more than a hundred yards or so away, market forces had failed to embrace this atmospheric quarter. Too steep for pedestrians, no room for cars – Janet guessed that these had been the inquest verdicts of those who'd been invited to invest in the area. So now the shop windows were either bare or filled with the rag-bag cast-offs that formed a display for a minor charity.

Janet paused to look into the window of one such shop – more junk than antiques – as Brigit herself had stopped to light a cigarette. Janet kept the girl in the very edge of her field of vision, so that when she moved off up a hidden terrace of steps the move did not confound her. Indeed, as she climbed the steps, her head rising to the next level of pavement, she could see Brigit's distinctive line in footwear planted in the doorway of a shop. Two more steps up enabled her to see the full picture – Brigit letting herself in through the front door of what looked like a bookshop that had gone out of business.

Janet paused for a moment, feigning breathlessness, but in fact logging details of the shop. There were no lights visible on the ground floor, where the two bay windows were filled with a higgledy-piggledy display of books. But then a light came on in the flat above, drab net-curtained windows suddenly enlivened by the orange glow from a table-lamp.

Janet stepped towards the bookshop, which shouted 'second hand' in every detail. In the top third of both windows was Sellotaped a rainbow of leaflets. She scanned them quickly, registering keywords such as 'therapy', 'holistic', 'workshop', and last, but by every means least, 'Glastonbury'.

But while most of the books in the window reflected the same alternative passions and practices, there was a distinct strand of mysticism woven through the selection. 'Stonehenge', 'mysteries', 'sacred Somerset', 'geomancy' and 'ley lines' were among the mental snapshots that Janet took quickly, before moving off back down the hill, happy that Brigit, the abandoned princess of the hill-fort, definitely belonged above this cheerless, plaintive collection of books and pamphlets.

Within two minutes, she was back in mainstream Frome, passing the bustle of the post office, and the bus queues of anxious pensioners outside Woolworth's. She saw the Pipe Shop, and wondered if Brennan knew about it. But as she looked at its defiant, manly window display of cigars, pipes, cutters, cleaners, pocket lighters and tobacco pouches, her question was answered – Brennan was already inside the shop.

'Every boy deserves a present, eh?' she whispered from behind.

Brennan remained focused on the cigars lying in the glass-fronted display cabinet, ranged like fat, spicy sausages in a butcher's window.

'I'll also need some serious sex to get over this disappointment,' he said through the side of his mouth. He turned round, determined to milk the joke.

'Oh, sorry – didn't realise it was you, Jan.'

'Where's the coffee shop?'

'About a hundred yards along on the left, where the road forks. Just follow the Buddhist chanting.'

Janet left him to buy his nicotine fix, trying to tell herself that it was no worse than Sherlock Holmes's cocaine remedy for that undiagnosed ailment, the detective's depression. At least he didn't smoke a pipe. Then she *would* divorce him.

When he joined her at the wholefood café, underneath the art gallery, Janet had already laid out two coffees and toasted teacakes, and had bagged the choice seat next to the log fire. Winter had now painted over the daylight outside, and the yearning for food, drink and warmth seemed less like a designer choice than a primitive necessity.

'She lives above a second-hand bookshop round the back of town,' she offered him as a tidbit. 'Occult, alternative history, mysticism, that kind of thing.'

'That figures. I can't see girls that young being drawn naturally to living in the Bronze Age.'

'A further indictment of Take That's failure to fulfil teenage fantasy. I couldn't see past Herman's Hermits when I was a kid.'

Brennan shivered at the memory of the Mancunian singer with teeth like a piano keyboard.

'Suddenly sleeping outdoors in a winter forest seems entirely reasonable,' he said.

'Is she your next bet – figuratively speaking?'

'I guess so. If I'm going to sell Stuart Gill this story, the Celtic Brotherhood have to be the main angle. I don't think I could get more than a hundred words out of the quarry on its own.'

'Will the police keep up the search for the lad's head?'

Brennan was aware of a certain frisson from the two old ladies at the adjacent table, and he gave Janet a pale smile as he leant close.

'Could you shout a bit louder please? Maybe offer a reward? No – I think once he's buried, that's it, as far as they're concerned.'

'Unless you find new evidence?'

'Even then I doubt if I'd shift Sergeant Harris into action. You know, there's an upside in living in the country when it comes to keeping the law. People see more, hear more. They get to know who the bad boys are, and because it's such a small world, the criminal is stigmatised far more easily. I mean, I bet all Len Trilling's neighbours, and all the people in whichever village he lives, will be watching him on telly tonight, judging whether he's telling the truth or not. The country community acts as its own judge and jury.'

'What's this got to do with Harris?'

'Well, the downside of what I've just said is that the police have to give priority to the most demanding voice in the village, which is usually the richest and most reactionary.'

'On that basis, they should have rounded up and shot the Celtic Brotherhood by now, shouldn't they?'

Brennan sipped his coffee, then shook his head.

'No, because they haven't offended anybody yet. This tribe is out of sight. They're not parading through the main street here on market day, or disrupting the local hunt. They've done a bit of damage to a company that doesn't want to make a public fuss, that's all. Until they step over the line, the coppers'll just leave them alone.'

'Which is good, isn't it?' Janet asked with a frown.

'Neither good nor bad. Just confusing. See, I don't get why they haven't moved them off that hill-fort. Why Roadstone are soft-pedalling. Or why Giles Castleton seems only mildly upset that his son is dead, when I'd be screaming for revenge. The justification for action is all there, but what's happening? Nothing. And I have to find out why.'

The Castleton family turned out in force, in all its generations and splinter groups, for the funeral Mass of Humphrey at a small, ancient Catholic church on the fringes of their estate, determined to put on a show of unity and feudal power. But for the severely black clothing and the absence of society photographers, it could have been a family wedding, such was the gathering.

Workers from the tenant farms, local suppliers and tradesmen were among the congregation which filed down an archway of sculpted, bottle-green-coloured yew trees to the church's great wooden door.

Brennan watched as the coffin was unloaded from the hearse and carried aloft into the church followed by the priest, and a flotilla of choirboys and deacons. He did a circuit of the church's graveyard, walled on three sides, with a great sweep of bare, brown earth rising to the horizon on the open side. Castletons abounded underneath these fading and crumbling stones, bordered by freshly trimmed grass. 'May he find eternal peace with God'; 'Asleep with Thee O Lord'; 'Futuram Civitatem Inquirimus', boasted the epitaphs.

'We seek a state that is to come,' Brennan translated to himself, dredging a sliver of O-level Latin from the recesses of his memory. This was the Anglo-Catholic establishment at work, and at rest here, not the brow-beaten urban scum, terrified into belief and ritual. A network of recusants, who had refused to bow to the common command of Tudor Anglicanism. They had been, and in many ways still were, a sect within a sect. Preserving each other's land, power and influence.

He heard the first chords of the organ soaring from within, and stared up at the church's four turrets, set with heraldic pennants against the pale winter sky. Now voices were singing an ancient hymn, whose cadences sprung fountains of memory in his mind.

'Can always put on a good show, we left-footers,' he thought to himself with a bitter smile. A mean, mysterious death for a child still grasping for manhood would be air-brushed into history on this ornate and beautiful day of astonishing winter colours.

He completed his circuit of the graveyard and made his way in quietly to the very rear corner of the church. The coffin lay across two wooden supports in front of the altar as the priest swished incense over it and prayed out loud.

> Grant O God, that while we lament the departure of this
>   your servant,
> We may always remember that we are most certainly to
>   follow him.
> Give us the grace to prepare for that last hour by a good life,
> That we may not be surprised by a sudden and unprovided
>   death, but be ever watching,
> That when you call, we may enter into eternal glory,
>   Through Christ our Lord.

Brennan felt like a man possessed as his right hand rose in reflex to begin the sign of the Cross. The curse was still with him. He hurried out from the church and immediately saw Brigit Parry standing over the open grave that would soon embrace the body of the father of her unborn child.

'Brigit,' he blurted unthinkingly, startling her, like a sparrow, into instant flight. She jogged off out into the open country, without turning to see that he was giving no chase. Brennan soon retreated too, as the coffin was brought out for burial. He would say his own farewell to Lovernios by finding out the truth about his death.

* * *

That night, despite a clear sky and a bone-chilling frost, Cernunnos and his warriors made their way across the fields and rivers, and through woods and copses, to the churchyard where Lovernios lay under a fresh mound of earth. With their bare hands they clawed the layers of soil and the clay off the coffin, and removed Lovernios's body from it. While four warriors quickly wrapped the corpse in a sheepskin and carried it off across the fields, Cernunnos and one of his lieutenants replaced the coffin in the grave and piled the soil, the clay and the pathetic floral tributes back on top of it.

Later, after they had trudged by starlight back to the hill-fort, they placed the body of Lovernios on the magnificent funeral pyre they had built that day, which, once lit, burnt so brightly that it seemed that the night and its demons had been banished for ever.

CHAPTER SEVEN

The morning after the funeral, Brennan gathered all his notes and his newspaper cuttings on the case, and took them down to the lounge on the first floor of the house, spreading out the various elements on the floor. Janet had gone to work in Bristol, Lester was at school, so he had the house to himself and therefore no excuse to avoid getting on with the case. To be precise, his aim was to see whether it was worth continuing. He'd offered a degree of posturing as a witness in the inquest, suggesting another means of death, without having the material evidence to support his claim. As John Major was always squeaking – it was 'time to put up or shut up'.

As ever, Brennan found that his thinking was liberated if he intoxicated himself with a dose of jazz. And there was no headier brew than Miles Davis's 'Flamenco Sketches' from the historic *Kind of Blue* album. Equally, the forms of jazz itself – spontaneous, elusive, elliptical – brought new shapes other than linear to his thoughts.

The structure of the band also had its parallels with the parties to the case. They had all combined, some randomly, some possibly with intent, to create a death. But who had written the score? Who had sounded the root note?

So he turned the volume up loud – it was a piece of such ethereal joy that the whole town should hear it – and began to circle his notes as Davis made his first appearance with a sound first celebratory, then haunting, the muted trumpet suggesting a tone of sadness.

He put his notes on Lovernios into one pile – this included the background on the family, such as it was, and the cuttings on Giles Castleton. The music swirled on. Now John Coltrane was sending out a bear-hug of emotion and hurt on his tenor sax. He piled up his notes for Cernunnos, the giant leader of the tribe, and in so doing recognised how little he knew about him. Who was he? Where was he? Why hadn't he come to the inquest? Questions spilled out from that corner of the brain which had been tapped by the music.

As Cannonball Adderly launched into his alto solo, a cheery, sexy theme, graced with two ecstatic cadences, Brennan thought of Lydia Pearson. He knew he was intrigued by her in a way that went beyond his usual instincts of wanting to beat lawyers at their own game. There was a flirtation there, and he sensed it was mutual, but he wasn't yet sure whether it was a device offered up by both of them to try to deceive or outwit the other. He made a note to go back to her, though not just yet – once she'd thought she'd got rid of him would be the time to turn up on her corporate doorstep.

As the bass of Paul Chambers floated effortlessly on, shaping the music and the response of the other players, Brennan began to feel a surge of optimism, that he could yet orchestrate the truth from this. Bill Evans's luscious, rolling piano chords echoed his euphoric mood. But suddenly the tone was changing – it was autumnal, valedictory. Davis's return, with a spidery, mournful, solitary theme, sobered his expectations. He'd get no help on this from the police or the security staff who worked at the quarry. He was out on his own, the ultimate soloist. The music gradually faded away to leave only the chilling hiss of drummer James Cobb's brushes on the cymbals, like the rustling of dead leaves in a forest. He looked out of the window down on to the town, still shrouded in its motionless January mist. Suddenly he felt lost again, a man without purpose. So it took him at least thirty seconds to break out of his trance and realise that his doorbell below was being rung urgently and insistently.

He slalomed down the stairs to the door. He could see the dark outline of a large figure through one of the frosted glass panels, and for a second he worried that Cernunnos himself might have been following in Lovernios's footsteps. But it was Tommy Preston on his doorstep, fresh out of Erlestoke prison, in cashmere roll-neck sweater and a smart tweed overcoat.

'Tommy!' he exclaimed, spontaneously throwing his arms around his old cell-mate. Tommy hugged him back.

'I thought you was trying not to answer the door,' he barked in his parched North London voice. 'I heard the music. Guessed you might have had a bird up there.'

'At half-nine in the morning? Come on in, Tom.'

Tommy stepped into the hall, sizing the place up, to see if it met his expectations of the way his chum should be living.

'Bit small, isn't it?' he asked brutally.

'Goes up three floors and you should see the view.'

'I had a nice view from Parkhurst once, and it didn't make the joint any better to live in.'

'Sit down. Want a drink?'

Tommy rolled his eyes at him theatrically.

'Did I just get out of the hospital or what?'

'Large whisky be all right?'

'Larger than the glass.'

Tommy took a seat at the kitchen table and took out a pack of Gitanes. Brennan thought about telling him about Janet's 'no smoking' order which excluded only his study, but he didn't have the heart. He poured the drink.

'I thought you weren't due out until the end of Feb?'

'Yeah, but the place is so fucking overcrowded they're having to chuck out all those coming to the end of their stretch. So God knows what they're gonna do when this government starts knocking remission on the head – look for another island the size of Australia, I guess.'

Tommy offered his glass. Brennan poured himself a quick Calvados and touched his glass against Tommy's.

'Santé,' Tommy toasted, lapsing into the French he used to speak when he was down on the Riviera in the 1960s, climbing into hotel rooms to relieve rich continental ladies of their jewels.

'So how's business?' Tommy said, retaining his ability to find the half-open window.

'Not great. I've got a story on now, but nobody's paying.'

'You offered it to anybody?'

'Not yet.'

'That would explain the absence of dosh, then, wouldn't it.' Tommy mocked up a paternal frown, one of the many gestures they had used as shorthand during the six months they had spent together, the thief with style, and the journalist with no constituency, two dying species in the same cage.

'How's the boy?'

'Fine. Settled at school. I think he may have got God, though.'

'Whatever gets you through the night,' Tommy said, shrugging tolerantly.

Brennan smiled. Tommy had an imperishable ability to cut through bullshit and angst, whether it involved demystifying prison policy or deciding if an individual needed a 'coating' to mend his ways. For all that, though, now that he was pushing sixty – he could have been older for all Brennan knew – Tommy had fewer options in life open to him. There was a chance he'd find a rich widow who'd keep him for the rest of his years, but women had only been transient figures in his life. He was unlikely to pick up a regular job, even in the improbable event of him wanting one. He would most likely exist on a diet of fencing knocked-off jewellery or fake Rolex watches. The days of the big heist, and the big celebration, were long gone now.

'What are you going to do, Tommy?'

'Finish this drink. Get you to show me round town. Have another drink. And then we'll take luncheon.'

Brennan nodded in self-admonishment. It was part of the unwritten code that you never asked such fundamental questions about life, just dealt with them as and when they came up. Forward planning, beyond the practicalities of a robbery, was not part of the criminal mind.

They talked of families and friends and later they made the descent into the town, Tommy breaking off to scoff at the exorbitant price of a piece of Edwardian jewellery in an antique-shop window. Then they took a window seat in the Dandy Lion, with a cappuccino and a Calvados each, and chatted and watched the traffic plough up and down Market Street, as Tommy reaccustomed himself to life outside.

'What's the story, then?' he asked at one point, with a sudden hint of interest.

'Young kid, living in a tribe, I'd guess you'd call it, protesting against a local quarry. Turned up headless in a trainload of stone at a depot in West London. They used to climb on board them, try and fuck with the brakes and whatever. So it looks like an accident.'

'Why should it be anything else?' Tommy asked pointedly.

'Well – there are two tribes. These kids who think they're defending their land as part of an historic heritage, from pre-Roman days, right? And the quarry, and their security operation. I went in with him two nights before he was . . . before he died, and they tried to beat the shit out of him.'

'Understandable.'

'This was more than doing their job, Tommy. It was a gut response, to something you don't understand, or which is so strange that you fear it. Like when a weird insect flies into your room – you pulp it to death rather than wonder what it is, or whether it can harm you first. These kids – well, they're men, some of them – have re-created a life for themselves which I think threatens what's now the conventional image of work, pay, hierarchy, wealth, exploitation. Like pitching hippies against Richard Nixon – it's as elemental as that.'

Tommy said nothing. Brennan knew he was no liberal, but the life he'd led had opened him up to a wider range of experiences than the old East End villains who never weaned themselves off their mums or jellied eels. He had seen, and embraced with passion, the continental life his work had brought to him.

'I can't judge. I don't like scroungers. But . . .'

'These kids are completely self-sufficient.'

'I was going to surmise that – what I hear is other voices. These security people – they've been taught to hate the opposition. To shit on them at every opportunity.'

'I think you're probably right.'

'Which means they're ex-Mob.'

'Army?'

'Well, I didn't mean the American Mafia. The first thing they do to a soldier is take his mind. And they tell him what a complete bunch of cunts he's fighting. So he doesn't stop to think, "Hang on, this feller's got two arms and two legs like me, probably got a wife and kiddies at home", he just gets on with the fighting, and the killing.'

'I remember that look in their eyes now,' Brennan recalled as the images of that turbulent night were summoned. 'They started to hate me as well, even though I was wearing a different uniform to the kid. That confused them. It was the first thing they picked up on – "Get rid of the designer walking clothes." '

'Mob,' said Tommy firmly as he went to the bar to order another round of drinks.

Brennan acted immediately on Tommy's educated guess, phoning Lydia Pearson from his window table to see if she would give details of Roadstone's private security operatives.

'You don't seriously expect me to divulge confidential company information such as that, do you?' Lydia Pearson said, laughing down the phone.

Brennan winked across to Tommy, who was still coming to terms with the fact that Brennan now had a mobile phone, eyeing him beadily like a disturbed passenger in a railway carriage.

'Well, I'll find out anyway,' Brennan said, 'so I thought you might just tell me straight out to save me the trouble. I'll throw in a lunch if it helps.'

There was a pause.

'You really have got some cheek, Mr Brennan, I'll give you that.'

'Was that a yes or a no?'

'A no, of course. My lunches are on company time. You are not on the company's Christmas list. QED.'

'Okay – make it dinner.'

'A drink will do.'

'Where?'

'Somewhere halfway. Do you know the Woolpack at Beckington?'

'I'll find it. Six o'clock tonight?'

'Six thirty.'

'Thank you, Miss Pearson. Bye.'

Brennan scanned the console of his phone and pushed the red

handset button which he thought ended the call. Roadstone International's number certainly disappeared from the display, and the light went out, so he guessed he must have done it right. Tommy watched him, exhaling fragrant blue smoke in a low cloud across the table.

'Sounds cosy. You tupping her?'

'Tommy – I've only just got the marriage back together. I do not "tup" any more. I never did anyway. Much. Least of all sober. This is a professional flirtation.'

'You mean she wants to get into *your* strides?'

'Possibly – I think it's more of a defence mechanism. I think that she thinks I won't go too hard on her company if she's nice to me. Because I think that she thinks the alternative to that, freezing me out, will get her a worse result, by antagonising me. See?'

'I expect you'll know when you ask her something really important – whether defending the company means more to her than upsetting you.'

'Right. I'll ask her something important, then.'

He checked his watch.

'What do you fancy for lunch? My treat.'

'The company's good here. And the view.'

'Dover sole suit you? Mashed spuds, two veg?'

'Sweet as a bun,' Tommy said, smiling.

Brennan ordered at the bar and came back with a chilled bottle of Chardonnay and two glasses.

'You don't have to do this, you know, Francis.'

'It's odd – the only other people to call me Francis are my mum and my parish priest.'

'Well, we presume you no longer talk to the latter, so that leaves just two, then.'

Brennan poured the wine and they drank, toasting each other again.

'You going to go back to London, Tom?'

'I'm a fish outside its bowl anywhere else. Except Cannes or Marseille maybe. And they ain't what they used to be.'

'Look – I can't promise anything. But I can put you on "the firm" if you don't mind.'

'I *do* mind. I only do favours for you, not jobs.'

'I'll pay generous expenses.'

'What if I get through a monkey a day?' Tommy teased.

Brennan shrugged.

'You don't need me, son. I can help you any time you want. But you mustn't kid yourself into thinking you need me. Nor that I need you. Just let it sit like that. Long as I know where you are, and you know where I am.'

Brennan offered a hand. Tommy took it in an arm-wrestler's grip, nothing so ordinary as a gentlemanly handshake. And then they lunched, drank some more, smoked a couple of Havanas which Brennan walked round to the off-licence to buy, and finished with coffees as the clock on the Catholic church opposite chimed three.

They walked back up to the house, and after Brennan had introduced Tommy to Lester, Tommy went for a kip on the sofa in the lounge. Lester waited till he was snoring before sidling up to his father.

'Is he really a criminal, Dad?' he asked excitedly.

'In the strictest meaning of the word, yes. But in the spiritual sense, he's one of the straightest guys I've ever met. Code of honour, that sort of thing. You ought to discuss that with your scripture teacher. Nothing's as black or as white as it seems.'

'Barabbas was a criminal. And he was saved so Jesus could be crucified,' Lester said thoughtfully.

'So . . . what does that tell us?'

Lester pondered.

'That we are all equal before God?'

'Something like that. But there's also this idea of judgment, isn't there? Yes, Tommy's a criminal in society's terms. But I know how kind he was to me in prison. And to other people.'

'Why don't you believe, Dad?'

'You pick your times to ask such questions, don't you, Lester? I can't say really. I just got out of the habit. Saw too much misery, too much evil to believe that there could ever be a heaven. Or a hell, come to that. These people I've been dealing with, the Celtic Brotherhood, they had beliefs before Christianity came along. But then the people they're imitating needed a belief to keep them going. To make sense of things. To take the fear away.'

'And you don't think we need that any more?'

'Not in religious terms, no. In human terms, maybe. If you think mankind isn't going to get better then all that's left is despair. I prefer to think we *will* get better. Stop killing each other. Help each other. Care for the poor and the sick. Share our wealth equally.'

Lester looked flummoxed. Brennan reached out and ruffled his hair affectionately.

'Take no notice of what I say, Lester.'

'But I do. You're my dad. And I love you.'

'Good. I love you too. Whatever you believe in.'

Janet's key in the door dispelled this moment of intimacy. But she was aware of an atmosphere when she walked in.

'Am I interrupting something?'

'Dad's got a criminal friend of his asleep on the couch upstairs. But I don't mind,' Lester said gamely.

'My old cell-mate, Tommy Preston got out of Erlestoke today. We've been drinking a bit.'

'Is he staying with us? I can make up a bed.'

'I haven't asked him yet. I'll offer. But I think he'll prefer a bed and room service at the Swan.'

Janet sniffed, smelling the once-fragrant cigarette smoke which had now turned sour.

'Maybe not a bad thing. He'll have dinner with us, I hope.'

'We'll see. Got a meeting before then. Quarry people.'

Later, when Tommy rose and washed, Brennan introduced him to Janet and they chatted earnestly about prison reform for an hour or so, before Brennan tapped his watch to signal it was time to go. He and Tommy walked out down the path, looking out over the town's lights, as the fog began to smother them.

'She's a good head, son,' was Tommy's verdict. 'You'd be mad to lose her.'

'I know that now, Tommy. I won't.'

The lecture was over. They got into Brennan's car and eased through the thickening mists to Beckington, a small village that had been liberated by a by-pass on the A36. At the centre of it stood the Woolpack, a pub smartened up by some enterprising people into a pretty country hotel, with a stone-flagged bar and a warm, upholstered restaurant. Tommy took a stool at the bar, acting as a listening-post for when Lydia Pearson arrived, while Brennan took a seat near the door. At six thirty on the dot, she was there.

Brennan bought her a vodka and tonic, while he stuck to a glass of wine.

'They are called Blue Chip Security, and they're based outside Westbury.'

'Thanks,' he said. 'All ex-army probably, yes?'

'I believe so. Just another reason why you won't get anything off them.'

'Maybe not, but I can ask.'

'Why are you banging on at this? The case is over. There's been a top-level review of security. It won't happen again.'

'Ah, but what won't? A beating up of protesters? Intimidation of innocent journalists? That's what squaddies are trained to do.'

'I meant incidents with trains. They're going to patrol the railway line now. As far as the tunnel anyway. And one of the guards is going to ride shotgun with every train driver.'

'Not literally shotgun, I hope?'

'Look – I could get the sack telling you stuff like this, Brennan. Be a little grateful.'

'Why are you telling me?'

'Because we've got nothing to hide, and you think we have.'

'How do you know you've got nothing to hide? You're a legal person. And a woman.'

'What kind of sexist crap is this?'

'I know how corporate men think. They put a pretty, clever young woman up as a front, tell her all is sweetness and light, and ask her to act accordingly.'

'I attend every board meeting,' Lydia said crisply. 'I see every policy document. I handled most of the flak we had during all the public inquiries. If there was shit there I'd have known about it.'

'And what would you have done if there had been?'

'I know where to draw the line. The company pays my wages, but it doesn't own my life.'

'Touching,' Brennan said.

'Don't patronise me.'

'Okay. Tell me the names of the guards who were on duty the night they caught me and Humphrey Castleton trespassing.'

Lydia said nothing.

'I'd also like to know who was on duty the night he died. But you won't tell me that, will you? Because you don't know. And they won't tell you, will they?'

'If you think I see that as a challenge to my authority, dream on, Brennan.'

'And you'd know, of course, if the company arranged any sweeteners for Councillor Giles Castleton in order to soothe away any worries for the district council?'

Lydia refused to rise to this fairly predictable bait. So Brennan took out a small sheet of paper. He wrote down his address, his phone number, his mobile phone number and the fax of the shop in Bradford he used for sending or receiving such messages. He pushed it across the table to her.

'One day soon you'll hear something. In the canteen, maybe, or down at the quarry where the "lads" get together for their tea breaks and their look at the page-three bird. And then you'll know I was right. And you'll have to decide what kind of woman you are.'

Lydia finished her drink and left, without taking his note with her. Brennan felt a shit for nobbling her like this but as a woman of apparent integrity she was the weakest link in any chain of deceit.

Tommy waited a moment and then wandered over from the bar and sat down at the table with his drink.

'I don't think she fancies you any more,' he said.

'I think I made sure of that.'

That night, Cernunnos and his small band of warriors prepared for a raid with their usual routines – a feast and a bonfire. A sheep had been claimed from nearby fields and decorated with a necklace of mistletoe before it was slaughtered and roasted on the fire. Some of the ale that Cernunnos had brewed and stored was drunk, and as he carved meat from the sheep's carcase on the spit, he marked the faces of his warriors with bold stripes of the animal's blood which had been collected in a ceremonial bowl when its throat had been cut. Each warrior ate heartily as the blood dried on his face in the heat of the fire. And towards the end of their feast, Cernunnos tossed some leaves of wormwood on to the blaze to create a cloud of fragrant, heady smoke.

Despite the freezing temperatures, their clothes of wool and animal skin held up well, and the food, ale and incense brought an intense inner warmth. Cernunnos went to the weapons store and handed out the pewter and iron daggers, blessing each one as he passed it over. And then they stood before the fire in silent prayer to Lugh, their god of the sun. Cernunnos bellowed out defiantly through the bare trees, brushing through the tangle of ivy and holly bushes to lie in wait for that night's infernal shipment.

But this time it was different. Before the steel rails began to sing of the train's approach, strange lights loomed out of the mist and the darkness up the line towards the quarry. And shadowy figures emerged, walking along the side of the track. There were more than a dozen of them, helmeted, body-armoured, and carrying prods that fizzed with blue sparks of light. Their high-beam torches played along the track, and then flashed up the banks of the hill. Cernunnos stilled his men and made them lie in the undergrowth, or bend their bodies behind the trunks of the trees.

A raucous shout of 'Come on out, you bastards!' echoed around the ravine. Cernunnos gestured for silence and signalled for his men to keep their positions. He was not so much alarmed by this new show of strength as by its likely tactics. Were they about to mount an attack on the camp, or were these centurions merely a bait for a bigger ambush should Cernunnos decide upon his own attack? His questions were soon answered as the first of the trains from the quarry clattered slowly through the ravine, waved on by the escorts, and disappeared into the tunnel. They held their places for the next hour as a further three trains lumbered and roared through the night. And then the guards retreated back down the line, shouting obscenities up to the warriors who they couldn't see but knew were there. Shivering with cold, Cernunnos led his men back up the hill and restoked the fire for warmth and cheer.

'Do not despair, my brave friends,' he said firmly. 'They wanted a battle tonight, because they had the numbers, and the strategy of surprise. But we did not give them one. We refused to fall into their ambush. *We* dictate when an attack takes place, not them! Our Celtic forebears forced the Romans to pour huge resources into their armies, and they still could not conquer our brothers. Next time, the surprise will be all theirs!'

He dutifully did the rounds of his men, like any good battle commander, to make sure that they were settled and warm. And then he took some more lamb and ale, wrapped himself in a blanket and sat on the ramparts looking down over the ravine. He was not just acting as lookout in case any of the enemy came back for an attack. He was planning his strategy for the decisive battles that he now knew to be imminent.

Over dinner that evening, Brennan, Janet and Tommy Preston had, despite their best intentions, ended up talking about the quarry and the protesters. And from their discussions – provoked by Tommy's posing of the most obvious questions – Brennan resolved to find out more about what Tommy called 'the key players' in the conflict. Tommy, from his knowledge of the East End in the fifties and sixties, suggested a parallel with the gang wars of that time, of which he'd been an interested spectator rather than a participant.

'You got two mobs here, each fighting over territory, each hating the other's guts by the sound of it. You got in with one of the fighters from one mob, but now he's dead, he's no good to you. And you haven't spoken to the top man. With the quarry firm, you know all the generals and none of the soldiers. So your whereabouts are not balanced, are they?'

'It isn't necessarily a question of balance, though, Tommy. My investigation, by its nature, is partial. I'm taking sides, I can't be a neutral observer, because of my suspicions.'

'Well, you're lining yourself up for a kicking, in that case. One side's out to stop you, one side thinks you're playing for them, not yourself.'

'Hang on – the protesters know I'll write what I find out about the story, not what they tell me.'

'I bet you they don't. Why should they come to you? Because you can get inside the other mob's operation, that's all. They expect you to get a result for them. They may even have set you up for it.'

'Tommy,' Brennan countered with irritation, 'I know my business. You think I can't tell when people are trying to exploit me?'

'That's for you to know, son. All I'm saying is, with the gangs in the fifties, if you moved between the two sides, as a broker, or as a peace merchant, or even as a deserter, *both* of them would look on you as a traitor. In fact, it was the quickest way to end up dead.'

'I think Tommy's got a point about this gang psychology, Frank. And if he's right, you're more or less a hostage,' Janet suggested.

'Oh, don't be so melodramatic, the pair of you. I could drop this thing right now, and what would happen?'

'You'd get bored in an instant,' Janet said, smiling triumphantly.

'Maybe, but I wouldn't be in any danger. The story would just go away, or would simply be covered in the same old television news clichés – a balance of views, no context, and certainly no passion.'

'But the one certainty when you've got two gangs, whether they're boy scouts or girl guides, is that it all has to end in a fight,' Tommy said, leaning back to sip his brandy like a high-table don.

'You don't think one death finishes it?' Brennan asked anxiously.

'As I remember, one death is just the start. Blood has to be spilt. That's the way it is, believe me. And you've got to make sure you're out of the way when it happens.'

Brennan slept badly that night. Tommy's street wisdom – insight into human nature would be more apt – always had the ability to cut through some of his own precious conceptions. He could see how his investigation, and maybe even his own well-being, could be compromised if he strayed too far to one side. His presumptions about the quarry protest were largely based on the attitude of those guards who had beaten up Humphrey Castleton, and on his admiration for Castleton's commitment. That had polarised his views. He himself, though, hadn't been able to deny, even at the inquest, that Castleton had attacked the guards first. Perhaps the violence had come, in the first instance, from Cernunnos and his tribe?

The following morning, after breakfast, he asked if Janet could get to talk to Brigit Parry, in order to find out more about life with the tribe, and about who Cernunnos was. She wasn't going into Bristol that day, and reacted as keenly as always. When Tommy came down, nursing the hangover that had put him off going to the Swan Hotel, and apologising for 'talking bollocks all night', Brennan asked him if he could think of a way of finding out more about the security company's operation.

Tommy, dunking his toast in his tea as if he were still in the prison canteen, suggested a briefer version of 'long firm fraud'. Janet frowned.

'It's an old thieves' trick,' Brennan explained. 'They set up a firm trading, say, in televisions, and order twenty and pay for them, cash on delivery. Then every month they up the order, but still pay cash. Finally they whack in an order for five hundred, but this time on credit. The suppliers have them down as good customers and prompt payers and so they deliver the goods, and then the firm does a runner with the lot.'

'I see that. But it's surely not a good trick to try on a security firm, is it?' Janet asked bluntly.

'Depends on how clever they are,' Tommy said with his first smile of the day.

'We go to them as customers, Janet. Buy some work off them, and promise more if we like what we see – but first they have to show us the goods, right, Tommy?'

'First, we have to show them we mean business,' Tommy corrected, before splitting another slice of toast and plunging it into his mug of tea.

CHAPTER EIGHT

Brennan judged that, in the circumstances, it was best to let Tommy take the lead. He knew, without having ever been given chapter and verse, that Tommy had done this sort of stuff before. There'd been half a story one night, told in the darkness of the cell, about setting up a jeweller's shop in Hatton Garden in order to have a base from which to break into a diamond dealer's safe in the building next door. He had never gone so far as to say whether the ruse worked or not, but it had, like several others Brennan remembered, suggested that part of his success as a jewel thief had always been due to his ability to be convincing as a businessman.

Brennan tried to rehearse him as they drove out to the address of the Blue Chip Security company in Westbury, having left Janet on the trail of Brigit Parry in Frome.

'Do you want to take my mobile phone in with you? In case it turns sticky?'

'Who am I gonna call?' Tommy asked with a laugh.

'What about a business card? We can stop somewhere and have one made up.'

'Then the first thing he'll do is find the address and number's false. *I'm* the customer, right? If he starts asking for that kind of gear, then he's tantamount, isn't he, to calling me a liar? Which is not a good way to conduct business.'

'I don't imagine they take orders from anyone off the street,' Brennan said with exasperation. Tommy shot him a glare of pantomimic disbelief.

'Do I look like someone just off the street?'

Brennan scanned the cotton piqué shirt, pure silk tie and cashmere overcoat that were Tommy's outward appearance.

'Jermyn Street, maybe . . .'

'Absolutely right. Now pull over while I make my appointment.'

Brennan slowed the car a touch, keeping an eye open for a lay-by or the opening to a field which might allow him to park. Inside a mile he found a lay-by, where a converted caravan was serving teas and hot bacon rolls to hungry drivers.

He handed Tommy the phone and switched it on for him, then stuck an adhesive yellow Post-it note on which he'd written Blue Chip's number on to the inside of the windscreen. Tommy peered at the number.

'Do you want a tea or anything?'

'No thanks – don't want to be peeing all through my meeting.'

'Do you want me to get out of the car?'

'You about to fart or something?'

'No. I just wondered whether you wanted to do your spiel alone.'

'Am I a member of the Royal Shakespeare Company or something?' Tommy asked sarcastically.

He dialled the number. Brennan looked out of the window, tensing more with embarrassment than with fear. Suddenly Tommy was speaking in the well-modulated tones of the English upper middle class.

'Good morning, young lady, I wonder if I could speak to your director of operations? Yes, of course. My name is . . .'

Brennan suddenly turned away from the window, thinking Tommy was about to say 'J. R. Hartley'.

'. . . Mr Thomas Preston. Well, obviously I can't go into precise details about what it concerns, but it's to your company's advantage. Thank you.'

He gave Brennan a reassuring wink while he waited to be put through.

'Good morning . . . Major Nicholls? . . . Yes, well, I'm in the area and I wondered if I might pop in to see you for a short while. Yes, of course you may ask – I'm a regular traveller between

Bristol and Amsterdam, and because of what I bring back from Holland I thought it might be wise to have a couple of strong young men alongside me, do you understand? You *do*? Excellent. Well, give me a time, will you, and I'll pop by . . .' He made a masturbatory gesture with his left hand, either as a comment on his own performance or as a reaction to the guff he was getting down the phone.

'Eleven – that's perfect. No, no – I'll find you. Thanks. Bye!'

He gave Brennan the phone so that he could switch it off.

'Where did you get the bloody accent, Tommy, RADA?'

'I spent most of my forties and fifties in the bars of the best hotels in Europe. Something other than cirrhosis was bound to rub off.'

'So what are you?'

'A diamond merchant, obviously. Amsterdam's not all dope, you know.'

'Did he buy it?'

'Stop worrying, Frank. What's the worst that can happen? He rumbles me. Then I tell him how impressed I am that he's passed my initiative test, and he can expect a bulk order for his goon squad from the Sultan of bleedin' Brunei.'

Brennan started the car. Working with Tommy might well turn out to be a major mistake, but for the time being it was worth it for the fun.

Janet had never feigned so much interest in books that she couldn't even pretend to understand. The appearance of them in the shop's window had suggested that they were second-hand, but on closer inspection it was obvious that they had just never been bought, and had been allowed to yellow and curl over God knows how many years of neglect.

'Need any help at all?' asked the permed-blonde middle-aged woman seated behind the counter.

'I think I might, actually,' Janet said innocently. 'My son's studying ancient English history at school this term. He's asked me to look out for books on Celtic ritual or mythology, anything in that line.'

The woman came out from behind the counter. She wore a

heavy woollen smock, and there were about four silver emblems hanging from her neck by chains. The absence of any make-up made her look older than she plainly was – Janet guessed at forty-five to forty-eight. She wore lots of rings but, conspicuously, there wasn't one on the third finger of the left hand.

'There's a few down here which should suit the younger reader. There's a lot of great stories don't get told so much these days.'

The woman gestured to a row of books on the bottom shelf, and then returned to the counter. No wonder she never shifted any books with such low-power sales pitches, thought Janet, as she bent down to scan the titles. Faced with such stodginess as *Britain's Celtic Past*, *Myths of Time* and *An A–Z of Celtic Britain*, she chose the latter, more functional title – at least Lester might find it useful. She took it back to the counter and handed it over for wrapping. The woman made no attempt to oblige, just looking at the pencil scribble inside the front cover.

'Five pounds, please.'

Janet handed a fiver over and that appeared to be the end of the transaction as far as the woman was concerned.

'Could I have a receipt, please?' Janet asked suddenly, hoping that this might reveal further details, but the woman simply took a standard-issue office notebook from a drawer, slipped a carbon paper underneath the top sheet, and wrote '1 book, £5 received', signing initials that looked like 'S. P.' Janet folded the receipt into her wallet and took a deep breath.

'Is Brigit around?'

The woman suddenly lost her previous apathy. She was alert, tense, and defensive in an instant.

'Sorry, don't know who you mean.'

'Brigit Parry.'

'Like I said . . .'

'Mrs Parry . . .'

'That's not my name.'

'What's the P stand for?'

'Look, who are you?'

'Brigit met my husband at the inquest last week. She told him about expecting a baby. The dead boy's baby.'

'Why isn't *he* here, then?'

'Because he thought this was a sensitive issue for a woman to talk about in front of a man. My name's Janet. Janet Brennan.'

She offered a hand.

'Sheila Parry.'

Sheila took Janet's hand in both of hers and shook it gently, as if she were a sister.

'I didn't mean to intrude. We just wanted to make sure that Brigit was all right. Frank, my husband, felt she'd rather been forgotten about in all the fuss over the inquest.'

'She's happier that way, I think. Would you like some tea?'

Janet nodded eagerly, and Sheila pulled aside the curtain that divided the shop from a small kitchenette and storeroom, which also featured the staircase up to the first-floor flat. She placed a stained tin kettle on a gas ring and then fished out three or four ˙˙˙s loaded with tea-leaves.

'Jasmin, rosehip, camomile or good old-fashioned Broken Orange Pekoe?'

'The Pekoe, I think, thank you.'

Janet took a pace towards the back room and craned her head round the door-frame. She could see a pile of cardboard boxes, marked with the names of obscure publishers. The kitchenette, tea jars apart, looked bare and functional. But underneath the rising staircase was a circular brick structure.

'What's that?' she asked, pointing.

'Oh, it's the old well. Used to be the only supply of water to the house in Victorian times. You can still hear water running down at the bottom some days.'

'Thank God for progress, eh?'

Sheila said nothing, calmly measuring out the scoops of dark tea leaves into the china pot.

'Is Brigit actually here?'

'No. She's out for the day.'

'Working?'

'Helping more like. Day centre for old people.'

She poured the boiling water on to the leaves and settled the lid on the pot, then arranged a tray with mugs, tea strainer and spoons, before bringing it out into the shop.

'It's none of my business really, but will she have the baby?'

Sheila glared at her.

'Why shouldn't she?'

'Well – her age. No father.'

'I managed to bring *her* up on my own. Don't need men around for babies, except at the beginning.'

'Sorry. I shouldn't have asked,' Janet said apologetically.

Sheila poured the tea through the strainer into the mugs. Janet waited for the offer of milk but it didn't come. She sipped the tea and it proved to be fragrant enough on its own.

'How did Brigit hitch up with Humphrey Castleton? I know they were at the camp together – but before that?'

'Batheaston by-pass. They met while they were camped out on Solsbury Hill, trying to save it from the road builders. He came and stayed with us here for a bit afterwards, and then they linked up with this anti-quarry group. He'd been at Solsbury too. Whatever his name is.'

'Cernunnos, I think my husband said. That's Celtic, presumably.'

Sheila pointed at the book that Janet had bought.

'I expect it'll tell you in that.'

'Yes, I'm sure. You didn't go to see Brigit at the camp, then?'

'Why should I? It was her business. She knew she could always come home when she wanted. And she did. You got children, Mrs Brennan?'

'A son. Thirteen.'

'He'll be going his own way soon, then. You can't stop them. The first night away's the worst. You just don't sleep with worry. But then you think back to what we did when we were young – pop festivals, hitch-hiking, sleeping on beaches in Greece. It's the last job of a parent to know when to let go.'

This homespun wisdom, for all its banality, had touched a nerve in Janet, given Lester's recent passion for religion. Like Sheila, Janet too had felt the first breakings of the link that had bound her to her son, almost since the moment of his conception.

'I wonder if Humphrey Castleton's family feel the same way?' she asked pointedly.

Sheila snorted.

'Didn't even show up for the inquest, I gather.'

'Have they been in touch with you? Offering any support or, well, money?'

'No. And I don't want anything from them anyway.'

'Might not Brigit, though?'

'No. That's why she's stayed quiet.'

'She told Frank about the baby. Why just him?'

Sheila shrugged.

'I dunno. Have to ask her that. Why didn't he tell on her?'

'Actually, I don't know that either. I guess Frank probably just wanted to protect her from what he knew his colleagues would do if they knew. Nobody's been around, I take it?'

'No. Till you.'

Janet sipped her tea. As a researcher, she was used to questioning people over the phone, having prepared notes, and with some sort of corporate identity behind her. Meeting people face to face, as nothing more than Brennan's assistant, was a less structured experience than she had hoped.

'I can't think of anything else to ask you, Sheila,' she confessed artlessly. 'Perhaps Brigit could give me a ring and talk about life in the camp?'

'I'll ask her.'

Janet scribbled down her phone number. It was the most she could do in the circumstances.

The first item to catch Tommy Preston's eye on the wall of Major Nicholls' office at Blue Chip Security was a nasty-looking curved dagger.

'That's a kukri, if I'm not mistaken,' he said as Nicholls came to greet him.

'Absolutely right, Mr Preston. Were you out there at all?'

'No – but I've seen them in action,' Tommy said obliquely, remembering the Hackney villain who made a point of carrying one around in his belt during the gang wars of the 1960s. 'Can take a man's head off at a stroke.'

Nicholls smiled.

'Actually, I think the Gurkhas were very good at generating

their own terrifying publicity. They only had to wave their swords to get a surrender.'

'All part of the game. Ninety per cent of winning is up here, isn't it?' Tommy announced, placing his index finger on his temple.

'I think you may well be right. It's certainly our company's belief that psychological warfare is preferable to the real thing. Take a seat, Mr Preston.'

Tommy began to remove his overcoat, but Nicholls stepped in to assist. A tall, thin man in his late forties, Nicholls was a classic collage of the ex-military style – Viyella shirt, Lovat tweed sports jacket, regimental tie, and commando-soled brogues. Tommy hoped that the combination of cashmere and silk in his own dress would be equally convincing for the guise of diamond dealer.

'Now how can we help you, Mr Preston?'

Tommy settled himself confidently on the sofa opposite Nicholls who was in an armchair.

'I'm a diamond merchant. Semi-retired, it has to be said. My travel usually takes me from Bristol to Amsterdam and back. But given my age, and the current climate of law enforcement, I've decided I should plan some protection for myself.'

'Very understandable. One of our services is to provide personal security, round the clock if necessary. As many men as you think fit.'

'Tell me about them. Your men.'

'All ex-army. All thoroughly vetted by the company. Trained in a variety of skills – communications, anti-terrorist, martial arts, intelligence.'

'Weapons?'

'Ah – tricky area, obviously. But, how can I put this, the technology is available to us if we need it.'

A secretary arrived with a tray loaded with coffee pot and cups – all best china – and a plate with a paper doily, stacked neatly with biscuits. Tommy let the secretary pour the coffee and leave the room before he resumed his performance.

'With respect, though, you won't be able to take a gun on to a plane, will you?'

Nicholls twitched a little, the pleasant façade momentarily darkening with irritation.

'Well, not in a literal sense, no. We are obliged to, and indeed *wish*, to operate inside the law. Without knowing your business precisely, I can't prescribe the right formula . . .'

'Two months ago,' Tommy interrupted dramatically, 'a Belgian friend of mine was ambushed in the car park at Schipol airport. They put a gun to his head, used a bolt-cutter to take the briefcase off the chain on his wrist and then chloroformed him and dumped him in the boot of his car. Could you have prevented that?'

Major Nicholls shifted uneasily. He was used to the paraphernalia of the company – the pukka name, the military connections, and the bespoke offices in a Georgian building – doing the hard work of establishing client confidence. Having to 'pitch' for work was an unusual experience for him.

'Well, let me see. We'd have had at least two men with you, possibly a third in a following car. All linked by radio. You'd never have been allowed anywhere near a car park, but simply taken directly into the terminal and into one of the private service suites. Had there been any sign of a planned ambush, the car would have whisked you straight back where you came from. Ah – and we might have had you down as a decoy, with the diamonds being carried by two of our other men.'

'Not bad,' Tommy nodded. 'But you still haven't told me what would happen if your men and I were confronted with a gun.'

Nicholls pulled on his lip for a moment.

'If I show you something, to reassure you, can I insist on complete confidentiality?'

'Of course.'

Nicholls rose from his armchair and crossed the room to a free-standing double-fronted library cabinet in what looked like cherrywood, which was positioned against one of the office walls. He took a key from an inner pocket of his jacket and unlocked the glass doors to the bookcase. He pulled at the two stacks of fitted shelves and they both swung outwards to reveal an inner compartment, where six pump-action shotguns were mounted on green-baize-covered racks.

Tommy tried not to smile – he'd seen hundreds of these fake cabinets in his time, although the contents he'd usually been in pursuit of had been jewels, not shooters. He thought about calling out, 'Standard three-way bolting system, operated by a nine-lever lock', but thought better of it. In any case, Nicholls had now reached into the recesses of the cabinet and was taking out a dark carbon-fibre truncheon of about three feet in length.

Tommy sat forward – this was something he hadn't seen before. Nicholls held up the truncheon. The handle was conventionally turned, but there was a switch. And at the top of the truncheon was a metal filament. Nicholls flicked the switch at the base and a spark of blue light arced across the filament.

'Electric stun baton, Mr Preston. Can render a suspect unconscious and disabled in an instant.'

'I bet the police wouldn't mind getting their hands on a few of them.'

'Only a matter of time, I believe. I have some videos of them in action. Nigeria, I think. Tested in combat, as they say. They're nasty but very effective.'

'Thank you – I'm sufficiently impressed. I take it your firm would only use them in the most extreme circumstances.'

'I can't go into operational details, but yes, you have the assurance that you could easily fall within those parameters.'

Tommy stood up in a business-like fashion and offered his hand to Major Nicholls.

'I shall be in touch within days.'

Nicholls was somewhat irked by the abrupt ending to the meeting.

'Don't you want to know more details, Mr Preston? Costs, for example?'

Tommy slung his overcoat over his arm and smiled.

'I'm reminded of the story of the guy in the Rolls-Royce showroom, Major Nicholls. He was told that if he had to ask the price then he couldn't afford the car. Thank you for your time.'

The secretary escorted him out down the thickly carpeted stairs to the front lobby, where a Blue Chip guard monitored four screens showing camera shots of the building's exterior facings. After checking each screen, he nodded to the secretary to open the door, and Tommy stepped out, taking care not to do anything that might register on the watching cameras.

He strode away with well-practised ease. 'Never run' had been one of the first lessons he had been taught by his criminal mentors when he started out as a seventeen-year-old bag-man. He thought about those long-ago days as he crossed the main square of Westbury to the small hotel where Brennan was waiting. He paused to look in a shop window to ensure that nobody was either following him or shadowing his moves in front. But all movement around him seemed innocent.

'Heavy-duty firm,' he said softly as he joined Brennan at the hotel bar.

'Did they rumble you?' Brennan asked anxiously.

'What's to rumble? Besides, if they did, or if they do, it'll get 'em all edgy, won't it?'

'But if they're as heavy-duty as you say, they're not to be messed with, are they?'

'Look, you're exactly the sort of geezer they can't handle. A man who can get them a lorryload of bad publicity.'

'But I've got none so far.'

'You have now,' Tommy said with a wink.

He waited until they'd had their drink and returned to the car before he told Brennan about the sighting of the stun baton.

'They'll deny it, of course, when you put it to them, but if you go in with a sworn statement from me, I'd lay you odds of seven to four that old Major Nicholls will cough up whatever it is you want to know.'

Brennan smiled in genuine admiration of Tommy's sheer balls.

'He's military, all right,' Tommy continued, 'but he's a desk man, or ideas, but he's never roughed it, in my estimation, that is.'

'That's good enough for me, Tommy. Thanks.'

Tommy and Brennan met up with Janet at the wholefood café in Frome, a venue that brought a curled lip of contempt from Tommy. But they soon adjourned to an Italian restaurant in the higher, older part of the town, where auction houses and serious antique shops lined the street.

Over lunch they pooled their news, Janet feeling reticent and faint-hearted about her achievements in comparison with

Tommy's apparently successful act of bravado. She detailed the miserable little shop, and the dead family atmosphere into which a new baby would be born in less than six months' time.

'We can't interfere,' Brennan insisted as he sensed her drift. 'It's all very unfortunate, but Brigit Parry getting pregnant doesn't seem like part of the story. I don't want it to be anyway.'

'I think Frank's right, Jan,' Tommy said, tucking his napkin into his shirt collar as his seafood spaghetti arrived. 'Unless her getting knocked up is part of some skulduggery, you have to drop the girl out. It's only fair on her.'

'Not just for the future, but for now too. If what Tommy's found out is right, there's a potential war between the quarry security and the protesters. We can't implicate her in that.'

'Okay, I see. But I still think we can help. The mother's brain-dead. Too much dope in the sixties, too much mysticism in the nineties. I'd like to talk to Brigit on her own, to find out what *she* wants to do.'

'Fine – but be careful how you proceed,' Brennan urged. 'She's an innocent bystander at the moment. Let's not turn her into anything more dangerous.'

Janet puckered her lips at him.

'An unwanted pregnancy isn't exactly innocence, Frank. It's a grave consequence. I think you should go to the Castleton family and tell them. It was their son's act. It's their seed that's been planted.'

Brennan gestured at his food, pleading for silence in which to eat it, which was exactly what Janet gave him for the rest of the lunch.

Brennan let Janet drive Tommy back to Bradford in the car after lunch, while he took a taxi from Frome out to Great Elm, asking the bemused driver to wait by the duck pond while he 'just went up to the camp on top of the Celtic hill-fort for a few moments.' He left a tenner to cover the initial fare and whatever the meter was running up.

He made his way along the footpath and took a quick look down the railway line. The ravine was bathed in shadow and the coating of frost on the wooden sleepers testified to the sun's absence. He shivered briefly at the thought that Humphrey Castleton's head might still be lying around somewhere in the undergrowth, before making his way up the hill towards the fort's ramparts. As he neared the top, heaving with a breathlessness that made him vow to give up cigars one day, he suddenly looked up to see that Cernunnos was standing on the ramparts, looking down at him, at an angle that made his six feet five inches seem doubled in size.

'What do you want?' Cernunnos asked.

Brennan paused on the slope, looking around to make sure that he wasn't being encircled.

'Cup of tea and a slice of fruit cake would be nice.'

'Flippancy doesn't become you, Mr Brennan,' Cernunnos announced.

'Nor does freezing my arse off on top of a hill. Can we talk? Now?'

Cernunnos looked around then held down a hand. Brennan took it and found himself very nearly pulled off his feet as Cernunnos hauled him on to the rampart. It was the first time he had seen the giant in daylight. He seemed older, and certainly less intimidating than darkness suggested. Behind the lattice of facial tattoos were deeply pouched eye sockets, and furrows ran across his forehead as if they had been ploughed there. More pertinently, he stank. A cocktail of garlic and vegetable odours combined to produce a dog's breath that could stun at six feet. Brennan tried to hide the fact that he was gagging by looking beyond Cernunnos to the encampment. There, a miserable circle of home-made huts and animal-skin tents stood cheerlessly. The cooking fire was virtually dormant, a wisp of smoke rising from the grey ashes past the charred skeleton of a sheep.

'I didn't notice you at the inquest,' he said slyly.

'We don't recognise your justice system. It stems from Roman law.'

'I thought you might have liked a bit of a publicity binge, make the most of Lovernios's death. Would have given the campaign against the quarry new momentum, don't you think?'

'We are not engaged in a propaganda war here, Mr Brennan. It is just a war, pure and simple. Either they lose or we do.

Nothing you can do or write will change that.'

'Did you know that Lovernios had come to see me, then?'

'He told me later, yes.'

'And you disapproved?'

'The tribe are free men. They can come and go as they wish. Lovernios had a naïve belief that publicity was the key to our cause. He was wrong, but that was for him to find out. I don't act as a censor.'

'What are you, then, exactly?'

'A leader. A Druid.'

'Eco-warrior, is that the term?' Brennan asked with a grin.

'This is about more than just ecology, Mr Brennan, I'd have thought you'd have realised that by now. This is about stopping an attempt to make a culture extinct.'

Brennan scratched an earlobe impatiently.

'Look, if that's all it is, why don't you apply to the National Lottery committee for money to become a theme park?'

He saw a sudden, hot flash of anger in the eyes behind the tattoos, the grime and the tangle of red hair.

'I thought you were worthier than that.'

'Sorry. Cheap digs are my biggest failing. Look – the reason I'm here is to ask about the security operation. I know for sure the quarry have tightened it up. What have you seen?'

'More guards. More armour. More aggression. And now weapons.'

'How do you mean?'

'Something electrical. A stick, or rod. It sends out blue sparks. I would think that it blinds or shocks. Typical Roman brutality.'

'Have they used them on you yet?'

Cernunnos shook his huge head slowly.

'We are changing our battle plans.'

'You know they're all ex-army lads. They're highly trained, well equipped, and they don't like people like you very much. I should think about that before you put anybody else's life at risk.'

'How do you think Lovernios died?'

'You tell me. Did any of you see it happen? Do you *know* what happened?'

Cernunnos didn't answer.

'I'm coming round to the view that the guards might have killed him. That he got cocky, or doped up on whatever it is you put on the fire. That he decided to prove himself to you and the tribe, and goaded them into taking him out. How does that seem to you?'

'It doesn't actually matter, Mr Brennan. There is no difference between life and death in our culture. Just this world and Otherworld. And this world is dying, raped and beaten by the pirates and exploiters. It has perhaps only a century or so left, and all because we couldn't follow our ancestors and learn to live with the woods and the water and the soil. We are all a part of the same elements, Mr Brennan, which is why Lovernios lives on now. He's in these branches above us, in the ivies below.'

'All things bright and beautiful,' Brennan chorused sarcastically. Cernunnos glowered at him fiercely.

'Don't mock our beliefs, Mr Brennan.'

'Well, they're hardly consistent, are they? If the planet's dying but you've got a cosy escape route sorted out, I'd be tempted to keep quiet about it if I were you.'

'You will never understand, will you?'

'I'm trying, believe me.'

'Come to our feast of Imbolc. That's your 1 February. We light fires to wake the sun from its winter sleep. We renew and purify. And the Earth responds.'

'I'll have to look in the Yellow Pages under "Wild Horses", I'm afraid.'

Brennan turned to go, but his attention was seized by a sudden movement from one of the tents. It was Brigit Parry.

'What's she doing here? Her mother thinks she's working in a day centre for old people.'

'Epona has rejoined us. She has rejected your vile world. She will live and work with us.'

'I should get some practice in on midwifery, then,' Brennan spat out, instantly regretting the remark when he saw Cernunnos's eyes narrow. And then his great painted face lit up with delight.

'Lovernios lives! Lovernios lives!' he bellowed across the camp. Bedraggled youths spilled from the tents and the huts and

Cernunnos ran towards Brigit and took her in a great bear-hug as the others gathered round.

'Almost touching,' Brennan mouthed to himself as he slipped away back down the hill. When he got back to the duck pond the taxi-driver had obviously had second thoughts about hanging around for some nutter climbing hill-forts, and had pissed off back to Frome. Brennan walked up the road, past the row of gentrified cottages, and held out his mobile phone until it registered a signal strong enough for him to call home.

Twenty minutes later, Janet and Tommy turned up in the car, having picked Lester up from school. Brennan wondered for one instant what memories his son would have of him, standing freezing on the roadside, apparently doing nothing to earn a living, just fucking about like a loon.

So he tried to sound purposeful when he got into the back seat alongside him.

'Right. The tribe leader – unbidden – has confirmed that these bastards are now patrolling with highly illegal stun batons tucked away in their uniforms. Which means I can go after them in a big way now.'

'Do you want me to call up some muscle?' Tommy asked in a matter-of-fact voice.

'I hope I won't need it, Tom. All I really require is the nod from Stuart Gill to do the story.'

'Call him now, why don't you?'

Brennan looked at his watch.

'Four fifteen. He'll only be on his second round of sticky drinks at the Ivy. I'm going up to London tomorrow. Catch him sober.'

'About time I said "hello" there as well,' Tommy said, realising that his time in Wiltshire had come to an end, at least temporarily.

'We can travel together,' Brennan said enthusiastically. 'There's a service from Westbury at five past eight that still does the full breakfast. Jan can give us a lift before she goes on to Frome.'

'Frome? What do I want to go back to Frome for?'

'Because Brigit's back at the camp. I saw her this afternoon. Bear-hugging with Big Daddy. So her mother is either lying to you or to herself.'

Janet's hands tightened around the steering wheel in anger, not so much at Sheila Parry, but at her own failure to get at the truth. Next time, she'd be harder.

CHAPTER NINE

Tommy and Brennan were late for the 8.05, but were relieved for once that the railway's traditional unpunctuality had come to their rescue, the excuse for the late-arriving train being announced at Westbury as 'adverse rail conditions in the Plymouth area', or frost for short. When the train eventually cruised in twenty minutes late, Brennan was able to bustle himself on board and bag a table for two in the restaurant car, while Tommy collected two free *Daily Telegraphs* from one of the other first-class carriages.

'Here's an idea,' said Tommy, settling in his seat. 'You publish your own crime or investigation reports every month or so, give 'em out free on trains and planes, and just cop for the advertising money.'

'Nice try, Tommy – but I'm very nearly obsolete already without burdening myself with production and distribution costs. Besides, papers are dying. There'll only be four or five left by the end of the century.'

'Better get your expenses claim in now, then,' Tommy growled. Without asking, he ordered two cooked breakfasts and a bottle of champagne from the stewardess, a tall, athletic girl with a dazzling smile. Tommy was smitten, and spent the rest of the journey to Paddington watching her every move and complimenting her every time she came to the table.

'If I had her as a greeter, I could open up the best bar in London,' he concluded as the champagne bucket was taken away.

'Is that your plan?' Brennan asked with a smile of admiration.

'It is this morning. I may feel differently by lunchtime.'

'I presume you've got somewhere to stay?'

'You're being presumptuous in even worrying about me. I'll be all right. If I'm not, you'll hear about it. And if you're not, I'll hear too. *Won't* I?' Tommy sat forward wearing his fierce inquisitorial look, probably poached from assorted detectives who'd tried to interview him over the years.

'Yes, of course,' Brennan said.

They shook hands spontaneously, departing from first-class decorum on account of the champagne and the suspicion that they might not see each other again for a while. Tommy embraced Brennan briefly on the concourse at Paddington, and promised he'd forward a number and an address once something semi-permanent had been secured. And then he was off, walking towards the cab rank with his head held high, a sixty-year-old man starting his life all over again. Brennan waved as the cab pulled away and then found an underground map so that he could plot the hitherto unfamiliar journey out to Docklands.

Janet loitered just out of sight of the bookshop, waiting for any signs of opening. The ancient cobbled hill seemed drearier and more cut off than ever on this grey morning. While she waited, she rehearsed some of the new questions she wanted to put to Sheila Parry. They were mostly her own, although Brennan had suggested a revised running order as she'd driven him and Tommy to Westbury station that morning. She tried now to 'cut and paste' the questions in her head, whilst retaining sufficient flexibility for surprise.

And then, just after ten o'clock, the single fluorescent light-strip in the bookshop stuttered into brightness, and Sheila Parry's hand reached around the yellowing net curtain and turned the 'Closed' sign round to 'Open'. Given that there was no evidence of a queue of New Age readers anxious to buy up all the back catalogue of unsold mystical books, Janet immediately made her way across and into the shop.

'You lied to me, I'm afraid, Mrs Parry,' she said brusquely. 'Your daughter's not here. She's back living at the camp, isn't she?'

'I don't have to talk to you, Mrs Whoever-you-are, so piss off.'

'Very Glastonbury, I don't think. What are you trying to hide, Mrs Parry? That you're a neglectful mother? That Brigit prefers camping out in squalor to living with you?'

'What's it got to do with you?' Sheila snarled. 'You're not here to help me. Just another shithead wanting to shop me to Social Services, aren't you? You even talk like one of them.'

Janet's recall of her list of questions was beginning to evaporate under Sheila's aggressive resistance.

'I am here to help you, you silly woman,' she insisted, hoping finally to assert herself.

'How can *you* help me? I'm stuck with this life now. Stuck in this bloody dead shop, stuck in this town.'

Janet noted that Brigit had suddenly dropped off the agenda. She sensed that Sheila Parry had to unburden herself of her own troubles before she would illuminate her daughter's.

'Can I have some tea? I'll make it.'

Janet moved towards the back room, but Sheila moved across in front of her.

'I'll do it. You sit down. I'm sorry. You just walked in on me when I was feeling low.'

Janet tried to work out whether this was another defensive act or the truth. She would withhold her apology until she was sure. 'Stay hard,' she implored herself, 'don't soften.'

'Okay. Tea, then. Pekoe.'

Sheila nodded obediently and went into the back room, filling the kettle from the tap and then lighting the gas.

'When did Brigit go back?' Janet asked around the curtain.

'She hasn't lived here properly for nearly a year now,' Sheila said without turning. 'She just comes and goes without telling me. Treats me like a doormat.'

'I think that's the fate of all mothers, isn't it?' Janet offered as consolation. Sheila turned; there were tears on her cheeks.

'She's not mine. Not my daughter. Never has been really.'

Janet advanced into the back room. The kettle was virtually the only noise, apart from the gurgling of the well.

'Did you adopt her, is that what you're saying?'

'No.'

'She's your step-daughter, then. The child of your husband by another marriage?'

Sheila nodded.

'Only we never got married. So she's not legally mine. Nor is this, the shop or the flat.'

'But she has the name Parry, same as yours.'

'She took it from her father.'

'And you did too?'

'No – I was already a Parry. I'm his sister . . . Brigit's father is my brother . . . so she's my daughter, and she isn't, if you see what I mean.'

She turned her eyes away from Janet. The kettle began to whistle on the stove. Janet stepped closer and put a reassuring hand on Sheila's back. The touch seemed to melt her and she fell on Janet's shoulder sobbing.

'Can you imagine what it's like – having a baby and not being allowed to love it?'

'Must be the ultimate hell,' Janet said softly. 'Is he still around?'

Sheila nodded.

'He controls her. Treats her as his own.'

Janet frowned as plus and minus signs began to form a coherent equation in her mind.

'The guy who runs the camp – that's *him*?'

'Only he doesn't have a proper name now. Cernunnos – that's what he calls himself. The Horned God of the Celts. And the worst thing is, he really believes it.'

Janet manoeuvred her back on to the chair behind the counter in the bookshop, and proceeded to make a pot of strong tea for both of them. While it brewed, she turned the sign on the door back to Closed – it would be just her luck for a customer to turn up at this sensitive moment. She returned to Sheila and poured the tea, handing a mug to her first.

'When did the relationship between you and your brother first start?'

'When I was about nineteen. He's a couple of years younger. He'd just been in trouble with the law. Spent a year in a home. When he came back he was even wilder than when he went in. I'd just started seeing someone – first time, like. He used to listen at the door while we were . . . I could tell he was there.'

'He became obsessive about you?'

'I think so. Dad had died. Mum had gone to stay at her sister's. There was only him and me in the house.'

'This one, here?'

Sheila shook her head.

'Only pitched up here seven years ago. We were down in Taunton before that. But there was a bit of trouble on the estate and we had to move. It was Clive's idea to open the bookshop, and take the flat above. So we could live as a family. Pretend, like.'

'Can I ask how you managed to get pregnant?'

'He raped me. Came back and did it again. And again. I had nowhere to go, nobody to turn to. He wouldn't let me get rid of the baby. So when she was born, I had to make out that I didn't know who the father was. Clive was just my brother. Looking after me. Us.'

'And you've lived together as man and wife since Brigit was born?'

'Man and domestic pet would be nearer the mark. I do my best to look after Brigit. Make sure she doesn't go mad like him. But now he's got her. Under his spell.'

'Does she know he's her father?'

'I never told her. But I think something in her bones must probably give away the secret. At least the baby's not his. Small comfort.'

She gave a pained smile. Janet sipped her tea, tormented by what she had heard.

'You won't tell your husband this, will you, Janet? If it gets in the papers, we've had it. Me and Brigit especially.'

'No – no, of course I wouldn't tell him. It's not what he's writing about anyway. He's only really interested in what happened to Humphrey Castleton. Promise.'

Stuart Gill came back from the members' bar with two pewter tankards of champagne. It was Garrick Club style *par excellence*, a joke about the plebs, drinking vintage champers out of a working man's vessel. Gill had the club's traditional salmon-and-cucumber tie on, though he'd worn one for several years prior to achieving membership finally. Brennan, in contrast, had had to borrow a spare tie from the club's doorman, a woollen tartan number that must have been at least thirty years old.

Gill looked around with self-satisfied ease. A couple of well-known actors patted him on the back as they made their way to the bar. He nodded across to a government minister who was drinking with the political editor of one of the more rabid tabloids.

'Taking a bit of a risk bringing me here, aren't you, Stuart?'

'Don't think so, Frank. Nobody remembers who you are now,' he said with a head-tossed-back chortle, a gesture that Brennan thought was not dissimilar to the preening routines of a flock of king penguins. He walked Brennan over to a quiet corner by the window, looking out on to the pre-lunch bustle of Garrick Street.

'I can only manage a drink, I'm afraid,' he said, confirming what Brennan had already suspected. 'Having lunch with David Mellor.'

'Lucky you. Writing a column for you, is he?'

Gill tapped his nose furtively.

'You'll know soon enough.'

'What does that make now – seven regular columnists per week, plus the odd guest appearance by Paula Yates or Angus Deayton. Pretty soon you won't have to run any news at all.'

'I'm all set for my usual dose of the view from the sticks, Frank. That lacerating insight into how we in London are getting it all wrong, sitting on top of the media dunghill, whatever. Must be half-day closing in Bradford-on-Avon, eh, otherwise you wouldn't have managed to pull yourself away?'

Brennan tapped Gill's paunch, which was thrust out proudly in club buffer style.

'The more weight you put on, Stuart, the lighter you get. I'll take this idea straight to the telly, then, shall I, if you can't find room for anything outside the M25?'

'Spin it past me. Quickly.'

'Big quarry near me, protesters adopt stance of being Celtic warriors from 100 AD, one of them turns up decapitated in a train-truck of stone, and the quarry company goes on overtime to make sure it's put down to an accident of the protester's own making.'

'And so what does Frank Brennan think?' Gill asked archly.

'A killing by the company's security firm, all ex-army, and now apparently not averse to using electric stun batons on anyone they don't like.'

Gill paused. The first stirrings of interest were visible in his eyes.

'Killing a crusty is strictly for Section Two of the *Guardian*, you realise. If you want my money, I'll need something more in the cake – any shagging, for example?'

Brennan paused. By rights he should have walked out there and then. But he needed the contact with Gill, and the money, or at least the prospect of it.

'Well, the kid who died has left his girlfriend behind expecting a baby.'

Gill wiped a line of champagne bubbles from his moustache.

'Could be handy. We're, er, taking a bit of a stand against this lone parent stuff. Shows up in all the market research as an issue with our readers.'

'Is that a yes or a no, then?'

'A maybe, Frank.'

'I'll need some money up front.'

'Pushing it these days. Even takes me a month and a half to get my exes back. I'll see if I can push a grand through. How's that?'

'Not enough.'

'Oh. Right. 'Bye then, Frank.'

Brennan looked away, feeling crushed, humiliated, angry – like he wanted to take an Uzi to the lot of them.

'Two grand by the end of the week, or I'll go elsewhere with it. Enjoy the lunch.'

He left his tankard unfinished on the window ledge and made his way out through the self-congratulatory throng in the bar. Self-doubt, he guessed, was something you left with the doorman, like a briefcase or an unsuitable tie.

He walked the short distance to his own, more amenable club, Two Brydges Place, off St Martin's Lane. It was relatively empty, so he took a seat at the bar and ordered sausage and mash and a half-bottle of Rioja. Before it arrived he made his way across to the club's public phone on the landing – he couldn't quite summon the nerve to use the mobile – and called Janet. He could tell immediately from the tension in her voice that something untoward had happened.

'Did you get anything new out of her, then?' he asked, trying to pin her down.

'Her brother's the bloke behind the tribe.'

'Cernunnos? What's his real name, then?'

'Er, Parry. Clive Parry.'

Brennan chuckled.

'Suddenly he doesn't seem quite so threatening, despite his six feet five inches.'

'I wouldn't be too sure about that actually, Frank.'

'Why? What did you hear?'

'Can I tell you later?'

'I hope it's not vital – I'm going to try and see the security firm on my way home.'

'It won't affect what you have to say to them.'

'You sound low.'

'Other people's unhappiness. Impossible not to catch it sometimes. How did you get on with Stuart Gill?'

'A begrudging grand is about all I can expect. He wants the sleaze angle. You know – teenage bride, shagging crusties, that sort of stuff.'

'You may have to think twice about that—'

Before he could quiz her, he heard the rapid bleeps of an impending cut-off.

'I've got no more coins . . . Janet, are you still there?'

'What happened to the mobile all of a sudden?'

'I can't summon the ego to use it . . . Jan?'

But the line was dead. He resumed his seat at the bar, persuaded Alfredo, one of the club's owners, to swap the Pet Shop Boys for John Coltrane on the stereo, and waited for his bangers and mash. Two hours later, fed and watered, he was on the 15.35 out of Paddington, back to Westbury. A real sense of euphoria surged as the train began to leave London behind. The Rioja and the promise of some money had a part in it, but he knew in his bones just how much going home meant to him now.

This time, the train was bang on time, and he took a taxi to Blue Chip Security's offices in the hope that somebody in authority would still be there at five in the evening, and that they might be feeling tired and a little vulnerable. He was lucky on both counts.

The guard manning the security screens made him wait at the desk while Major Nicholls came down to meet him. In the meantime, Brennan browsed through one of the company's glossy promotional brochures, showing men in suits practising unarmed combat on swarthy ne'er-do-wells. The list of corporate clients prepared to endorse Blue Chip's services included Roadstone International. He wondered how many of these companies would be screaming to be removed from the brochure once his story had come out.

'Mr Brennan?'

He turned to see the man he promptly recognised as Major Nicholls from Tommy's description – 'Viyella Man, right down to his underpants.' He offered a handskake, but Nicholls' right hand produced a typed sheet of paper.

'This is a statement by Blue Chip Security regarding the intrusion, at your behest, of a Mr Thomas Preston, a convicted felon, at our premises yesterday.'

Brennan tried to gather his thoughts – he'd got over-confident, sloppy; he wasn't prepared for them to attack first.

'I think we should go to your office to discuss this, Major Nicholls.'

'We're having it swept at this very moment, Mr Brennan. Your file suggests you're one of the few technophobes among left-wing journalists, but we'd like to be sure that Mr Preston didn't leave anything behind.'

'I'm happy that you acknowledge my colleague's visit, Major, because it forms the centrepiece of serious allegations I may have to make against your company. Mr Preston is swearing a statement about his visit before my London solicitors today.'

'I think you'll find that the only statement he'll be making will be to the Metropolitan Police when they pick him up. Several valuable items are missing from my office, and I'm afraid Mr Preston's criminal record is rather damning in that area.'

'Look – nice try, Major. Impressive almost. But you didn't manage to screen him before he got in. And there was no deceit involved – he used his own name, and his own profession. He didn't steal anything.'

'How do you know? A character assessment based on spending six months in a cell won't impress the authorities.'

'You know why I'm here, do you?'

'I don't care to think. The fact that you tried to penetrate our confidentiality is all I need to know.'

Nicholls was beginning to flush. Brennan sensed that a few more exchanges would have him puce with exasperation.

'Tell me about the stun batons, Major.'

'I've no idea what you're talking about.'

'They'll feature very heavily in Mr Preston's sworn statement, so I'd advise you to catch up.'

'I'm gratified that you've mentioned that statement twice now, Mr Brennan, which confirms to me that no taping or wire-tapping of my conversation with Preston took place.'

Brennan smiled to try to keep the bluff in place.

'I was saving that for later.'

'There is no later, Mr Brennan. I want you off our premises now.'

'I have eyewitness reports of the batons being used – correction – *sighted*, in the hands of a security patrol along the quarry's freight line. Your company provides that service, doesn't it, Major Nicholls?'

'Yes, but your "sightings" are nothing more than figments of the imagination. We do not possess, or use, stun batons.'

'Well, I'm sorry you deny that, because it will make it all the more embarrassing when my story is printed.'

'Please go ahead and try. We pride ourselves on our contacts with Fleet Street. We'll make sure they get to hear our point of view first.'

'There's nobody left in Fleet Street, actually – they've all moved.'

'Goodnight, Mr Brennan. I look forward to demonstrating some of our company's legitimate technical and surveillance skills to you over the next few days.'

Brennan produced his mini tape recorder from the top pocket of his jacket and showed Nicholls the rotating spools.

'That sounded like a threat to me,' he said with plodding irony. He switched the tape off. 'I should update your files on me if I were you, Major Nicholls.'

He let himself out and gave a cheery wave up to the security camera that craned down from the wall above him, knowing that the image would be played directly into Major Nicholls' view. The thought of this kept him tickled all the way back to Bradford.

But his good humour lasted only until he saw the sadness in Janet's eyes. Fortunately, Lester was upstairs watching *Top of the Pops,* so Brennan and Janet were at least able to talk about it there and then, rather than holding back until after his ever-later bedtime.

'Brigit Parry is the product of a long-standing incestuous relationship between Sheila Parry and her brother, Clive, who you know as Cernunnos,' she said solemnly.

Brennan sat down, utterly deflated.

'Christ Almighty,' he sighed. He shook his head in dismay.

'Who are you feeling sorry for, Frank, yourself or Brigit?'

'What do you think?'

'It doesn't impinge on your story.'

'It bloody does if I'm trying to make out a sympathetic case for the Celtic Brotherhood, and their leader's been shagging his own sister.'

'Keep your voice down.'

'I can't help it. I feel like shouting. I've just gone out on a limb against this security firm, partially on the basis of Cer-fucking-nunnos being a credible witness.'

'Frank – he could never have been that anyway. He's a drop-out. A fantasist. A loser. Even before we knew about any of this other stuff.'

Brennan got up to pour himself a glass of wine.

'Is there any evidence for all this, Janet? I mean, have you checked out Sheila Parry's story, with the registrars, births, marriages and all that?'

'I was waiting to talk to you. But I happen to believe what she said was true.'

'You believed her yesterday when she was lying to you about Brigit's whereabouts. Check it out – okay?'

'*Please.*'

'Shit, I'm sorry, love. I've had Stuart Gill putting me down in a big way today, and I was really counting on sticking his champagne tankard up his arse with this story.'

'You've lost me.'

'He took me to the Garrick Club for a drink, which just happened to involve quaffing champagne from a tankard.'

'I thought sticking tankards up each other's arses was a condition of membership for the Garrick?'

Brennan smiled and exhaled.

'What a shambles.'

'Look – the key to the story is still what happened to that poor kid. If you can prove that the security guards had something to do with it, and that the quarry's management were implicated, it doesn't really matter about this Cernunnos bloke. He's a side issue. He's in the background.'

'But if Sheila's allegations are true I can't ignore him, Jan. I have to be aware of the implications, both for what I write, and for what happens afterwards. Say I get the story nailed down? Persuade Stuart Gill to run with it? The follow-up is bound to involve the Parrys' sordid past, and that will then discredit me and my writing.'

'I've given her my word that you wouldn't write about it. To protect Brigit. She doesn't know.'

Brennan shrugged and slapped his palms on the kitchen table.

'Then I'm stuffed. Boxed-in. Banjaxed.'

'Can't be that bad, Frank.'

'It can if I've just gone out of my way to antagonise a security firm staffed by ex-soldiers with access to all kinds of hi-tech hardware. I mean, I can think of better people to pick a fight with, with only an ex-con and an incestuous nutcase for back-up.'

'You've got me as well.'

He took her hand and kissed it.

'Look, I might give Robert a ring. A dose of his Buddhist meditations and a couple of large Armagnacs might allow me to think my way out of this. Do you mind?'

'No – long as you make love to me later.'

'That's one commission I can honour, I think.'

The Brennans had dinner together, and allowed Lester to dictate the course of the conversation in order to avoid the vexed subject of how each parent's work was going. So they skirted around an equally vexed subject of how Lester's schoolwork was going, but it didn't yield much beyond 'All right' or 'Okay, I think'.

'I really like the teachers here,' Lester said. 'They're not like the ones in my old school. I never felt they were interested in me. Just passing time.'

'Who's your favourite, then?' Janet asked innocently.

'Mr Parker.'

'He's the RI man, isn't he?' Brennan asked suspiciously.

'Well, not just that. But I like the way he's enthusiastic about religion. All religions. He makes it come alive.'

'Don't be in too much of a rush to sign up with the guitar and sandals brigade, will you?'

'Is that supposed to be a dig at Christians, Dad?'

'An observation, that's all.'

'Nobody in our Bible studies group wears sandals.'

'Not in this weather, no. I'm just talking in terms of image, Lester, that's all.'

'He means stereotype,' Janet said.

'All I'm saying is listen to them, by all means, but in the end, make up your own mind. That's what education should be about – creating a mind with questions, not one with answers. And the trouble with religion is that it's about getting rid of the questions.'

Lester looked a little glum, taking the disapproval personally. Janet put an arm around him.

'Take no notice of him tonight, Les. He's a bit down. Right – bathtime.'

Lester rose from his chair and came round to Brennan.

'Goodnight, Dad.'

Brennan pulled him towards him and kissed him on the forehead.

'As long as you're happy – and if you're not, tell us.'

'Right.'

Lester made his way towards the staircase.

'Mum – can I have a look at that book you bought?'

'It's on the shelf behind the telly, I think.'

Brennan raised his eyebrows questioningly.

'A little something I picked up at Sheila Parry's bookshop, an alphabet of Celtic culture.'

Brennan got to his feet and hooked his winter jacket from the coat-rack in the hall.

'"I" is for "Incest" . . . I'll only be an hour.'

He slipped out of the front door on to the footpath. Another frost was forming on the paving stones and brickwork, and there were white haloes of cold air around the bulbs of the street lamps as he made his way down into the town.

Robert was already in the Dandy Lion, ensconced near the fire in the back room, away from the juke box and the youngsters who filled the main bar. Brennan found Robert stimulating company, albeit in small doses. He admired his bookshop in The Shambles, the oldest part of Bradford, and regarded his work as being close to heroic in the face of the onslaught from the multi-media corporations. But while his Buddhist thinking could frequently give Brennan a new perspective on a tangled story, the eerie placidity that went with it sometimes made it seem that this life was a passing triviality. So Brennan had to correct the cheery assumptions of their opening chit-chat.

'Actually, I've hit a major problem with this new case.'

'Legal, factual?' asked Robert mildly.

'I think it would be classified as ethical – whether to use information that will help me sell my story, but which I know will hurt, and maybe seriously affect, the lives of a particular family.'

Robert absorbed the information calmly. Time seemed to take on a slower pace in his company, such was the sense of equilibrium he conveyed. Nothing was rushed or garbled, nothing was strung out beyond its natural worth. Brennan wondered if Robert's skills could ever have been harnessed into bowling for England, because if they had, his line and length of delivery would have been unvarying.

'If this family is involved in your investigation, I presume there's a possibility that they may have done wrong.'

'Yes, but it's not strictly relevant to what I'm writing about. That's the problem.'

'That doesn't matter. You may now simply be the instrument of justice that failed to act before. I mean, I wonder how many other crimes police solve when they sometimes think there's only one?'

'Depends what force it is and how keen they are to manipulate their clear-up rate.' He touched Robert's arm. 'Sorry, I didn't mean to be glib. I take your point – that the nature of investigation is single-minded in theory, anything but in practice.'

'You will always find fish in your net other than the one you most want.'

'Exactly. Did you just make that up, or is it, you know, an aphorism?'

'I can bullshit with the best of them, Frank. So – forget the family. Let them take the consequences. Does that clear your path?'

'Yes, it does. You see, it didn't help me that Janet was taking their side. Protecting them. But I think I can see a way of squaring it now.'

'For them, or for you?'

'Both, I would think.'

He leant close.

'Do you mind if I go into detail?'

'No. I can keep a secret.'

'There's a teenage girl. She's pregnant by a youth who has since died. She's also the result of an incestuous relationship between a brother and his sister.'

Even Robert looked pained at this combination of circumstances.

'Does the girl know?'

'Apparently not. She knows her mother, but thinks this man is just the uncle.'

'The psychological damage of such a revelation could be enormous. I see what you meant by a major problem.'

'It gets worse. The girl's run away to live with this man now, under his care, I mean. But you never know if lightning can strike twice.'

'Do you not think you should hand this over to the social services?'

'What could they do, Robert? It was all in the past. Besides, the girl's living in a kind of New Age camp. She's out of the reach of social services.'

'It has to catch up with him some time, though. The laws of natural justice will see to that. You can't offend against them and not face the consequences.'

'You sound a bit like him now, actually. He's protesting against the expansion of one of the big quarries outside Frome. *He* talks in terms of nature gaining its revenge. Calls himself Cernunnos.'

'The Horned God of Celtic mythology.'

'Which signifies what, exactly?'

'As I remember, fertility, in the sense of woods and trees, rather than human reproduction.'

'Must have read the instructions wrong,' Brennan said ruefully.

'I have a few old books in the barn, I'm sure, if you want to find out more.'

'Janet bought one at this family's shop in Frome the other day.'

'Frank, you're not talking about the Parrys, are you?'

Brennan looked baffled suddenly.

'Yes. But how . . .'

'There aren't that many bookshops in this area. We tend to find out about each other, even if we don't meet.'

'Christ, I'm slipping – I never even made the connection. So have you met them?'

'Once or twice only. The woman seemed a bit – how can I put it? – down-trodden. Now I know why.'

'And what about him, Clive Parry?'

'Big bloke?'

'That's the one.'

'I don't remember much. It was a book fair. We weren't really working in the same areas. He was all Druids and Avalon, Celtic Britain, that sort of stuff. I went to the shop once – it seemed suspicious and, dare I say it, slightly menacing. Odd man. Seem to recall that he'd spent time in prison, or there was a rumour about it.'

'Speaking as an old lag, I can check that.'

'But I thought you wanted to avoid embroiling his family?'

'On balance, I think I've got no choice.'

He went to the bar to replenish their drinks. Talking to Robert had helped show him how skewed his pursuit of just one target had been. So by the time he had finished the second pint, and had listened to Robert confirming the righteousness of his exposure of Blue Chip Security, he left the Dandy Lion in high spirits.

He climbed up Market Street with renewed energy and swung left past the Priory Barn, where a meeting of the Arts Association was breaking up. He crossed to the shadows on the other side of the road to avoid being collared by Moira Backhouse for yet another talk. But the detour also took him up past the car park, away from the paved edge of the hill up to Tory. And as soon as he drew level with the rough, unlit space, two men in balaclavas stepped out in front of him. Brennan turned to run, but the drinks had slowed his reactions, and the next thing he felt was the swish of something through the air towards his head. A blue spark ignited just above his left eye, and then all was darkness as his body folded on to the hard, frosty ground.

Chapter Ten

Brennan had been found by a neighbour, shortly after eleven. A coating of frost had already started to form on his jacket, but the neighbour had at least been able to ascertain that he was alive before running home to phone for an ambulance. On the way back, he'd knocked at Janet's door and let her know. Janet, in turn, had been able to get Moira Backhouse to sit in at the house while she went down to attend to Brennan.

He had been completely unconscious, and the fall, or a brush with a car park wall, seemed to have left a nasty cut on his forehead. Janet, once her initial panic had subsided, had to admit to herself that he smelt of drink, but she couldn't believe he could get so smashed in an hour and a half – not these days anyway.

The ambulance had been forced to reverse up the hill – no easy task with the frost coating the road surface – and once the paramedic had checked Brennan's vital signs, the ambulance crew wrapped him in a shiny thermal blanket and loaded him on to a stretcher and then into the ambulance. Janet had climbed in with him, and it then made the short journey up Mason's Lane to Bradford's community hospital.

The doctor on duty had been a little on the sarcastic side when he'd examined Brennan, initially because of the smell of beer. But Janet's defence of her husband had jolted him into taking the most constructive form of action, transferring him to the accident unit at the Royal United Hospital in Bath.

While this was being done, Janet had returned home and roused Lester, and they both took a taxi into Bath. By the time they located Brennan, in amongst the victims of pub fights, domestic arguments and road accidents, he had regained consciousness.

'What the hell happened?' she asked, raising her voice in order for it to be heard above the accident room clamour.

'I can't remember,' he said groggily. 'What am I doing here anyway?'

'You were found on Conigre Hill. Unconscious. Freezing. Another half-hour and you might have succumbed to hypothermia.'

'I remember none of that. I had a couple of drinks with Robert. Passed Moira Backhouse outside the Priory Barn. That's it.'

'How did you get the cut on your head, Dad?'

Brennan reached up and felt the dressing on his forehead.

'Didn't even know it was there. Shit, I feel terrible. Sick. Groggy. Bleary.'

'Let's check your jacket. You may have been mugged.'

Janet gestured for Lester to get his father's jacket from the cabinet next to the bed. He went through the pockets.

'Nothing.'

'The nurses might have taken stuff,' Brennan muttered.

'Lester – go and get one of the ward nurses. Ask about your father's personal effects.'

Lester left the curtained booth with relish. This was a bit of excitement, he thought, with the welcome by-product of a day off school extremely likely.

'Has a doctor examined you?'

'Somebody in a white coat shone a torch into my eyeballs. Does that count as treatment these days?'

'You're probably concussed. You need to rest, love.'

'Can't afford the time.'

Lester poked his head through the curtains.

'All Dad's stuff is in the office. Wallet, money, keys. Nurse said we can collect it on our way out.'

'Can you remember how much you had on you, Frank?'

'Yeah – about two million quid. Don't let them short-change you.'

Janet leaned over and kissed him.

'We'd better get back. Lester's got school tomorrow.'

Lester grimaced.

'Get some sleep. I'll be over first thing.'

'Right. Thanks, love. Sorry to be an embarrassment.'

'What – after those ten years of fishing you out of the gutter when you were pissed?'

'Nice to know I'm on an upward curve, eh?'

Lester gave his dad a kiss and a handshake, and then Brennan was left alone. Despite the clatter of trolleys and the shouts of 'Nurse!' all around him, he soon fell profoundly asleep.

The next morning he woke to find himself in a ward, with Janet sitting at his bedside.

'Jan . . .'

'You've been out for nearly nine hours. Nurse reckons it's the shock. Feel any better?'

'Don't know yet.'

'I've had a look at your charts – you seem stable.'

'Makes a change.'

He eased himself into a sitting position and looked around blearily. He touched the dressing on his forehead, and then felt the area over his left eye and round his temple.

'Sore?'

'Something like that.'

'Do you want me to get the police in?'

'What for?'

'If you weren't mugged, and you didn't fall over drunk, somebody must have bopped you one.'

He shrugged.

'I could have slipped, I suppose. It was getting icy.'

Janet took his hand.

'Talk me through it again.'

'Don't I get some tea and toast?'

'When you've finished. You'd just passed Moira Backhouse outside Priory Barn . . .'

'Right.'

He stared at the ceiling.

'I crossed over when I saw the arts mob. I knew she'd try and collar me for something if I got too close. It was dark on the other side of the road. I turned up Conigre Hill. Stayed close to the wall. It was cold. Then I got to the car park . . .'

He paused.

'That's where we found you,' Janet said. 'You couldn't have been hit by a car or anything, could you?'

'I don't remember any noise.'

He strained to think. His brain felt like putty.

'A swish of air . . . I heard it. Felt the movement here, by my eye . . . and a blue light. Like a spark!'

'What?'

'Janet, it was those fuckers from the security firm. A stun baton. It gives off an electrical charge. Wave it close to somebody and they black out. The bastards must have decided to give me a demonstration. Where's my phone?'

'At home. Why?'

'I need to call Major bleeding Nicholls and tell him how impressed I am with the weaponry at his disposal.'

He swung his legs out of the bed.

'You got any coins, Jan?'

'You're not walking anywhere now?'

'Only to the phone.'

'I'll get the one on the trolley. Sit down.'

He leant closer to her.

'With respect, my dear, I don't particularly want the rest of the ward in on the call.'

Janet submitted and helped him off the bed. She held his arm while he slid his feet into his slippers, and then helped him on with his dressing-gown. They walked down the ward and out into the corridor. There was a pair of wall-mounted phones about twenty yards away.

Brennan couldn't recall the Blue Chip number, so went through directory enquiries. But when he got through, he was told that Major Nicholls was out of the office and couldn't be contacted. He did not leave a message.

Lydia Pearson went back to her office to check her diary. She'd been passing the Roadstone International boardroom on her way back from the ladies' when she'd glimpsed not just Len Trilling, but also Steve McMichael from the London office and Major Nicholls of Blue Chip Security taking coffee at the sideboard. And then, as she'd moved towards the door to say 'hello,' McMichael had smiled but closed it in her face.

Her diary showed no special entries for that day. She called her secretary, who confirmed that no memos or faxes about new meetings had been received. She then phoned Len Trilling's secretary who simply said that he'd had to call a meeting at short notice and didn't want to bother her.

Lydia put her phone down. Through the glass walls on the executive floor, she could see Trilling's empty office. But the wooden Venetian blinds, which screened off the boardroom, were down. She made a note of the time in her diary. Over one and a quarter hours later, Trilling finally emerged, and escorted McMichael and Nicholls to the lifts. She watched them all shake hands and pat each other on the shoulders, and she couldn't help but think of freemasons.

A few minutes later, Trilling put his head round the door of her office.

'You didn't miss much there,' he said calmly.

'I'm sorry – I was available if required.'

'Yeah, I know – but it wasn't worth bothering your pretty little head with.'

He seemed impervious to the insult. It was just boys' chat as far as he was concerned.

'So what did I miss that wasn't much?'

'Just some ideas for this year's West Wiltshire Show.'

'In *July*? It's only January, Len.'

'Yeah, but Nicholls has got a few thoughts about putting on a joint display – how his firm and ours team up, a lesson to other industries, that sort of thing.'

'Win back some public confidence, eh?'

'I didn't think we'd lost any, Lydia. It's all sweetness and light as far as I can see. Catch you later.'

'Len – you'll send me the minutes of the meeting?'

'Sure.'

'Only there wasn't a secretary in with you.'

'I've made mental notes. I'll circulate them later. *Ciao*.'

Trilling closed Lydia's door and prowled back to his own office. Lydia watched him through the glass partitions as he began to make notes on his executive pad.

Brennan was released from hospital after lunch. An X-ray had revealed no damage to his skull, and though he still felt groggy he was more than happy to come home and free up a bed that the hospital evidently needed quite badly. Indeed, even while he was getting dressed, an orderly was changing the sheets. The pharmacy issued him with some painkillers, and with the dressing on his forehead renewed, he strode out looking fifty per cent better than when he'd been brought in.

Janet drove him back to Bradford, taking the car right up to the car park on Conigre Hill in order to minimise the walk. Once he was settled in an armchair, she left to take the car down to its usual parking place on Newtown. When she got back, Brennan and his mobile phone had gone, leaving a note asking her to chase up anything she could get on Clive Parry.

Janet stormed out of the house, angered by this act of schoolboy treachery. There were three routes down to Newtown from Tory, and as Janet's preference was always for the road on Conigre Hill – it was more public and therefore safer – Brennan had easily slipped away down one of the two, narrow flights of stone steps. By the time she reached Newtown, he and the Renault were disappearing over the rise by the Priory Barn, and down into the town centre. She cursed him all the way back up to the house. When she opened the door, the phone was ringing. She snatched at it.

'Yes?'

'Sorry – I knew you wouldn't let me go if I asked.'

'I don't care, Frank. Kill yourself if that's what you want.'

'I have to stay on the case while it's still warm, Janet. If I lie in bed for a few days, it all goes.'

' 'Bye, Frank.'

She slammed the phone down on him. She wasn't just angry about his irresponsible behaviour. She hated the fact that when his adrenalin began to flow on a job, she was always relegated to back-room duties such as phone calls and searches of public records. One day, she'd show him she could do it just as well as him, if not better.

Brennan parked his car within sight of the main entrance to Blue Chip Security. He didn't particularly care whether the cameras picked him up or not, although he hoped that they would. He phoned several times in the next hour, each time being told that Major Nicholls was not available. Each time he left his name and his mobile phone number, though he guessed they would probably have it already.

He eased back his seat and tried to stop himself dozing off while he watched. As the boredom set in, he wondered what else he could usefully do. He decided to phone Lydia Pearson, and was surprised to get through to her.

'Hello, I just want you to know that I'm sitting outside Blue Chip Security waiting to speak to Major Nicholls, after two of his expensive thugs knocked me out with an electric baton last night.'

'Busy life you lead, Mr Brennan. In your imagination at least.'

'This was all real, Miss Pearson. I don't have any imagination. I wonder if you've seen one of those little clusters of chaps talking to each other in whispers? Or maybe there's been a sudden meeting – to which you'd have been invited, of course?'

There was silence.

'Hello – look, I can't be breaking up, this is one of those digital jobbies, and I'm not on a train. Answer me, Miss Pearson. You know that something's amiss, don't you?'

'That same pub. Tonight. Six.'

The line went dead before Brennan could even reply. He put the phone on his lap and resumed his surveillance. As time passed, he wondered whether Major Nicholls might be out hunting. Or having a long lunch with his secretary before rogering her on the office rug. And he wondered what Lydia Pearson looked like naked, but then stopped himself.

By four o'clock is was almost dark. January was in its last week, but the endless days of grey, cold skies obliterated any sense of liberation brought by the knowledge that the nights were shortening. The gloom seemed everlasting. And it was only six weeks or so till the Cheltenham Festival, the one week of the year that Brennan always tried to take off.

As the darkness descended and the car began to chill, he thought about the camp. He was going off the idea of the protesters' nobility. They must all be barking mad to live the way they did. The windscreen was misting up as his hot breath hit the increasingly cooler air. There was nothing else to do but wait outside. He needed a piss in any case.

He pocketed his phone and locked the car and ploughed up and down both sides of the street where Blue Chip's offices were. There was no sign of a public toilet and it had been a long time since he'd been forced to have a slash in an alleyway. At least two months. He ran his gaze along the row of shops and offices. He couldn't see himself getting away with 'Excuse me, I'd like to send a fax and use your toilet if I may' in the stationery shop. He was also aware that his hospital dressing, smack in the middle of his forehead, probably put him in the Rab C. Nesbitt class of domestic violence as far as any passers-by might be concerned.

And then he had a brain-storm. He knew that Nicholls was aware that he was outside, and guessed that, short of finding a hidden clause in the Criminal Justice Act relating to door-stepping journalists, there was nothing Nicholls could do about moving him on. Being brazen was as much a part of surveillance as being secretive, especially when quick pressure was to be applied. And letting them know you weren't going to go away was a key part of that pressure. There was, lastly, the outside chance that Lydia Pearson would now join in the fun and remind Nicholls who was the employer and who the employee. Brennan took out his phone and called the Blue Chip number one more time.

'Hello, this is Mr Brennan calling again for Major Nicholls. I know he's trying to avoid me so I'd just like to let him know that I'm going to the toilet for a few minutes. I'd be grateful if he didn't take advantage of that to leave the building. Could you give him that message, please?'

He switched the phone back to stand-by and slipped it into his pocket, whereupon it promptly rang. It was Nicholls, terribly apologetic for being busy, and inviting him in to use the facilities and have a drink. Brennan accepted with good grace, and a few minutes later was sitting in Nicholls' office, being offered whisky from a cut-glass decanter.

'Is it churlish of me to ask if this is drugged?' he asked.

'I don't think we'd try that on someone as clever as you, Mr Brennan,' Nicholls said, pouring a generous measure of malt for him.

'We're not going to get very far if this is just an attempted schmooze, Major Nicholls. I'm happy to negotiate a settlement with you, but not to buy one.'

'What are you offering?'

'No complaints to the police about being zapped with one of your stun guns last night, and no mention of your possession of them in any piece I write.'

'In return for?'

'A face-to-face interview with the guards who were on site the night that Humphrey Castleton met his death.'

Nicholls looked at a file open on his desk.

'Mr Brennan, at close of business last night your current account was overdrawn by £4578 78p. You have an outstanding loan of £3000 with a finance company, and you have an unpaid tax bill for £6536.'

Brennan gave him a cheeky wink.

'Marvellous the things you can do with computers these days. Did you get the balance of my Tote Credit account too? Or my annual subscription to *Big Knockers* that I have to pay for with postal orders?'

'This isn't about your character profile, Mr Brennan. It's about your debts. We'd like to offer you a chance to clear them.'

Brennan chortled out loud.

'A bribe?'

'A settlement, as you said.'

'And I get to talk to the two guards?'

'Ah – we thought that as we were offering to reimburse you with far more than a newspaper would, you might not bother persisting with your enquiries.'

'I see – of course not, silly of me. Does that mean you won't go around hitting me on the head again?'

'I don't know what you're talking about. But if you are worried about your personal safety, we could loan you one of our operatives at very competitive rates.'

Brennan sat back, sipped some more Scotch, looked around the well-upholstered room.

'Okay – you've got a deal.'

'Really?' Nicholls looked genuinely surprised. 'Well, that's marvellous. Are you sure, now?'

'I don't know. It's my first ever back-hander.'

'Now, how do you want this?'

'Does it matter?'

'Well, cash, a cheque payable to you or your wife, a transfer to a private deposit account, we can arrange any of these.'

Brennan fell silent.

'Last-minute doubts? Wrestling with the conscience? Much of public life is run on this basis, it seems to me, so no need to feel ashamed. You're offering a service.'

'Or not, to be precise.'

'Shall we say five thousand now, and a further five in three months, after the expansion of the quarry has been approved, and all the fuss has died down?'

'If it gets the go-ahead, you'll have your hands even more full, I'd have thought.'

'I think you'll find your unwashed friends are soon to be served an eviction order.'

Brennan drained his Scotch and stood up.

'Come on – get on with it, then. I'll take a cheque. Now.'

Nicholls opened one of the drawers in his desk and took out a fat Coutts and Co. chequebook. He began to write, blowing on the wet ink when he'd finished.

'I just need to get this countersigned.'

He wandered out into his secretary's office, and Brennan heard another man's voice before he returned and handed him the cheque inside an open envelope.

'There. Thank you very much for your time and your energy, Mr Brennan.'

Brennan pocketed the envelope and left the room. He paused at the door.

'This agreement is instantly void if any of your head-bangers come near my wife or child. Understand?'

Nicholls said nothing. Brennan left, went straight past the security console without looking and returned to his car. Once inside, he kissed the envelope.

Cernunnos was preparing a rich soup with Epona, while the other tribe members were out collecting wood for the camp's fires. To the sheep bones he had added spring water, scallions, great handfuls of wood mushrooms which he had collected after the feast of Samain and then dried in order to preserve them, barley and bundles of herbs. Epona stirred the cooking-pot as it hung above the fire.

'That should keep everybody warm tonight,' she said with a smile.

Cernunnos looked at her with great affection.

'I think your time at the camp is over, Epona.'

'Why?'

'In your condition, it is not a safe place to be any more. The nights are cold. We are in constant danger of attack and, I have to say, disease. The enemy are stronger now too. Soon there will be a final battle.'

'Women can fight too.'

'I know – and you have fought bravely in the past. But you must leave this place, and rejoin your mother. I command it.'

'But I don't want to be Brigit again. I like Epona. I like being here with you.'

Cernunnos held her close, smothering her in his arms.

'Brigit is a proud name. The great feast of Imbolc is dedicated to our St Brigit. So don't be ashamed of it. I named you, you know. All those years ago.'

'Will you still come and see us?'

'If I survive the great battle, yes. Your mother will care for you, don't worry.'

'But will we all be together again one day?'

'Yes, or course – if not in this world, then in the Otherworld. And there, we will suffer no pain, no cold, no wars. We will be as one with the animals, the trees, wild flowers and the water springs.'

'I like the idea of that, Cernunnos,' Epona said as she nuzzled into the giant's chest.

'Precious child,' he whispered, with tears forming in his eyes, 'you are too good for this world.'

When Brennan arrived at the Woolpack in Beckington, Lydia Pearson was sitting at the bar drinking a vodka and tonic. She smiled when she saw the white dressing taped to his forehead.

'Walking wounded.'

'Tribute to your security people.'

'What'll you have?'

'Scotch – same as I've been drinking with Major Nicholls.'

She ordered the drink from the barman, and asked him to put it on the dinner bill. Brennan wondered if he'd misheard.

'You expecting somebody?'

'Yes – you. I figure that if I'm busy compromising my job prospects I might as well get a dinner out of it.'

Brennan looked at his watch.

'Go ahead. Call your wife. You'll be back by nine thirty. She can have a night off the cooking.'

'I doubt if she'll see it that way.'

He walked out into the hotel's lobby and found the pay-phone, trying to work out the right phrases. Echoes of the bad old days came back to him – 'Just a quick one with the editor', 'I'll be back in time for dinner, promise', 'No, I've *not* got a bird with me'. Janet heard the same echoes too as he tried to explain the situation.

'No, of course it's okay, Frank. You get smacked on the head, I run backwards and forwards to hospital all night, so it's perfectly understandable that you should go out to dinner with another woman.'

'It's just work. My head's throbbing. I wish I didn't have to do it, but I think I'm close enough to a breakthrough to make the effort.'

'And did she call you or did you call her?'

'I forget. Look, I'll be back by nine. Maybe earlier.'

'Please yourself.'

Lydia was hovering when he put the phone down.

'There. Might as well stay and enjoy yourself now.'

The hotel's dining-room was a sumptuous, richly coloured affair, with cushions and swags all over the place. Candles on the tables added to the aura of warmth and intimacy. Brennan watched with growing unease as Lydia dithered over her selection.

'Shall I have duck – or do I deserve a steak, I wonder?'

'Look, would you rather I left you the money, and you could eat with someone you wanted to be with?'

'I'm with you.'

'What about a boyfriend?'

'I haven't got one – I work too hard for the frigging company to have the time.'

She broke off to order – the pasta to start, the roast duck as a main course.

'I'll have the same,' Brennan said without having looked at the menu.

'Wine, sir?' asked the waiter unctuously.

Brennan scanned the list quickly.

'The Beychevelle, please.'

'Would sir like it decanted?'

'Just in the glass, as soon as possible, please.'

The waiter scurried away.

'Forty-five quid on a bottle of wine. I *am* being spoiled,' Lydia said tartly.

'Why are you behaving like this?'

'Like what?'

'Like some sad divorcee who hasn't been out for ages.'

'Maybe because that's exactly what I am. Only I never got married.'

Brennan fished in his inside pocket and brought out the envelope with the corporate cheque from Blue Chip Security. He took the cheque out and showed it to her.

'Five grand? To you?'

'That's what it says.'

'But why?'

'Well – you decide. Is it because I'm corruptible and easily bought off? Or is it a sign of the desperation of Nicholls and his firm to have me out of the way?'

'Nicholls gave you this?'

Brennan nodded.

'Best piece of evidence I could get – it's got guilt written all over it. I'll get it framed tomorrow.'

'But he thinks you've accepted it.'

'I think I'll find that Major Nicholls will have issued a stopping order on the cheque already. And in the meantime, he'll be compiling some faked video or document which suggests that I demanded money from him.'

'So you're stuffed.'

'No – because I know I didn't ask for this. But I also know he was prepared to offer it to me.'

'As a trap, though.'

'I think that's just a back-up in case I refuse to stay quiet. He'd rather I banked this. It's neater all round. So – does this square with your view of things? Is there something worth paying money to hide?'

A duo of waiters appeared to deliver bread, first courses and wine, which they insisted on pouring with great solemnity, offering it to Brennan to taste after swirling it around the glass in the candlelight.

'Any chance of just drinking it? I'm sure it's fine. If it's not I'll tell you.'

The waiter filled Lydia's glass then Brennan's and after a chorus of 'Enjoy your meals' they were left alone. He watched her pounce on the pasta. The poor woman had probably worked right through lunch while her male colleagues had gone off to the golf club bar.

'How old are you, Lydia?'

'Not a very gallant sort of question.'

'Sorry. Is this your first job?'

'First with a pension and private healthcare, yes.'

'Then why are you prepared to risk losing it?'

She shrugged.

'You were right. There are little conclaves of men all the time. I sort out the messes they make, but they no longer let me in on the decisions. I don't want to spend my life like that.'

'So why don't you just leave? Find a friendlier environment.'

'Because I worry about something call integrity. I trained as a lawyer. At Bristol. Got a good degree. Not much point in doing all that if you find that the company you're in regards the law as an obstacle to its progress.'

'I have to say that Roadstone don't seem like a bent firm. No more than any other I've come across.'

'Well, they take pride in their image. I mean, they have to, or the public wouldn't let them dig holes in the ground. But they find ways to get what they want.'

'Does their use of a private security firm bother you?'

'Yes. I think we should have our own people. Train them. Tell them what's on and what isn't. By going outside, they can get round that. Say one thing, mean another, and let the security firm worry about what it means. So if anything goes wrong, we stay clean.'

'Do you know what happened to Humphrey Castleton? How he died?'

'No. I happen to agree with the inquest jury. But . . .'

'But what?'

'They knew about the body being discovered that morning you came in.'

'Who – Trilling, you mean?'

'Trilling, me, the public affairs director in London. We were all shitting ourselves that we'd just got the police on to you at the worst time for the company.'

'You'd found out who I was, presumably?'

'The phones were ringing all Sunday once your CV had popped up. But we couldn't tell the police we'd dropped the charges against you till Monday morning. Then we had the body to deal with, and you got the red carpet rolled out for you.'

'But if you believed it was accidental death, why all the fuss?'

'We knew how the publicity would stink. This protest campaign had us all on the edge of insanity. We couldn't strong-arm it, because we knew we'd lose public support. So it was all softly-softly, combined with keeping our fingers crossed that nothing went wrong. Then, boom – they had a martyr.'

'I can see all that. Understand it even. So what's gone wrong since?'

'Just pressure. Like the fact that the dead boy was the councillor's son. The same councillor who'd supported the expansion against local opposition.'

She hesitated.

'You have something to hide there, right?'

'It's a little thing. A detail. But it bothers me in the context of what's happened.'

'Think carefully before you tell me. I can't promise I can protect you.'

'I don't need your protection, Mr Brennan. Giles Castleton used to be a major Name at Lloyds – gullible and prat being two of them. He's taken a caning over the past three years. All he's got left is the house and the estate.'

'Poor man – down to his last two thousand acres.'

'Some of the senior people in our parent company used to go shooting on his estate at weekends. It was part of the normal currency of local business and local politics. Nothing sinister. But when we heard of his troubles, Trilling has this idea of helping him with his losses. We bought into the estate. Made it ours to a large extent. A gaff for entertaining the Yanks when they come over. Castleton's effectively our tenant now.'

'Which of course doesn't affect his independence of mind when it comes to voting.'

'You'd have to ask him that.'

Brennan's mood darkened, his appetite dying in an instant.

'You realise that was probably the real reason Humphrey Castleton left the family home? The ultimate consequence of which was his death?'

'Come off it. Nobody could have forseen that, Brennan.'

'If it bothers you now, how come it didn't bother you then?'

'Because there was a different context. I can see it is just one of a number of little treacheries which slowly accumulate.'

'And from which you are excluded? Are you sure you're just not jealous of what the boys are getting up to?'

'If I was in there with them, it wouldn't be happening. I think women have a moral stance on corporate governance.'

'So what are you going to do – resign, or wait till they sack you?'

'I'll stay on board. Find out what they're planning next. Nicholls, Trilling and McMichael were all in conflab today.'

'Yes. The day after I confront your security firm with serious allegations. The morning after I get beaten up. They're closing ranks, Lydia. And you're not among them.'

The rest of the dinner passed in gloomy chit-chat about Lydia's position within the company. Brennan urged her to hang on in there – not just for his own purposes, but because he felt that her presence in the company, as its moral front, would limit the rogue element's sense of what it could get away with. Without Lydia Pearson, there was no telling what they might do.

He paid the bill as promised and walked her to her car to make sure she was safe.

'I don't suppose you want to come back?' she asked suddenly.

Brennan looked at her fondly.

'Lydia – that's the nicest offer I've had in ages. But I've just spent the last year stapling my marriage back together. You can do better than the likes of me. You deserve it.'

'All I had in mind was some uncomplicated sex.'

'No such thing,' he said with a smile, kissing her on the forehead. 'If you hear any more, or just want to talk, please call me.'

She nodded and got into her car. Brennan watched her drive away into the darkness which dropped like a curtain at the edge of the village.

Janet was already in bed when he got home. There was a list of phone and fax numbers scribbled all over a pad on the kitchen table – district registrars, Prison Service. She'd been busy. His head was aching again, probably not unconnected with the Scotch and the wine. He could use an early night himself. For all his pains, he could at least console himself with the thought that he'd made progress that day, and secured a valuable informant inside the opposition fortress. With a bit of luck, he felt, he could nail them within a few days.

The first shift of loading shovels and dumper trucks pulled out of the sheds just after 7 a.m., and began to lumber their way down to the base of the quarry, where a new face had been opened up by the previous day's two 'shots'. Now, as the big-muscled machines grabbed at the ground with their huge tyres and advanced on the latest pile of dislodged limestone, the lead vehicle paused by the quarry's pumping station. The loading-shovel driver appeared on the ramp that ran around his cab, gesticulating at the small, green-coloured lake that adjoined the pumping station. As he clambered down the metal ladder of his vehicle, the other drivers also stopped and got out of their cabs. For it was plain to all of them that a body was floating face down in the water.

CHAPTER ELEVEN

'May I ask who's calling?' Janet asked protectively, knowing that pre-9 a.m. phone-calls for Brennan usually meant trouble. Her face puckered across the kitchen at him, and she covered the phone with her hand.

'It's your date from last night . . . Lydia Pearson.'

He wiped a dollop of marmalade from his lip and crossed to the phone, seeing Janet's glowering expression of accusation.

'Hello,' he said, turning away from Janet, who watched keenly for messages emitted by body language.

'Oh, Christ, no,' he uttered with real dismay. Janet moved closer to him, alarmed no longer by the imagined threat from the younger woman, but by the obvious sense of grievous news.

'Are they sure it's her?'

He cupped his hand over the mouthpiece momentarily.

'Brigit Parry was found drowned in the quarry this morning,' he whispered to Janet, who clasped a hand to her mouth in horror.

'I'll be over at the police station as soon as I can. Thanks for calling.'

He hung up and backed up against the wall in defeat.

'The first shift of drivers found her face down in the run-off from the pumping station this morning.'

'God, that poor girl. Does Sheila know yet?'

'The police are getting her now. Lydia identified the body initially, from the last inquest.'

'What should we do?'

'I'll have to go to the police and see what they say. Offer them what I know. Two deaths in the space of three weeks is more than just coincidental.'

'Will it compromise things if I go to see Sheila?'

'I can't tell. There'll have to be another inquest now. The story becomes *sub judice* again. You want to come over to Frome with me?'

'I better had. I think Sheila had decided to trust me. I owe it to her to be there if she needs me.'

They quickly got themselves ready for this suddenly uncertain morning, and set off for Frome with a cold dread in their hearts. The death of a young girl and her unborn baby touched all levels of grief, from the personal and the public to the quasi-religious. And mystery was almost certainly overshadowed in the first stages by an overpowering sense of misery.

Brennan parked outside the police station, and as he and Janet made their way into the lobby they saw Lydia Pearson and Len Trilling pacing the corridor, faces taut with genuine sadness. Trilling was too preoccupied to wonder how Brennan had heard the news. Janet introduced herself to Lydia, in the absence of any gesture from Brennan.

'Have they got the mother in yet?' she asked her.

'Talking to her now.'

'Any idea how she is?'

'Well, she was still walking. Looked more dazed than grief-stricken.'

Brennan took a step towards Trilling.

'Mr Trilling . . .'

'There'll be a press conference here with the police at ten thirty, Brennan.'

'I was just going to say I was sorry.'

'Before you jump back on the bandwagon?'

'Look, this is out of my hands now. All I do is ask the questions that the police haven't. But it's their case from today.'

'We'll be co-operating with both police and media to get to the bottom of this, won't we, Len?' Lydia said firmly.

Trilling nodded silently.

Brennan caught a look of determination in Lydia's eyes which suggested that, for now at any rate, she'd wrested power from Trilling.

'Do you know where the loo is?' Janet asked her.

'I'll come with you.'

The two women moved across the lobby. Trilling shuffled away from Brennan, trying to avoid any eye contact.

'I presume the coroner's been informed?'

'Police's job,' Trilling said without turning. 'We did it all by the book. Police, ambulance were called without delay. I've issued an order to stop all blasting and crushing at the quarry till further notice. As a mark of respect. Terrible thing. But they will keep trespassing, eh?'

He turned to challenge Brennan with a stare but Brennan declined the fight for now.

In the ladies', Lydia and Janet washed their hands side by side, unsure of each other's reactions.

'I'm sorry I kept Frank out last night,' Lydia suddenly said as a peace offering.

'I'm used to it.'

'It *was* just work.'

'I know,' Janet said with a piercing look.

'Can you tell Frank that Trilling had a complete shit-fit this morning when he heard the news. I thought he was going to explode. I made him call a meeting with the security company this afternoon. I think I can persuade them that it's in all their interests to play this completely straight.'

'Good for you. What does it look like, then? Another tragic accident?'

'From what I overheard this morning I suspect that the police will try to put it down as suicide. Having just lost her boyfriend, you know.'

Janet weighed Lydia up, laying aside any personal or professional animosity. She seemed to be a girl on the level, forceful but not over-confident. And trustworthy too.

'You may as well know this, because it will come out after the post-mortem – she was pregnant.'

'God, this gets worse and worse. They'll slaughter us now, whatever the inquest verdict.'

175

'Well, your security people certainly have some questions to answer, even at the basic level of protecting the site.'

'Tell Frank I won't be letting them off the hook. What's the mother like, by the way?'

Janet shrugged defensively. She wasn't ready to give up Sheila Parry's secret without her permission.

'A bit drab and down-trodden. She runs a sort of New Age bookshop, so the press will probably give her a kicking as well – irresponsible lone parent, doped-out hippy mother, that sort of stuff.'

'I'll try to make sure the company doesn't sell that angle too cynically. There's bound to be an element that'll try.'

'I'm sure. We'd better get back. And Lydia – thanks.'

Lydia smiled and opened the door for her.

Sheila Parry nodded mutely. She could barely see through the gauze of tears in her eyes, but the body on the mortuary slab was plainly Brigit. She was amazed at how peaceful she looked, how it looked for all the world as though she was just asleep. Only the creamy pallor and the swollen, blue-coloured lips indicated that anything was amiss.

DI Blackwell nodded for the attendant to re-cover the body with the hospital sheet.

'Don't cut her open, please. She's got a baby inside her. I'd like them to be buried together. As mother and child. Please.'

Blackwell gave the pathologist a look that said 'Just pretend' before he ushered Sheila out of the cold, silent room. The pathologist began a silent count to sixty, to allow her to clear the area before the whine of the chest-cutter started up.

Out in the corridor, a bizarre normality continued. Nurses and doctors walked cheerfully about. Visitors passed with bunches of flowers. Sheila watched it all as if through a distorting lens.

'Do you want a cup of tea, love?' Blackwell asked kindly.

'I can wait.'

'We'll, er, need to ask you some questions when you feel up to it.'

'I don't mind doing it now. Nothing matters now, does it.'

'Forgive me asking, but is Brigit's father still with you?'

Sheila didn't even blink.

'No – he went a long time ago.'

Blackwell walked her out into the car park where a uniformed WPC helped her into the back of the car that would take her across to the police station. He followed in his car, and decided that he'd deal with the press conference first, while Sheila Parry was being comforted, as far as possible, by the WPC.

There was a sombre atmosphere in the briefing-room as Blackwell, Trilling and Lydia Pearson took their places along the desk. Blackwell made the briefest of statements, confirming a death, the identity of the girl, and the due process of post-mortem and coroner's inquiry. He would not take questions.

Trilling gave a factual, timed account of events as far as the people at the quarry had been concerned, and said that Roadstone International would be co-operating fully with the police and the coroner. He offered the company's condolences to the relatives of the deceased, and confirmed that the quarry would be closed for the entire day out of respect.

When the TV journalist from the previous inquest tried to question him, Blackwell intervened to insist that the inquest must be the first course of any inquiry. Lydia Pearson then leant towards the microphone to say that any floral tributes to Brigit Parry could be laid out at the main entrance to the quarry, and would later be transferred to the site of her death. She too offered her condolences.

As the briefing broke up, Brennan asked Janet to see if she could get to talk to Sheila. He was going to try to get up to the camp and see Cernunnos before anybody else did. He edged his way out quickly before any of the younger hacks could cotton on to what he was doing. He knew that they'd been watching him, asking about him, and by now, maybe they even knew who he'd once been – the hack all the others would never allow to be the last in the bar, or first into a press conference, because they feared he'd have the real story before they did.

He jogged across the street to his car and was already driving away when the TV reporter came out to greet his crew, who had set up their news camera on a rostrum. Brennan guessed that they would go up to the quarry first, which bought him another half-hour or so at the camp.

He gunned the Renault out into the country, down a now-familiar route, and within ten minutes was parked by the duck pond. He skipped over the stile with practised ease and crossed the footbridge up to the base of the hill-fort. He paused – from the top of the hill came the solemn, steady beat of a drum, and when he listened he could hear chanting or prayers accompanying it.

He climbed quickly, flicking branches away with his forearm. He clambered over the ramparts. The tribe were seated before Cernunnos, who again wore what Brennan guessed must be his funeral mask, beating the crudely made drum which was wedged under his left arm. Everything suggested that they had heard the news already. The site of Brigit's death was less than a mile away, and members of the tribe probably watched the comings and goings of the quarry like Apache scouts, discerning news before it was even rendered into words or pictures.

He waited respectfully to one side while the ceremony drew to a close. Cernunnos slipped off his mask and eyed him.

'I came to offer my sympathy.'

Cernunnos marched towards him.

'You are not welcome here.'

'I knew her too, and I'm sorry she died. Anyway, there will be others coming here soon to ask questions. Almost certainly the police as well.'

Cernunnos's eyes were narrowed with suspicion and grief. Brennan took a step towards him.

'Look, could I talk to you? At a less sensitive time, obviously . . . Clive.'

Brennan saw his eyelids flicker briefly in reaction, as though a distant memory had entered his consciousness.

'Brigit had come back here, hadn't she?'

'Her name was Epona – after our goddess.'

'Well, whatever. She was back at the camp until yesterday – so how come she's dead now?'

'She left yesterday evening. To go back to her mother's. I told her this was no longer a safe place for her.'

'Was she depressed, angry, worried?'

'She wanted to stay here with me, but I said no. She was unhappy about that.'

'So did you take her back, yourself?'

'She knew the way.'

'Any normal father would have made sure she got home all right,' Brennan said petulantly.

Cernunnos's right hand flashed out and snatched Brennan by the front of his jacket, claiming a handful of skin on his chest as well. He winced in pain.

'Is this what foreplay with Sheila was like?'

Cernunnos smashed the back of his left hand across his face.

'Do not defame me. I am Cernunnos, God of the Woods.'

Brennan struggled to break free of his grip.

'Clive, I've got news for you. The real world is closing in on you. The game's almost over here.'

'This is not a game, Brennan. This is my life.'

With that, he thrust Brennan back over the rampart, sending him tumbling through the bracken before he broke his fall against a tree. He slowly got to his feet. There was little point in going back up to continue the argument. Cernunnos seemed to have left Clive Parry behind now in all but the most lurid of memories. As with a schizophrenic, one personality had gradually smothered and killed the other. Brennan brushed the mud off his trousers as best he could. He would be glad to see the back of this hill and its tribe as soon as possible.

The WPC ushered Janet into the interview room where Sheila Parry was sitting on a bench against a wall. She sat down next to her and held her, wordlessly, for several minutes. She could almost feel the agony racking Sheila's body, as if pain and grief had their own form of malign electricity, which she was trying to siphon off, woman to woman. But nothing could soothe her.

'Do you want a hot drink, Sheila?'

'She's had plenty of tea,' the WPC said.

'I'm all right. I just keep wishing time would go backwards. So I could have stopped her.'

'Sheila – I'll stay with you if you want.'

She shot a look at the WPC, who shrugged in response.

'That'll be up to DI Blackwell, ma'am.'

Right on cue, Blackwell appeared, accompanied by Sergeant Dean Harris. They each carried notebooks, and Harris had two blank cassettes which he snapped into the interview recorder.

'Mrs Parry – if you're ready to talk.'

Sheila crossed to the desk and took a seat opposite Blackwell and Harris. Blackwell looked across at Janet.

'Are you a relative?'

'Friend.'

'Could we ask you to leave, then, please?' Harris said.

'I'd prefer to stay. Make sure she's all right.'

Harris looked to Blackwell for confirmation and got a grudging nod. Blackwell set the tape machine rolling, confirming time, date and interviewee.

'Mrs Parry – I'm Detective Inspector Blackwell, this is Sergeant Harris, who is here in his capacity as a Coroner's Officer. Because your daughter's death was suspicious, Sergeant Harris has to prepare information for the coroner and the inquest. And I'm here just in case anything pops up which requires the police to take more urgent action. Do you understand?'

Sheila nodded.

'Now you have formally identified your daughter, Brigit Parry,' Blackwell said, 'do you have any information which you think might shed light on the circumstances of her death?'

Sheila wiped her nose with a tissue which she held tightly in her hand.

'I don't know. I can't understand why it happened.'

'Your daughter had been, from time to time, a protester against the quarry, hadn't she?' Blackwell asked quietly.

'Yes.'

'And you now say that she was carrying a baby believed to be fathered by Humphrey Castleton – the young man who died in an accident with a quarry train?' he continued.

Janet thought about pointing out that the coroner hadn't specified that, but she knew any comments would see her removed from the room.

'She said it was his, yes.'

'So it's reasonable to assume she was depressed by his death?' asked Harris.

'I suppose so – she didn't talk about it too much.'

'Perhaps she was hiding her feelings from you, Mrs Parry,' Harris suggested bluntly.

'I don't know.'

'When was the last time you saw her?' Blackwell asked, resuming his more formal line.

'Three days ago. She told me she was going back to the camp.'

'This is the protesters' camp at Tedbury?'

'Yes. She said she felt they'd look after her.'

'Was she on friendly terms with them, then?'

'Obviously – they were his friends too, Humphrey's.'

'Is there anyone there that you knew?'

Sheila's eyes flicked a brief look across at Janet.

'No, nobody really.'

'But you thought she was safe there, did you?' Harris added, with just a hint of sarcasm, which was only the prelude to the real thing. 'A girl expecting a baby, sleeping rough, with, what, a dozen or so strange men around her. That was safe?'

'It's what she wanted.'

'How old was Brigit?'

'She's . . . she was sixteen last birthday. June the eighth.'

'Was Brigit a strong swimmer, Mrs Parry?'

Sheila nodded.

'I taught her. When we lived in Taunton we were quite near the river. I always worried about her.'

Blackwell patted Harris on the hand. He'd heard enough for now.

'One of our WPCs will drive you home, Mrs Parry. Sergeant Harris will contact you about the inquest. I'm afraid the coroner will expect you to be a witness.'

'When will that be?'

'Three or four days, I should think. I'm pretty sure there won't be any jury on this one.'

Janet registered the policeman's certainty, their swift progress towards confirming what they already suspected.

'One last thing, Mrs Parry. Brigit didn't leave you a note or anything?'

'Note?'

'He means as in suicide, Sheila,' Janet said tartly, collecting a glare from Harris in response.

'I haven't seen anything.'

'Well, when you go through her things at home, when you're ready to, that is, if you find anything, please let us know. It's very important.'

'Right.'

The policeman stood. The WPC escorted Sheila out and Janet followed.

Brennan was outside, pacing the lobby of the police station. Janet broke way from Sheila for a moment.

'I'm going back with Sheila for an hour or so.'

'Right. I saw Clive,' Brennan said quietly. 'He's going off his trolley. See if you can find out any more about him.'

Janet nodded and turned away to return to Sheila. Unfortunately, Sergeant Harris had seen the little cameo between the woman who'd been in the interview room and Brennan. He sidled up to him and hissed in his ear.

'I'll have you for perverting the course of justice if you start interfering with a coroner's witness.'

'She's my wife, Sergeant Harris,' Brennan said patiently. 'She's a friend of Sheila Parry's – not against the law is it?'

'I'll find out. But if you write anything, or withhold anything, which might affect the outcome of the inquest, I'll have you charged, understand?'

'Good luck with your investigations, Sergeant Harris. I'm sure you'll conduct them with your usual enthusiasm and vigilance.'

Harris stalked away and disappeared inside the body of the police station. Janet and Sheila were outside, getting into a police car.

The media pack had moved on, presumably to file their initial reports. Brennan decided that the most useful thing he could do was to visit the quarry again.

When he got there, the gates of the main entrance were closed, and arriving lorries were being rerouted to another quarry three miles away. A couple of cheap bunches of flowers had been tied to the gate as a memorial for Brigit, whether by staff or locals

Brennan couldn't guess. He parked on the grass verge a hundred yards past the entrance and walked back. There were four guards from Blue Chip manning the gate, while a quarry foreman and his assistant were dealing with the lorries and their frustrated drivers.

Brennan didn't recognise any of the guards as the two who'd ambushed Lovernios and himself.

'Can you stand to one side, please, sir. There's lorries turning here,' one guard said to him politely.

'I'm supposed to be meeting Lydia Pearson of Roadstone International.'

'Walk down to the gatehouse and report there, please, sir.'

The guard showed Brennan through the pedestrian entrance, and he took the sweeping turn that brought the road to the gatehouse and to a panoramic view of the quarry. He crossed to the railed platform. Down below he could see the artificial lake cordoned off by police tape. Two white police vans were parked up, and three scene-of-crime officers were walking about, taking measurements, and tracking footprint trails. The huge quarry vehicles were parked in formation to one side, and an eerie silence hung over the chasm where normally so much noise was generated. Brigit had succeeded in stopping the quarrying, but only for one day.

'Yes, sir? Can I help?'

It was one of the guards from the gatehouse.

'I'm meeting Lydia Pearson.'

'She's not here, sir. Back at the office, I think you'll find.'

'Right,' Brennan said, standing his ground.

'Bloody shame isn't it, the young girl.'

The guard nodded sympathetically.

'One of the drivers thought he could feel a pulse apparently. Tried to give her the kiss of life, but she was so cold he couldn't get her back.'

'How deep is that?' Brennan asked, pointing down at the lake.

'No more than three feet. Do you want me to call Miss Pearson, tell her you're here?'

'No, it's okay – I'll ring her on my way. Thanks.'

Brennan knew his chances of getting any more information

were limited, and retreated back up the road, through the gate and across to his car. Another two empty lorries thundered past, denied their load of stones, and now hungrily searching for them elsewhere.

On the drive over to Roadstone's offices, his phone rang. He pulled over to the side of the lane and answered.

'It's me. Sheila's just had a call from Blackwell. The pathologist says death was due to drowning. No signs of any violence, any struggle, or sexual assault.'

'That's one blessing for Sheila I suppose,' he said, thinking of the fears of what Clive Parry might have done.

'No sign of any note, then?'

'We haven't really looked yet. She's gone for a lie-down. She's in shock.'

'Okay – thanks, Jan. I'll call you later and pick you up.'

Len Trilling paced the boardroom, pulling on an earlobe. Lydia and Steve McMichael watched him, waiting for a pronouncement.

'What about a meeting with the protest groups? Set up a joint working-party to stop these dangerous incursions?'

'The trouble with that is that while it's good for PR, it signals that we're prepared to concede power to them. And once we do that, they'll be at us all the time,' Steve McMichael said, making a note of his own remarks.

'I think we should acknowledge our security lapses,' Lydia suggested. 'We pay a lot of money to Blue Chip to police the quarry, and now they appear to have failed disastrously twice within one month.'

'Doesn't that offer a hostage to fortune, though?' Trilling asked. 'It would only encourage more incursions if they see what trouble it causes us.'

'Well, I think a sacking or two would not only look good, but would actually be the right thing to do,' Lydia asserted.

'Hang on,' McMichael cautioned. 'If we admit security lapses, doesn't that open us up to claims for third-party injuries? If the protesters get some smart-arse leftie barrister, they could sue us for failing to protect the public or something, couldn't they?'

'It's a possibility,' Lydia admitted. 'But there are sufficient warning signs around the quarry, and there should, in theory, be sufficient policing, to make only a wilful act of trespass possible, and therefore dangerous. I think we should read the riot act to Major Nicholls this afternoon – we have to be seen to be doing something before the coroner recommends it.'

Trilling and McMichael looked at one another and nodded their approval of this consideration. Lydia felt a surge of pride and power. She was controlling the bastards for once, and it felt really good. Brennan would be proud of her.

Brennan had tried to phone Lydia, but the usual brush-off of 'She's in a meeting' seemed perfectly genuine in this instance. He thought through his options, which were restricted by the pre-inquest inquiry, and found only Giles Castleton as the loose end that could most likely be tied up in a few hours. So he drove over towards Wells and, after locating the estate on his Ordnance Survey map, found himself at the entrance to a long drive lined with pollarded willows. There was an entryphone at the gate, which presumably controlled its opening. He leant out of the window and pressed the button that activated the speaker. Moments later, a woman's voice crackled out of it.

'Hello?'

'Hello – my name is Frank Brennan. I'd like to have a word with Giles Castleton about Roadstone International.'

'And who are you exactly?' fluted the voice.

'I'm a journalist. I want to confirm a few details of my story with Mr Castleton.'

'We've had enough of the press, thank you. Goodbye.'

The speaker went dead. Brennan pushed the button again.

'Would you go away, please, or I shall call the police.'

'I'll call them for you if you like – they'll be interested in what I have to say about Roadstone's purchase of this estate.'

There were a few muffled noises through the speaker, as though the handset at the other end were being passed around like a lit firework. And suddenly there was a buzz and the gates hummed into life and slowly swung open. Brennan put the Renault back in gear and drove up towards the house, a handsome eighteenth-century manor in Bath stone. On either side of the drive were immense paddocks, one lined with show-jumping fences, the other being grazed by sheep. A large gravel forecourt fronted the main door to the house. Brennan parked alongside a pair of matching Jeep Cherokees. By the time he got out, Castleton was already waiting for him on the steps of the house.

'This is as far as you get, Mr Brennan.'

'That's all right, Councillor. I'm a journalist not Loyd Grossman trying to go through your keyhole. I don't give a shit about your furniture.'

'Are you always so offensive?'

'Usually worse.'

Brennan took his pocket tape recorder out and made a great play of setting it up for an interview.

'Would you like to tell me about your involvement in Roadstone International, Mr Castleton?'

'In what way? Some of their people have been here on a social basis.'

'I was thinking more in terms of them bailing you out of your losses at Lloyd's of London. I don't have the syndicate details but I can get them.'

'What other evidence do you have to support your monstrous accusations?'

'Information, that's all. I thought you'd be keen to set the record straight.'

'Who do you work for?'

'I'm freelance.'

Castleton smiled for the first time.

'Unemployed, then?'

'Not in this instance, no. I am being paid by a national newspaper to investigate the background to your son's death in a protest against the Roadstone International quarry.'

'There's been an inquest. It was an accident.'

'I know all that. But the background to that was your son, Humphrey, leaving home.'

'I made a statement after his death. That's all I've got to say.'

'But it's true that he opposed the quarry expansion, and that you, in your capacity as a district councillor, didn't.'

'We had our differences of opinion, that's all.'

'They contributed to him dying, to him being in the wrong place at the wrong time.'

'That was his decision.'

'Did he find out about the monies Roadstone paid to you?'

'No money was paid to me.'

'On your behalf, then.'

'I have no knowledge of that – do you?'

'From a reliable source, as they say.'

'But no evidence?'

'I'll get whatever's needed. It's easier for you if you do the honourable thing.'

'I'm not taking lectures in morality from a fucking journalist. I deny your allegations. And if you persist with them, I shall take the strongest possible recourse at law.'

'Are you sure you want to do it this way?'

'Damned right. Too many people in public life are brought down by allegations, without anything ever being proved. You lot are like some medieval witchfinders, prowling the country condemning and sentencing people without evidence, and without due process. Now please leave.'

'I'm sorry you feel unable to co-operate, Mr Castleton. I'll be in touch when I write my story.'

'You'll be hearing from my lawyers well before that, Brennan.'

Brennan handed over a business card.

'You can contact me any time you change your mind. May I ask what those are in that third paddock over there?'

'Ostriches – we farm them for their meat.'

'Big demand, eh? My sub-editors will have a lot of fun with lines like "head in the sand", you realise?'

'Piss off.'

Brennan clicked his tape recorder off. Castleton slammed the large oak door shut. Brennan retreated to his car, content for now with having inflicted a flesh wound rather than a direct hit.

Lydia was convinced that the meeting with Major Nicholls had been scheduled for 3.30 that afternoon, but when she arrived in the boardroom and found it empty she felt she ought to check with her secretary. But she in turn confirmed that this was the correct time.

She went down the corridor to Len Trilling's office, but she could see from ten yards away that it was empty.

'Not back from lunch yet,' his secretary said, miming a wine glass.

'Who'd he go with?'

'Mr McMichael.'

'Where?'

The secretary looked a little embarrassed.

'Mr Trilling asked me to make a booking for Bishopstrow House in Warminster.'

'For how many?'

'Three.'

'The third person not being me, obviously,' Lydia muttered, before stomping back to her office. She sat there waiting for Trilling and McMichael to return, but she knew that they wouldn't be back today. They'd have been wined and dined by Nicholls, plied with brandies and cigars, and no effort would have been spared by Blue Chip Security to keep their contract with Roadstone International on track. Any proposals that Lydia might have made that morning would almost certainly have been deemed too extreme and too precipitate once the three-course lunch and the expensive wine had soothed McMichael and Trilling's executive anxiety. She knew that they thought women didn't really understand how business was done sometimes.

As it approached five, with the office emptying, she phoned Brennan on his mobile.

'They blew me out,' she said. 'Switched the meeting with Nicholls without telling me.'

'Slippery,' Brennan said.

'Where are you?'

'On my way home. I got blown out too – Giles Castleton denies any allegations of financial links with your company, and will sue if I say so in my story. You are sure of what you said last night, aren't you?'

'Positive. Have a look in your post tomorrow.'

She hung up and took out her set of master keys for the office safe. The executive landing was deserted now, the secretaries having left on the dot once they knew their masters were still out lunching. She crossed the corridor to the records office and opened the safe, by key and combination. She found the Castleton file promptly and walked round to the photocopier, making sure she duplicated everything of value for Brennan, including a copy of the banker's draft for £324,000 payable to a Lloyd's syndicate. She then replaced the file in the safe and found a despatch-sized envelope for the photocopies. She would have to wait till she got outside the building before writing Brennan's address.

Sergeant Dean Harris was not impressed. This was not his idea of The Job, as the police federation's magazine described their work in its title. Poxy travellers' camp, New Age drop-outs crawling with crabs and head-lice. He would have to think about dropping this Coroner's Officer lark if things like this kept coming up.

It wasn't that he was frightened. He had his two-way radio crackling on his shoulder, so he could call out back-up in a second. He also had his new extending night-stick already in his hand if any of them got too lippy. And he had his big beamed torch raking the undergrowth and the trees on the hill so that the bastards couldn't spring any surprises on him.

But as he drew within torchlight distance of the overgrown ramparts of Tedbury Camp, the beam caught something that wasn't vegetation or human. He stopped moving and panned the beam back in the direction of whatever it was he'd just glimpsed. Suddenly the light locked on to it in full – the recently severed head of a big, black-faced ram was mounted on a stick, its glutinous blood still dripping from the gaping hole where its neck had once been. The animal's glazed, dead eyes seemed to be staring back at him as they reflected the light. Harris felt his pulse racing. He'd sorted pub fights in Frome on Saturday nights, he'd handled road smashes where a family of four had been crushed into a space the size of a suitcase, but this – this got inside his mind.

So he backed away down the hill, playing the beam across the undergrowth as if it were a flame-thrower in the Vietnamese jungle. 'Nobody found on site,' he'd report to the coroner. Nobody would give a toss. This was only about another dead hippy after all.

CHAPTER TWELVE

By the time of the inquest on Brigit Parry, Brennan had abandoned his notion of co-operating with the police in attempting to solve both this and the Humphrey Castleton case. The secretive attitude of the Trilling–Blue Chip alliance, which had excluded Lydia, and thereby Brennan, from its deliberations, and Sergeant Harris's subsequent refusal to accept that he should be a witness at the Parry inquest, left him with no choice but to take, as they referred to it in legal circles, 'the contrary view.'

He was quite prepared to acknowledge that Brigit's death had, in technical terms, been due to drowning, but what had been the run-up to that? Had the security guards been malevolent again, or had their operational failings simply provided Brigit with the dramatic and emotional circumstance for her final gesture? What had been Roadstone's reaction to Blue Chip over a second highly public death on a site they were supposed to protect? These were some of the questions to which Brennan hoped the inquest would provide answers, as he and Janet took their seats on the public benches.

One answer had been delivered already. Despite the presence of a score of silent, banner-holding women protesters outside the court – mostly of the cropped-hair and cardigan variety – there was still no sign of any of the Celtic Brotherhood, nor Cernunnos. Maybe he did just hold modern law in such contempt that he refused to deal with it. But Brennan couldn't help suspecting that Sergeant Harris, now seated to one side of the courtroom, had done as little as possible to provide testimony from the other side.

Sheila Parry was escorted in by a WPC, while Len Trilling arrived with two of his quarry drivers, with Lydia trailing behind. She directed a quick, rueful glance at Brennan before taking her seat. Once the pathologist had arrived, Sergeant Harris closed the doors and the clerk summoned the coroner to the bench.

Without a jury, the pace of the inquest was much brisker, since the coroner essentially had only himself to satisfy. Brennan took it as no accident that the pathologist – Dr Scott again – was called to give his testimony before Sheila. No doubt he had pressing engagements on the golf course, or at the Rotary Club, which precluded working too close to lunchtime.

Scott duly trotted out his uncontroversial findings, being allowed far greater leeway to indulge in techno-medical jargon than if a jury of ordinary people had been present. The drowning had shown all the expected features of a freshwater immersion – dilution of the blood causing the red cells to burst, consequent release of potassium which in turn had provoked death by cardiac arrest.

The presence of diatoms – small single-cell plants – had been found in the deceased's brain and liver, confirming that, since they needed circulation to get there, death had occurred in the water, and not beforehand.

Allowing for the cooling effect of the water, Dr Scott estimated time of death to be between 4 a.m. and 6.30 a.m., the relatively short span of immersion making the post-mortem an easier process than it might have been had the body been undiscovered for a week or so, by which time putrefaction would have set in. The preservative effect of the icy water was particularly helpful in showing that the body had not suffered any other injuries or contortions – no violence or sexual assault had taken place prior to drowning.

Finally, Dr Scott confirmed that the deceased was carrying a foetus of about ten to twelve weeks' gestation. This last revelation had the hacks scribbling furiously and whispering to each other, while Sheila Parry began to sob quietly. The coroner thanked Dr Scott with a fraternal smile, and called up the first of the two quarry drivers to have found the body.

The story of the grim discovery was relayed in clipped, rustic phrases. There was a sense of sadness in the man's voice, but he might equally have been describing the finding of a squashed pet by the roadside. The second driver, though, with some first-aid training, had tried to apply the kiss of life, having thought he could detect a faint pulse. He and his colleague had pulled Brigit out of the water and laid her on the ground, wrapping her in one of the nylon coats they wore for their work. But the resuscitation attempt had been in vain.

'Her lips was cold as stone,' the driver said, with unintended irony. The coroner commended him for his manful efforts and asked, as a by-the-by, that the company be prepared to provide both employees with trauma counselling if it was required. Lydia Pearson rose to confirm that it had already been offered to both men.

Janet leant across to whisper in Brennan's ear.

'Are you sure she's on your side?'

Brennan nodded discreetly.

Sheila Parry now arrived at the bench. The coroner adopted a grave and sympathetic demeanour, coaxing rather than forcing out of her details of Brigit's final days and her state of mind. Sheila couldn't give much detail on the pregnancy – but was she, as a mother, pleased or dismayed by it, the coroner asked.

'Oh, pleased, of course. Though it was sad about the boy dying.'

'You believe the father to have been one Humphrey Castleton, do you not?' asked the coroner, consulting the notes that Sergeant Harris had prepared for him.

'Brigit said so. I've no reason to doubt her word,' she said wistfully.

'Mrs Parry, I'm sorry to ask you this, but do you think that the death of Humphrey Castleton might have disturbed your daughter mentally in any way?'

'Mentally?'

'I mean, by way of depression, anger, bitterness, self-doubt, perhaps even anxiety.'

'She was saddened, that's all. She knew she could stay with me and have her baby.'

'Ah, but she didn't, did she? Stay, that is.'

'No.'

'Why not?'

'I don't know. I didn't throw her out or anything.'

'But she preferred to rejoin this camp of protesters?'

'They were her friends. And they'd been his. So I suppose she just wanted to be with them.'

The coroner turned to address the court.

'I must point out to the court that my officer has attempted to bring members of the camp to this court but was unable to serve a *subpoena ad testificandum* upon any of its members, as they appear to have moved on.'

Brennan shook his head and shot a glare in the direction of Harris, who was staring at some point on the rear wall of the courtroom.

'Was there anyone at the camp, apart from the late Mr Castleton, to whom Brigit was attached, or wished to be with?'

Janet sat forward, watching Sheila keenly.

'No,' she answered. 'I think she just wanted to be part of the gang. Always been a bit of a tomboy, Brigit. Just like her . . .'

Her voice tailed away. The coroner was too immersed in his notes, or perhaps already indifferent to Sheila, to pick up any nuances. Janet, though, turned to Brennan.

'Why is she still protecting Clive?' she whispered.

'Don't know. Fear, embarrassment?'

'Should we say something?'

'It's not our secret, Jan.'

The coroner looked up from his notes, and turned to Sheila again.

'Finally, Mrs Parry, I must ask if your daughter left any note or correspondence to indicate her state of mind prior to her death?'

Sheila shook her head.

'You may step down, Mrs Parry.'

Sheila walked, head bowed, back to her seat, where the WPC comforted her with a hand on her back.

The coroner made more notes, then scanned his list of witnesses.

'Mr Trilling – Roadstone International.'

Trilling took up his seat and was sworn in.

'This is the second time within a month that you have been before me to help explain a death on your company's property, isn't it, Mr Trilling?'

'Yes, sir – I'm aware of that sad fact. But my company is taking all possible measures to protect the quarry site, and thereby also protect members of the public.'

'Have you any idea how this girl, Brigit Parry, was able to get into the quarry?'

'It is a very big site, sir. It would need five hundred men to seal the perimeter. She obviously went in under cover of darkness, possibly in an empty rail truck returning to the railhead.'

'I presume that none of the guards on duty that night had a sight of her?'

'No, sir. We've interviewed all staff. Nobody saw anything amiss.'

'Had you or your security operation seen Miss Parry before at any time?'

'Well, yes – she was part of the protest group that had been camped up in Tedbury for more than a year. She was on our files.'

Trilling opened a ring-pull binder which he had with him – blurred photos of members of the tribe, enhanced from security videos, were sealed inside plastic sheets.

'There she is.'

He held the photo up for the coroner and the court to see.

'So it's more than likely that Miss Parry knew her way around the site?'

'Yes, sir.'

Brennan whispered into Janet's ear.

'He's trying to exclude the possibility of an accident.'

'Mr Trilling, was there any sign of sabotage or damage, or even a slogan, or a note of protest around the site on the night of Miss Parry's death?'

'Nothing was seen, sir. It was a very quiet night by the usual standards.'

'How did she get in then?' Brennan hissed through clenched teeth.

'Now, Mr Trilling, the run-off from the pumping station? This is a permanent feature of the quarry?'

'Semi-permanent – there's not much there in summer. But we are quarrying way below the water table, so the pumping operation is always in action.'

'And the depth of the run-off is what?'

'No more than three or four feet at most.'

'In other words, not the sort of depth that would present obvious difficulties for anyone stumbling into it in the dark?'

'You could virtually paddle across it, sir.'

'Thank you, Mr Trilling.'

There was an adjournment for coffee, and after this the coroner briefly took evidence from a forensic scientist, working with the police, about the site of Brigit Parry's death. He had been able to find a line of her footprints leading into the lake, which suggested no dragging or physical enforcement had taken place, although the footprints of drivers and other workers were also in evidence around the water.

After another brief adjournment to consider his notes and his verdict, the coroner returned and announced that, despite the absence of a note, he would have to conclude that Brigit had committed suicide. He could find no evidence that her death had been accidental – she knew the site, had been many times before, but wasn't part of a protest that night. He thought, then, that the sole purpose of her visit had been to kill herself in a fashion that she might somehow have construed as bringing her closer to the deceased father of her unborn child.

He then ordered Trilling to stand and began a stony-faced lecture about making sure no further accidents or misadventures happened at the quarry.

'I charge you with the responsibility of making this site safe, even for those who intrude upon it for their own purposes. I am minded to write to the Department of the Environment to alert them to the dangers which this particular quarry seems to generate. Unless the public can be given a guarantee that the site is secure, I suggest that there is a real possibility that an application for its closure, or at the very least for a scaling down of its operation, will be moved.'

Trilling's face was a mask of barely controlled anger as a hum of comment echoed around the courtroom. This was his worst nightmare – that these kamikaze protesters would, indirectly, win an argument that they had legally lost.

'With respect, sir, we spend millions of pounds policing this site. All possible measures and procedures are taken to keep it as safe as possible. We have a very low accident rate, considering the danger of the work and the volume of traffic. These two deaths have come about through wilful acts of trespass. Our security company is doing all it can, and any failings are readily punished. The guards who were on duty on the night Miss Parry died have been sacked as a matter of course.'

The coroner glowered at Trilling, and gestured for him to be seated, making a note of his comments. But his head rose again as he saw Lydia Pearson now standing to seek his attention.

'You have something to add, Miss Pearson?'

'Yes, sir – Mr Trilling's last sentence, about the guards being dismissed, is untrue.'

There was a loud hubbub around the court as Lydia's dissent became obvious. Trilling pulled at her sleeve to get her to sit down, while Brennan elbowed Janet excitedly.

'No disciplinary action has been taken. There has just been a meeting between two directors of public affairs and the managing director of the Blue Chip Security company – over a long lunch at Bishopstrow House.'

Trilling stood up.

'With respect, sir, Miss Pearson wasn't at the meeting to which she refers. She cannot know of what was said.'

'I have seen the minutes of the meeting—'

'They weren't circulated to you—'

'Nevertheless, I have seen them – all they did was agree to put up a publicity screen about tightening up procedures.'

Now Brennan stood up and pointed at the coroner.

'Why don't you ask what that means – more violent attacks on protesters?'

The coroner slammed his gavel down several times.

'The court will come to order! Order!'

Gradually, the uproar subsided and the coroner stood up and announced the court closed, commanding Sergeant Harris to summon police assistance if an orderly dispersal was not forthcoming.

As the coroner filed out, Trilling gave Lydia the thinnest of smiles.

'Don't bother coming back to the office, Lydia.'

'You can't sack me. You haven't got the authority.'

'I'll get it.'

'I'll have asked some more questions by then.'

Lydia stalked away. Brennan thought about going to congratulate her, but guessed such a gesture would make life even harder for her. In all the uproar, Sheila Parry had been almost forgotten. Janet moved round to take a hold of her arm, with the WPC assisting Harris in clearing the court.

'I'll walk back with you.'

Sheila nodded her thanks. Janet turned to explain to Brennan but he could see what was going on. He tucked himself in behind the media pack as they set off in pursuit of Trilling. Outside the court, Trilling was cornered, but would add nothing more than that security at the site was being constantly reviewed. In the background the women demonstrators booed him. He broke away to get to his car, and Lydia was now caught and surrounded, microphones were thrust into her face, and the questions flew at her.

'Were you saying that Roadstone were lying about sacking the guards?'

'Yes,' Lydia said curtly.

'Why should they do this?'

'It's part of their culture. To sack somebody is to admit defeat.'

'Will sacking you be a defeat, then?'

She smiled.

'Yes. But I haven't been sacked yet. I'm hoping that the company will take a more open stance in the light of these two unfortunate deaths. That's why I spoke out.'

'What do you expect to happen next?'

'It depends what I can organise. I'll let you know.'

She squeezed her way past the clutch of journalists and the two local television camera crews and found the sanctuary of her car. Brennan watched, admiring her courage, but knowing that she'd signed a death warrant as far as her corporate career was concerned.

Janet made a pot of strong tea and poured a little drop of brandy from the half-bottle she'd purchased on the walk back from the coroner's court. Sheila sat by the counter staring at all the books that offered to demystify human life, both ancient and modern. None of them, she felt, could help her cope with her daughter's death. Janet brought the tea out.

'There's a little something in that. Just for warmth.'

Sheila took the cup, hugging it against her chest.

'Ta. You're very kind, Janet.'

Janet shrugged.

'You'll begin to feel better once the funeral is over.'

'I haven't even thought about that yet.'

'Let the company do it all for you. Will you want a church service?'

'Doesn't seem right in the circumstances. Not one of God's children, was she?'

Janet said nothing. She watched Sheila carefully, with a mixture of pity and, if not contempt, then a certain anger.

'Why didn't you mention Clive in your evidence?'

'Make too much fuss, wouldn't it. People'd start asking questions. Maybe they'd even find out the truth.'

'Brigit's got nothing to hide now.'

'Yeah, but I got a life. I remember what it was like when Clive got himself on the wrong side of what people think.'

'This was back in Taunton?'

Sheila nodded.

'What happened exactly?'

'Young girl on the estate got murdered. Raped and stabbed, like. Clive was one of the blokes who got interviewed. So all the locals had him down as guilty. Got dog-shit through the letter-box. Somebody tried to set fire to the house with me and Brigit in it – she was just a baby at the time. Even when Clive got off, they wouldn't let him be innocent. They'd decided he was the one.'

'So they hounded you out?'

Sheila nodded.

'They'd have killed us if we'd stayed. So we started our new life here. Opened the shop, took another name.'

'A new name?'

'Wasn't much of a change – from Berry to Parry. We kept our first names – people like us wouldn't be smart enough to hide them.'

She gave a rueful smile. Janet took this as a sign of improvement and drained her cup.

'I'll pop out and get you some shopping, shall I?'

Sheila smiled her gratitude.

'What do I do, Janet?'

'Well, the hospital morgue will release the body to the funeral directors once you've chosen one.'

'No. I meant after all that. What do I do for the rest of my life?'

Janet sighed.

'I'd get out of here. Sell the books. Better still, burn them. There's no answers in this stuff. Find yourself a new place to live. Start again. You've done it once.'

'Clive has his name on the deeds of this place.'

Janet shrugged.

'Frank saw him the other day.'

'He didn't say anything about . . .'

'No, no – I'm sure not. Anyway, Frank thinks he's going mad.'

'Was already, really.'

'So get a lawyer on to it. Say your husba— Clive's gone. You'll be down as next of kin. Clive doesn't strike me as the will-making kind of guy. I doubt if he'll come back now anyway. Seems to have settled for living out this fantasy to its bitter end.'

'I can't believe I'm ever going to be free of him.'

'Oh, you will, Sheila. One day. Nothing's for ever. Keep telling yourself that when it feels hopeless.'

Brennan had adjourned to the wholefood café to catch up on his notes, sipping cappuccino by the log fire. He knew he had Giles Castleton bagged and tagged, but that was only a tail-piece to the whole story. On the Richter scale of sleaze, it would probably only register in fractions rather than whole numbers. He also had Blue

Chip Security fairly well nailed – Tommy Preston's sworn statement about the stun batons was vulnerable not only because of Tommy's record, but also because legally he'd entrapped Nicholls, a dubious practice for the law enforcement agencies, but a distinct no-no for ex-lags a few days out of their most recent stretch. Brennan had Clive's eyewitness account, but that looked increasingly open to a sanity test. But the cheque, the attempted bribe, would make the other two pieces of evidence look more substantial, together with the fragments of tape containing Nicholls' threats and bluster.

What he really needed now was for Lydia's public stand to open up a rift between Roadstone and Blue Chip – to get them shafting each other as self-preservation became the dominant instinct. To his great embarrassment his mobile phone suddenly started to ring in his pocket. Short of ordering a mixed grill, he couldn't have done more to attract hostile glares in this wholefood environment.

'Hello?'

'It's me,' said Lydia with a hint of intimacy.

'Well done this morning.'

'I've only got the rest of the day, I reckon, before they get Head Office to slaughter me. How can I be useful?'

Brennan stood and edged away from his table, aware that a dozen or so herbivore grazers were ear-wigging his end of the conversation. He talked as he moved out into the hall, climbing the stairs of the art gallery to get a stronger signal.

'Call Blue Chip to a meeting. Your place, not theirs. Tell them I've levelled serious allegations against them and Roadstone, which you, as Director of Legal Affairs, are trying to sort out. Don't tell them I'm coming to the meeting, but insist that I'm allowed in when I turn up. If I can crack them today, I may be able to save your job.'

'I'm thinking of taking a year off right now.'

'Be strong, Lydia. It's nearly over. Call me when you've got them gathered.'

'I will.'

Brennan tucked his phone away and returned to the café to find Janet at the bread counter.

'How is she?' he asked.

'Bearing up – just stocking up for her.'

'Don't get too close, Jan – I may end up writing something that will hurt her.'

'You think there's anything left to hurt?'

He apologised with a gesture.

'Look – you take the car. I'm waiting on Lydia to get me into a meeting at Roadstone. It could be a long day of hanging around.'

Lydia Pearson's first strategic move was to occupy the top-of-the-table seat in the boardroom and to work from there, with her secretary alongside her. The image of a woman taking charge of events quite unnerved Len Trilling. He phoned McMichael in London, begging him to get her the sack, but there was a sudden coldness down the phone which Trilling knew to be McMichael cutting him adrift. So it was a local fight now, directly between Pearson and Trilling, with Major Nicholls sure to weigh in behind Trilling. At least that's how it seemed, which was why Lydia had phoned Nicholls, demanding his immediate presence, irrespective of anything that Trilling might later say to him. She teased him with references to trying to save his company's contract in the light of the two inquests and now some serious allegations that couldn't be dealt with over the phone.

By the time Nicholls arrived, he had already picked up on Trilling's edginess in a phone call that was meant to bolster their male confidence, and had therefore decided that a switch of allegiance might be necessary. Certainly Lydia Pearson looked to be in charge, seated calmly in the chair reserved for the chairman when he visited, and with her secretary alongside her making notes.

'Sit down, Major Nicholls,' Lydia commanded. He did as he was told.

'Tell Mr Trilling Major Nicholls is here, will you?' she said to her secretary, who promptly left the room to summon him.

'Bit of a flap on, is there?' Nicholls said archly.

'The last thing I can do for this company before I leave it is to at least sort out its moral stance.'

The secretary returned with Trilling in tow.

'Thanks, Sally. Could you call Mr Brennan for me on that number I gave you, and make sure he's sent right up when he arrives?'

'Yes, Miss Pearson.'

'Are you completely off your rocker, Lydia?' Trilling asked.

'We'll see, won't we. Now, let me sum up. This company has found itself indirectly involved in two deaths within the space of a month. Whatever the motives of the protesters, having people die on your property is not good PR. Nor does it suggest a value-for-money security operation.'

Seeing Nicholls about to speak, she waved a hand at him.

'Before you say "It's a big site to protect", I've heard it. *Ad nauseum*. Now I, and Head Office in London, want to know what's really been going on. You two have been able to busk it so far – boys' lunches, sympathetic gestures, propaganda about the protesters, lies about sacking security guards. This is that awful day when you have to tell the truth.'

'Lydia, do you realise that in effect you're disputing the findings of Her Majesty's Coroner by opening all this up again?'

'Yes, I do. But the evidence he's been given has been so skewed it's hardly surprising that the result is a travesty.'

'Forgive me – I wasn't present at the inquests—' Nicholls said.

'I'd noticed that actually,' Lydia interrupted. 'Wouldn't have looked too good if we'd had ex-army personnel lined up against civilians, would it, Len?'

She gave Trilling a piercing look.

'I was able to speak for the company, Lydia. Had the coroner's office requested the presence of any of our security people, we would, of course, have complied.'

'How much did you bung Sergeant Harris, by the way?'

'That's an outrageous accusation!'

'Well, it's an outrageous fact that this company – you, to be specific, Len – bailed Giles Castleton out of his Lloyd's debts to keep him on our side. *That's* true, isn't it?'

'He was already a friend of the company's – he came to us with a problem . . .'

Sally the secretary poked her head round the door.

'Mr Brennan's on his way up.'

'Thank you,' Lydia said, smiling.

'I think this is ridiculous, if you don't mind me saying so,' Nicholls blustered. 'Inviting a journalist in to a meeting like this.'

'It will help concentrate your mind, Major Nicholls. You might also like to think about what will happen when Mr Trilling here is dismissed by the company, and you no longer have a chum batting for you. A new Director of Corporate Affairs might well take a dim view of your overly close relationship with him.'

Nicholls looked at Trilling, trying to gauge the likelihood of his survival. For once, there was no smug assurance in Trilling's eyes.

The door opened and Brennan walked in.

'Take a seat, Mr Brennan.'

Brennan sat two spaces away from Lydia, enabling him to have a full-face view of both Nicholls and Trilling. He took out his tape recorder.

'Now hang on!' protested Trilling.

Brennan calmly emptied the batteries out of the back of the machine.

'I think we'd all prefer this to be settled in an open and civilised manner, wouldn't we?' he asked superciliously. 'Besides, I think I know most of what's got to be said.'

Nicholls eyed Brennan with pure malevolence, and he responded immediately by taking out the cheque that Nicholls had written him. He unfolded it for the benefit of both Lydia and Trilling.

'This was meant to be a little gift from Major Nicholls, in return for my silence.'

Nicholls sat forward.

'The fact that Brennan was prepared to accept it shows that he's a bent journalist.'

'Ah, but I was kidding, you weren't. Anyway, that's not really the issue. Tell Miss Pearson about the stun batons.'

'I deny their existence,' Nicholls said.

'Christ, is that what you've been using on them, Nicholls?' Trilling asked.

'Interesting, Lydia – is Mr Trilling genuinely shocked, or has he just decided to distance himself from the use of these weapons?'

'I think it's genuine. He didn't know, did he, Major Nicholls?'

'I gave them strict instructions as regards what they could and couldn't do. Why do you think we chose ex-army people? Because we needed a disciplined response to the provocation of these protesters. I could have got fifty big lads from the pubs round here for two quid an hour if I'd just wanted a few heads kicked in,' Trilling said in an attempt at executive frankness.

'You saw them, though, didn't you, Mr Trilling?' said Brennan. 'Perhaps that first afternoon at Blue Chip after the long lunch when you first approached Major Nicholls. A few more drinks. Stories about what his boys got up to in Belfast. Then he goes to his secret cabinet and shows off his collection of – what's the trade name? – "persuaders". And you thought – we've got the right people here. Serious. Heavy-duty. And, yes, disciplined.'

Trilling looked at Lydia with contempt.

'Do you recommend I answer that, Lydia?'

'Yes, I do.'

'Major Nicholls did indeed show me an electric baton. And I said I wanted nothing to do with them.'

'With respect, Trilling, you left operational matters entirely to us,' Nicholls snapped, as the alliance finally collapsed. 'You never once came down to see what my lads had to put up with in the middle of the night. Bloody madmen. Stone Age warriors with daggers and clubs. So I authorised the use of the batons, but only in extreme circumstances, and by my most senior men, with maximum restraint.'

Brennan offered Lydia the follow-up question, but she nodded for him to take it.

'Did these batons have anything to do with the death of Humphrey Castleton?'

Trilling and Nicholls looked at one another. Trilling shrugged first.

'No. At least that's what we were told by the duty guards,' he said. Nicholls nodded.

'If I remember, the pathologist said that Castleton had scratches on his arms. Could they have been caused by a stun baton, Major?'

'As I recall, they leave a small burn.'

'I recall that too,' Brennan said acidly.

'So what happened that night?' Lydia asked pointedly. 'I mean really.'

'Over to you,' Trilling said, gesturing to Nicholls.

'What's the deal here?' Nicholls asked. 'It all seems rather one way at the moment.'

'Perhaps that will change once you've told us the truth, Major Nicholls.'

Nicholls took a deep breath.

'I got a call at home just after three thirty in the morning. Not best pleased, obviously. But it's a measure of our dedication to the job that my men felt able to ring me at all hours.'

Brennan scratched his nose to stop himself laughing.

'Carry on, Major,' Lydia said.

'They'd found a body. Castleton's. Just by the wheel-wash for the lorries. It was already headless. Just dumped there.'

Lydia and Brennan shared an anxious look.

'And, well, frankly, they were panicking. Wanted to know what to do. Whether to call the police or not.'

'Not being the conclusion.'

'After I'd phoned Len, yes. We both knew how bad it would look, whatever the cause of death. So I suggested they dump the body in a rail truck before it was loaded up. That way, at least, it would look like an accident, which it undoubtedly must have been.'

'Bollocks,' snapped Brennan. 'If you dumped the body, you must have hoped it would get lost. Buried under another stretch of motorway or something.'

'No – that wasn't in our thoughts, I promise. We needed time to think, and yes, to ensure that it would be viewed as an accident. Castleton and his pals had ambushed our trains on a regular basis. It was, it still is, the most plausible explanation. He fell under the wheels, or he was hit by a cable, or he fell through one of the hoppers.'

'The wheel-wash is a good twenty yards from the railway line,' Lydia said emphatically.

'Look, if we'd wanted to get rid of him completely, we could have dropped him into the primary crusher. He'd have come out of there as dog-meat. We just needed time to get our response organised, knowing what an accident like this could do to inflame an already volatile situation.'

'Do we believe this, Lydia?' Brennan asked.

'I hate to say it, but I'm afraid I do,' Lydia said with a sigh.

'Which leaves us where?' Brennan said promptly.

'Well, legally speaking, Major Nicholls and Mr Trilling are guilty of perverting the course of justice. The same certainly applies to the guards involved. If we accept this new evidence as being true, we have a duty to go to the coroner and report it to him. He may call a new inquest, as well as asking the police to press charges. It wouldn't necessarily mean a different verdict, but it would at least have the virtue of being the truth. What it would do for the company's image – both companies, to be precise – God only knows. But it seems the only move available. And we should, *you* should, in the first instance, sack the guards in question and offer your own resignations for your part in the cover-up.'

Nicholls shifted in his chair, twitching with anger.

'Come on, Len. I think you should assert your authority here. I mean who's calling the shots – you or her? We've done nothing wrong – it wasn't our fault these protesters got themselves killed. All we've done is fiddle around the edges a little. I think we should negotiate a deal about how much of this stuff actually needs to come out.'

'You're not in a strong position,' Lydia said.

Brennan sat forward.

'We're in danger of losing sight of the real issue here – which is simply how did these two kids die?'

'It was nothing to do with us, Brennan. Can't you get that into your skull?' Nicholls spluttered.

'Look – if you can help me work my way through this, I may be prepared to drop certain elements from my story. The baton attack on myself, for example.'

'I didn't authorise that, Brennan,' Nicholls said.

'I didn't say that you had. But something you said must have filtered down to your troops. Two of them took it upon themselves to do it. Are you sure they weren't capable of taking similar renegade action against Humphrey Castleton? I mean *really* sure?'

'What do you want?' Nicholls asked quietly.

'A face-to-face interview with the men who were on duty the night Castleton died. Were they the same two who beat him on the Friday I was with him? Were they the two who put a stun baton to my head to warn me off? You know, don't you, Nicholls. Every officer has head-bangers in his platoon. They're a pain in the arse to control, but very useful when there's a nasty, shitty little job to do.'

Nicholls looked at him defiantly.

'Say I decide to stand by my men. And to deny your allegations.'

Brennan took out his mobile phone and switched it on. The keypad and display panel lit up. He pushed several buttons, then showed the phone to Nicholls.

'That's the direct line of Stuart Gill, my former editor. I can start filing copy in the next half-hour, particularly on your possession and use of banned weapons. If you don't deliver up the guards, that story will be in Gill's paper tomorrow morning, and then all the other papers' "rotters" will be swarming around your offices. Now they may only have pens and notebooks and mobile phones, but they'll beat any army you care to put up because, like your worst enemy in battle, they basically don't give a fuck.'

His finger hovered over the green call button.

'So do I make that call?' he asked, staring at Nicholls.

'I'll call them to a meeting. My office at ten tomorrow morning. How's that?' Nicholls offered.

'Oh, no,' Brennan scoffed. 'I'm not giving you sixteen hours or so to get your stories straight. I want them delivered here as soon as possible, without being forewarned by you or any of your staff.'

'Well, I'm not sure . . .'

'Do it,' Brennan commanded, pushing one of the conference table phones towards him. 'Nobody leaves until I've heard their testimony.'

Nicholls exhaled deeply and then picked up the receiver. Brennan watched as he dialled the Blue Chip number.

'It's Nicholls. I'm at Roadstone's offices. Can you get Cooper and Henderson here a.s.a.p. – their home numbers will be on my Rolodex. And tell them it's urgent.'

He put the phone down with an ill-tempered slam. Brennan smiled.

'Thank you, Major Nicholls,' he said with mock courtesy.

Lydia stood.

'I'll get some coffee organised. This could be a long night.'

CHAPTER THIRTEEN

Henderson was the first to arrive, just after six, looking considerably less menacing without the uniform and truncheon he had used to beat up Lovernios on the night of Brennan's visit to the quarry. Now there was, if not fear exactly, then certainly confusion in his eyes as he was escorted into the room by Lydia to see his boss sitting down with the 'enemy'.

'Take a seat, Henderson,' Nicholls instructed.

'What's this about, sir?' he asked stolidly.

'All will be revealed.'

'What's he doing here?' Henderson asked, pointing at Brennan with contempt.

'Just think of me as your ghost writer, Mr Henderson. You have a story to tell and I'm here to help you express it.'

Lydia poured coffee for the new arrival, and they all sat and waited, fidgeting silently. Twenty minutes later, the entryphone to the Roadstone offices buzzed and Cooper was admitted and escorted up to the boardroom. Brennan enjoyed the spreading paranoia on the faces of the guards. It was no consolation for the electric beating they had given him, but as a man disinclined to violence, he clung to the satisfaction of an imminent victory for brain over brawn.

'You'd better explain to them, Major Nicholls,' he said.

'I want you to tell Mr Brennan about the night you found the boy's body at the quarry.'

'Sir?' Henderson parried in puzzlement.

'Tell him what happened. What you saw. What you did.'

'Are we on a charge here or something, Major?' Cooper asked pointedly.

'No. This isn't a court. More a hearing,' Nicholls said impatiently.

'But you know. We told you, sir,' said Henderson.

'Tell me,' Brennan said firmly.

Henderson shrugged.

'We found him, that's all. No head. Just a body sprawled out by the wheel-wash.'

'Time?' asked Brennan.

'About three fifteen or so. We'd just had a tea break in the quarry office. Decided we'd do a quick tour of the two gatehouses. There'd been no nonsense or anything that night, so we were, well, a bit shocked to see it. Him.'

'Did you know who it was?'

'Not exactly,' Cooper said. 'But you could tell it was one of them from the clothes. We weren't about to conduct a search for his wallet and credit cards.'

'And then what did you do?'

'Called Major Nicholls.'

'Not the police?' Brennan asked.

'We wanted Nicholls to know first,' Henderson said. 'Find out what to do.'

'Didn't you know? I mean, if you stumbled on a headless body in the street, wouldn't you have called a policeman?'

'Yeah, but this was different obviously. We had standing orders. Anything big went down, refer upwards. And this was big – and nasty.'

'What did Major Nicholls say?'

Nicholls nodded for them to go on with their story.

'He'd call us back. We waited around.'

'Did you see anything else or anybody else?'

'No.'

'Did you conduct a search of the area?'

'We had a look around for his head, if that's what you mean. No sign. Then Major Nicholls called back. Told us to dump the body into one of the outgoing railway wagons. So that's what we did. The driver was still having his breakfast. Nobody saw us.

We spread a bit of dirt over the ground where the body had been . . .'

'Why was that?' Brennan interrupted.

'There was a bit of blood around.'

'You mean the corpse was still exsanguinating?' Lydia asked with a look of horror on her face.

'That's a posh word for leaking,' Brennan said helpfully. 'So he'd been freshly killed, had he?'

'They aren't pathologists, Brennan, give them a break,' Nicholls barked.

'Sorry. So, you dumped the body. The train pulled out with its load and you finished your shift and went home to bed.'

'That's more or less it,' Henderson said calmly.

'Weren't you disturbed by what had happened?' Brennan asked, sitting forward so he could see Cooper's eyes.

'Mr Brennan, I once saw a private have his head blown off by an IRA sniper. This was nothing.'

'Did you form any opinion about how the boy died?'

Both Henderson and Cooper shrugged simultaneously.

'Who cares?' said Cooper. 'He was probably lucky to have lasted that long after surfing on so many trains.'

'And you never did find the head?'

'Nope,' Henderson said, his confidence restored. 'Could have been snatched by a fox, I suppose,' he added with a laugh.

'Mr Henderson, Mr Cooper,' Lydia said, addressing them formally. 'Tomorrow morning I will be going to the coroner to report your statements, and those which Mr Trilling and Major Nicholls made earlier. It is more than probable that he will order the police to interview you, and he will almost certainly press for charges on the grounds of perverting the course of justice.'

Henderson smiled arrogantly.

'We were, as they say, only obeying orders. So we won't be alone in the dock, will we?'

He looked at Nicholls and Trilling with sudden contempt.

'Did you kill him?' Brennan asked abruptly, hoping the surprise might ruffle their complacency.

'No,' Henderson said firmly. 'If I'd wanted to kill him I would have done. And I wouldn't have left a body behind. Like kicking shit, dealing with that lot. All you get is dirty boots.'

'I'll pass your sympathy on to his family,' Brennan said sarcastically.

'In the meantime, both of you are dismissed as of this moment,' Lydia said. 'Major Nicholls will no doubt sort out the details.'

'Hang about,' Cooper protested. 'What about these two?'

'Mr Trilling and Major Nicholls are considering their positions.'

'The one consolation for you is that I won't be pressing charges for assault,' Brennan said.

'Just as well because you couldn't prove it, could you?'

'I could try,' Brennan warned. 'And I will if you even think about threatening me or my family. Understand?'

'Fuck off,' Cooper said succinctly, standing and nodding to Henderson. 'Fuck off the lot of you.' He directed a specially intense glare of contempt at Nicholls as he and Henderson made their way to the door.

'Thanks for your support, sir,' Cooper said with leaden irony, saluting Nicholls. 'You won't have anybody left on the payroll once the rest of the lads hear about this. If we get shit, we'll make sure you get double shit.'

They left the room, slamming the door so violently that it rattled the panes of smoked designer glass in the boardroom's partitions. Nicholls hung his head. Trilling looked as though he was in shock.

'Come on, I'll see you out,' Brennan said to Lydia. She gathered her papers and he picked up his phone and tape recorder, putting the batteries back in.

'I'll be seeing you gentlemen in the coroner's office,' he said as he left.

Once Lydia had gathered her coat and briefcase, he escorted her down to reception.

'Well done, Lydia. You did the right thing.'

She sagged on to his shoulder.

'All this misery for one silly accident.'

'It wasn't the accident which caused this, Lydia. It was the lies. If they'd all played it straight, they'd still have their jobs. Come on, I'll buy you a drink.'

She opened the main door and let him out, before moving

through herself and letting the door spring shut. They walked into the floodlit car park.

'Is that it, do you think?' she asked.

'Depends on the coroner, and on the police,' Brennan said with a shrug. 'Depends on how much control he has over them too. I think I'd back him to nail it all down, though. They're lawyers too, you know, just like you.'

She smiled. He put his arm round her shoulder and walked her towards the company car which she'd soon have to surrender. A small price to pay for her integrity.

But as they drew close, he could see that the rear window of her car had been smashed in. And a quick inspection revealed that Cooper and Henderson had inflicted an identical petty revenge on Brennan's Renault, Nicholls' Range Rover and Trilling's Mondeo. Quarry stones wrenched from the ornamental borders of the car park had been rammed through the windows of all four vehicles.

'I suppose we should have expected this,' Brennan said glumly.

'Will they come after us?' Lydia asked.

'I wouldn't rule it out,' he said. 'Come on back to ours if you're worried, though I think you'll find they'll be more angry with Nicholls than us. Nothing the squaddies hate more than being pissed on by an officer.'

'I'll take you up on the offer if you don't mind.'

Brennan walked her down the main road, where they were able to hail a taxi within a few minutes. They got the cab to pause at the Woolpack in Beckington for ten minutes while Brennan bought Lydia a celebratory glass of champagne, before resuming their journey to Bradford.

Cooper and Henderson hadn't finished yet. They'd adjourned to one of Frome's less salubrious pubs and got stuck into several pints of lager. Cooper had taken time off to ring round a few of the boys and tell them of Nicholls' treachery. In groups of twos and threes, these lads had turned up to commiserate and apportion blame. After Nicholls had got a slagging, Cooper and Henderson had agreed that one night soon they'd go back and give this cunt Brennan another going-over, and then find out where that snotty bitch Lydia Pearson lived so they could get round there and all line up and take it in turns to give her one.

By closing time – not that the landlord was brave enough to call it – the nine ex-squaddies had built up an overwhelming drunken momentum for violence. And Cooper knew exactly who would be on the receiving end.

'Look – if we're losing our fucking jobs and the company's losing its contract, we don't have to fart-arse around with those smelly wankers up on the hill any more. We can take the cunts out now.'

The idea had gone down well, and an instant war party had been assembled in the pub's car park as they pooled the weapons they routinely carried around in their cars – baseball bats, hunting-knives, a shotgun – and crammed themselves into two of the vehicles. They'd set off in a squeal of tyres, immunised by the drink to any notion that they might get caught or stopped. Ten minutes later they had parked up in a lay-by opposite the main exit to the quarry, taken Communion in the form of a mass piss against the gate, and then set about searching for the enemy. At the last minute, Cooper had returned to his car, opened the boot and taken out the electric stun baton that he'd so enjoyed using against Brennan.

Now, as they moved off into the darkness, clambering down the railway embankment to the line itself, all the old drills and disciplines came back by instinct, despite the fog of alcohol. Cooper and Henderson took one side of the track each, with the other men strung out in two lines behind them. There were enough torches to go around, but Cooper ordered that they should be used only as a last resort. This was to be a surprise attack.

The nine-man raiding party paused as it began to file through one of the old quarries and enter the ravine. The darkness of the night intensified here, as did the sense of controlled anxiety. Cooper felt images of Ulster swim back into his mind – the night patrols across open fields where every hedgerow might have hidden a killer with a rifle or a radio-controlled bomb. Then he reassured himself that all they were dealing with here was a bunch of hippies, who'd never been in a fight in their lives. This would be fun.

The men paused for a breather, whispering their disappointment that they hadn't caught the bastards in the act of vandalism. Didn't quite seem fair ambushing them while they slept. They'd probably just run away rather than face a good old-fashioned tear-up.

Cooper called them into a huddle.

'Right. We're going up. Four of you go with Hendo on this side. You three come with me up here.' He checked his watch by the beam of his mini-Maglite torch which the lads in the regiment had bought him as a leaving present.

'In the old days we could get up there in two minutes – but I'll give us four, right? Smack on, Hendo, you charge in, give 'em every fucking thing you've got. Drive 'em our way. Then we'll steam in and back 'em against the edge of the cliff. I want to see these bastards shit their pants, right?'

There was a ripple of collective giggles and a counter-wave of 'shushes' before the men split into two groups and began a silent ascent of the hill. Cooper switched on his baton, and an arc of blue light spread across the filament, while Henderson popped two cartridges into his shotgun and snapped it shut.

Within thirty seconds the two lines of men were out of each others' sight, hearing only the breathing and the faint rustling of bracken as the pincer movement took shape. Up above, the glow of a bonfire was becoming visible. But there were no silhouettes of lookouts on the ramparts.

Cooper paused for a moment, listening. There were no sounds of life above. He resumed his forward movement. The second step of this had him screaming in agony as a metal-jawed animal trap clamped on to his right leg. His party gathered around him as he tried to stifle his yell, and then from the shadows of the trees there was a sudden, swift movement and two of the guards were beaten to the ground with axe-blows to the legs. The third was clubbed to the ground with a rock to the head.

An inferno of noise split the night air as Cooper and his men shouted for help. Cooper waved his baton into the darkness but hit nothing. Then, as one of his men scrambled around and switched on a torch, they saw five of the tribe, their faces and chests painted in blood, closing in around them.

'Hendo! Get over here with that fucking gun!'

There was the sound of a shotgun blast in the near distance, but a kick to the face put Cooper down again, stifling any hope of rescue. One of the Celtic warriors picked up the baton and sent a jolt through his body, rendering him unconscious in a second. And then they retreated up the hill.

Henderson and his four men thrashed through the bracken, with all their torches switched on, and found the scene of the ambush. Cooper was out cold, his leg still wedged in the animal trap, two of the guards were clutching their calf muscles, with blood soaking through their jeans, while the last lay groaning with the bone of his nose shattered and protruding through the flesh around it.

Henderson reloaded his shotgun.

'Get them back to the cars. I'm going to kill these bastards.'

With that, he charged headlong up the hill towards the ramparts, roaring in bravado as he ran. He scrambled over the top, panting for breath, and levelled the shotgun in readiness. In the light of the bonfire, he could see nobody in the immediate vicinity. He stepped out into the camp, swinging the gun round in an arc, from his right hip. As he advanced on the first hut, he emptied both barrels into it, and then kicked the flimsy structure down. There was nobody in there. He took two more cartridges from his belt and reloaded before moving through the camp.

'Come on out, you smelly fuckers!' he roared, breaking into a trot. He blasted another two shots into what looked like a food store, and then broke the gun to reload. In that instant, Cernunnos's huge bulk exploded out from behind the hut, and his tattooed face sped towards Henderson, launching a sickening head-butt into the guard's face. Henderson fell to his knees. Cernunnos picked up the gun and swung it high in the air. The last thing Henderson saw as he looked up through his blood-stained hands was the stock of the gun crashing down towards him.

Along the railway track the remnants of the raiding party carried their wounded back towards the safety of their cars.

Suddenly there was a thud on the line and then several more, as cricket-ball-sized rocks rained down from the darkness above them. The four uninjured guards tried to fend off the deadly shower with their arms, but couldn't prevent themselves being hit.

'Scalpings – they're bombarding us with the fucking stuff we guard,' Cooper groaned as he limped on, with the rocks bouncing around him. By the time they reached the embankment, rocks had hit all eight of the men several times, cutting open heads, breaking fingers, bruising shoulders and arms, and they dived into their cars comprehensively routed.

'What about Hendo?' asked one.

'He'll be all right,' Cooper said. 'I'll wait here for him. Get these other lads to hospital.'

Cooper wrapped himself in a jacket and limped across to the quarry gates as the cars sped off like ambulances. As he reached the gatehouse, one of his fellow Blue Chip guards shone a torch at his face.

'Jesus Christ, Coop – what happened?'

'We got beat,' Cooper said, before leaning on the guard for support as he was led back to the gatehouse. 'Can you get the site's medic out to me? Can't go to hospital. Got to wait for Hendo.'

Back up on the hill, the tribe of the Celtic Brotherhood celebrated its victory with the last of the ale that Cernunnos had brewed for them. They congratulated each other for the cunning they had shown in preparing traps and ammunition for the attack Cernunnos had always told them would come one day. Now their leader stood before them and called for silence.

'My brave warriors, we have won a great victory this night. The Romans could not defeat us. They will never defeat us. Now they are in disarray. We have won!'

The tribe cheered this announcement, and toasted their leader with their ale.

'Hail Cernunnos – scourge of the Romans!'

Cernunnos held a hand up for silence.

'But as much as this victory means to us, we must always be ahead of our enemy, never behind. Which is why it is time for you all to become leaders yourselves. You are battle-hardened warriors. You know how to fight and organise against Roman expansion. So you must go out into our country and each recruit a new army, the same way that I summoned you, and you answered. Our Gods demand this service of us – we must protect our earth, our rivers and springs, our trees, for they are as one with us. I am proud to call you my brothers. And what joy there will be when we all meet again in our Otherworld!'

He took his animal-headed dagger from his belt and held out his left palm. He drew the blade of the knife across it and a line of blood appeared.

'He that wears my blood will never fear again!'

Cernunnos moved among his warriors, smearing his blood on to their faces as he passed each in a solemn ritual. When they were all anointed, he stepped back.

'So now we sleep, and when dawn comes it will be the eve of the feast of Imbolc. Tonight, wherever you are, you will light fires to wake the sun from its winter sleep, and our earth will be purified and reborn. The God Lugh will smile on us as we defend our land against rape and despoliation. Our land! Our earth!'

'Our land! Our earth!' they chanted in response, before dispersing to the shelters for sleep. Cernunnos made one last circuit of the camp's ramparts to see that all invaders had been beaten off. He had come to love this quiet, elevated wood which echoed with the lives of the Celtic warriors who had camped here two thousand years ago. He felt their pain and their confusion and their terror in the very branches of each tree and rock. But now he had one last blow to strike against the Roman stone-takers, and if he could please the gods with a gift, they would surely help him in his quest to seal up the great quarry for ever.

Lydia had slept well in the spare room at Brennan's house, and enjoyed meeting Lester at the breakfast table. Spending time with families usually reduced her to tears of boredom, but this short refuge – a hearty supper cooked by Janet, Brennan filling her full of wine – had helped calm her fears of what life would be like without the Roadstone International company as the significant other in her life. There was something apart from work, and something apart from brain-dead domesticity, and the Brennan family seemed to have found it.

Lydia told Brennan this as they went back to the Roadstone offices in Frome to organise the repairs for their damaged cars, and to prepare for their visit to the coroner with the new evidence.

'I've only just rediscovered it,' Brennan confessed. 'The first time, when my son was just a child, and we were living in a small flat, I couldn't face going home, so all I did was work. And that was too much for me. I became an alco-work-aholic, if such a phrase exists. Nearly destroyed the lot. But don't be in a rush, Lydia – too soon can be just as bad as too late.'

The corny homily lasted only as far as the car park of the Roadstone offices, where two police cars were already standing outside the main entrance. Brennan paid off the taxi-driver while Lydia went into the reception area, where two uniformed constables were on guard. By the time Brennan had joined her, she was halfway through receiving the story from one of the constables.

'They won't say how it was they got their injuries, but we're assuming they must have had a run-in with some of the quarry protesters. Anyway, one of them, Henderson, is still on the run with a shotgun, so Mr Trilling asked us to make sure he didn't get in here, something he might try to do in the circumstances.'

'Seems like Cooper and Henderson went on the rampage with some of their colleagues last night. Five of them have been detained in hospital with stab wounds and head injuries,' Lydia passed on to Brennan.

'What about the protesters at the camp? he asked anxiously.

'Nobody's reported anything, or been into hospital, sir,' the constable said. 'I think Detective Inspector Blackwell is planning to go up there this morning, see what damage these hooligans might have done. We've had the cars towed away to the police pound for safety, by the way.'

'Thank you,' Lydia said.

'We'd better go and see Blackwell later,' Brennan told Lydia, 'after we've seen the coroner.'

'Can you tell us where the coroner's offices are?' she asked the constable.

'On the hill up towards the Radstock roundabout, on the left by the church. He's part of a firm of lawyers, don't know the names.'

'Thank you.'

They set off into Frome, and after ten minutes' walk found a brass plaque on the wall of a Victorian red-brick building, adjoining a churchyard, which boasted the legend 'East Somerset Coroner's Office' among the names and legal qualifications.

They walked in, and after explaining the urgency of the situation to the receptionist were ushered into a conference room lined with legal books and leather upholstered chairs.

'Takes me back,' Lydia muttered as she read the titles on the spines of the legal textbooks.

'Makes the Ten Commandments look pretty concise, doesn't it?' Brennan observed wryly.

The coroner arrived, in his solicitor's pinstripe suit, looking considerably younger and less forbidding than he did without his formal robe.

'Robert Magee, Miss Pearson,' he said, offering a hand to Lydia, although he was slightly less polite to Brennan, remembering his outbursts at the inquests.

He asked them to take a seat at the conference table while he collected a yellow legal pad for his notes. Lydia then carefully took him through the new evidence that Brennan and she had accumulated, concerning the true location of Humphrey Castleton's body and the conspiracy to dump it into a rail truck. She also brought up the issue of the use of electric batons by the security company. She finally pointed out that neither of the two guards had come forward at the inquest. Brennan suggested that it had been neglectful of Sergeant Harris not to have interviewed anybody from the protest camp prior to the inquest.

Magee seemed quite taken aback by this catalogue of deception, as he instantly referred to it. He wanted names and addresses for the guards, and contact numbers for Nicholls and Trilling, so that they could all be served with new subpoenas for what he felt sure would have to be a reopened inquest. He needed, though, any papers and statements that Lydia could supply to support the new evidence.

'I should be able to manage that – you will realise that my job prospects at Roadstone International are fairly sketchy at the moment,' she said.

'Well, I can't intervene directly,' Magee said, 'but I would have thought they stood to benefit much more from you exposing the truth than having you toe the line.'

'Does that apply to me too, Mr Magee?' Brennan asked.

'All I ask is that you don't, in anything you write, pre-empt a decision which the new inquest might make. The police are the proper investigative agency for this, despite your reservations about certain officers.'

Brennan put on his most sincere expression.

'I will, of course, abide by the coroner's wishes,' he said solemnly.

Once outside, however, he told Lydia he was off to see DI Blackwell.

'Don't worry – it's in the coroner's hands now. He may not look like it, but he's got a lot of clout when it comes to getting people in line. You should relax now. You've done your bit.'

'All feels like an anticlimax,' Lydia confessed.

'It's not over yet,' he promised her, kissing her on the cheek before they parted.

Blackwell sipped at his coffee in its plastic container, watching Brennan carefully.

'So it's now likely that the coroner will insist on another inquest. He may even press for charges to be brought. I don't think Sergeant Harris is going to come out of it too well.'

'And what's the verdict likely to be?' Blackwell asked chattily.

'Accidental death, I suppose.'

'Same as the last one,' Blackwell said pointedly. 'I could almost charge you for wasting police time.'

'I think you manage a good enough job of that without my help, Mr Blackwell. You've been up to the protester's camp yet?'

'No – these security boys are saying nothing. They got into a ruck with persons unknown.'

'They were carved up.'

'Serves 'em right from what you've said. We can't do anything about it unless they talk, or press charges.'

'How do you know they haven't injured or killed any of the protesters?'

'How do I know it was them that they had the fight with? You don't understand police work, do you, Brennan? I've had a five-year-old girl battered to within an inch of her life overnight – do you think I should drop the search for her assailant while I sort out what two bunches of arseholes did to each other?'

'Why does it always have to be a trade-off?'

'Because there aren't enough of us. There isn't enough money. They could eliminate crime in a year if they trebled the amount of police. But who'd pay for it? And who'd want it that way? We have enough work as it is without going out looking for more. So unless the coroner tips us the wink, that's all that's going to happen for now.'

'Could you at least do one favour for me?'

'Possibly.'

'The bloke who leads the protesters is called Clive Parry. I hear he might have been in a bit of trouble once. Taunton way. Do you think you could have a look in your computer . . .'

'And what – let *you* know? What are we – a service industry for the press?'

'I meant only that you might find something which broadens your picture of events.'

'If I'm interested, that is.'

'What about Henderson – has he shown up yet?'

Blackwell shook his head.

'They were all pissed out of their brains. He's probably sleeping it off under a bush somewhere. In the meantime, I am wasting valuable manpower sticking officers on Trilling and Nicholls as a safeguard.'

'I am trying to help you – believe me. To ease your burden.'

'Well, I'm sorry, Mr Brennan, but it doesn't ever seem like that.'

Brennan withdrew from the police station, feeling flat and depressed by their obduracy. He was going to have to do this all by himself. Thank God he'd had Lydia to help otherwise he was sure he'd have given up. He returned home and sulked for the afternoon, then snapped himself out of it in time for Lester's return from school.

He made him a mushroom omelette with oven chips to get him over the gap until dinner. He watched Lester assiduously unpack his school-bag and pile up his books and notes on the breakfast table.

'You take after me for tidiness,' he said.

'I've seen your office, Dad. It's like one of them cardboard cities.'

'No extra scripture lessons tonight, then?'

'It's tomorrow. And it's comparative religions. I've got them to read some of that Celtic history book that Mum bought. They had religion too, you know?'

'Tell me about it,' Brennan said.

'Okay, well, it seems—'

'No, no – I was being ironic. Sorry. I've had all sorts of mystical spouting over the past few weeks. I think I know it all by now.'

Brennan saw his disappointed look.

'Sorry, son. I'm sure I must have missed something. What do you find interesting about it?'

'Well, they believed that there was no single god, but a whole lot of individual ones who looked after the sun, nature, rivers, animals – that sort of thing.'

'Hardly surprising that, is it? When so much was unknown, things like the light and the warmth of the sun, fresh water, the harvest, all must have seemed like strange gifts from a benign presence.'

'What's benign mean?'

'Kind, gentle, loving – somebody or something which cares.'

'Why did they offer sacrifices to gods, then, if they thought they were kind?'

'Sacrifices? Where's it say about that?'

Lester took the book out of the pile and found the relevant section.

'It says that the Celts sacrificed living animals at their festivals, and then killed human beings too sometimes – stabbed them, ripped their guts out, cut their heads off, set fire to them or drowned them. Not very benign, eh?'

Brennan took the book and looked at it, flicking through the text. The various authors seemed learned enough, with lots of degrees after their names.

'I don't think they saw it as punishment, more as a gift to the gods, Lester.'

'But how can you call killing somebody a gift?'

'Isn't that what happened with Jesus – for God so loved the world he gave his only begotten son? A sacrifice.'

Lester nodded.

'I suppose so. Must have been really weird living in those days.'

'You can see why people needed religion then, can you?'

'And why they still do too.'

Brennan completed the cooking of his son's meal, brooding about the nature of sacrifice in Celtic culture, and what it might say about Cernunnos's state of mind. He mentally scrolled through the big man's utterances and behaviour, and his apparent descent into insanity. But then the sacrifices that the book described were, at the time, seen as rational acts of worship. So Cernunnos could claim that all he was doing was being faithful to Celtic rituals, of which the most potent was the taking of human life in order to appease the gods.

But then he suddenly began to feel a sickening dread in the very pit of his stomach. What if the urge to kill had simply been grafted on to Celtic worship, because it was so accommodating to his instincts? He thought of Clive Parry, the woman-beater, the rapist, the committer of incest. The man was already more than halfway to achieving the perfect harmony between his personality and identity – becoming a killer priest would complete the process. Only Brennan's own selfish, professional self-denial – what would this mean for his story? – prevented him from calling up the police there and then.

But now, through the fog of his mental confusion, he heard the phone ringing. He answered it, taking a moment to recognise both Blackwell's name and purpose.

'That check you wanted . . . on the Parry bloke.'

'Oh, right – yes?'

'Nothing – no form listed, either locally or on the CRO computer. Whoever he is, he's a nothing, Brennan. Sorry to ruin your story.'

The line went dead before Brennan could even think of a

question. If Parry had no criminal record, then Sheila Parry's account of their life together might also be flawed, or even a complete fantasy.

He mooched around the house while Lester watched consecutive Australian soaps on the television. He thought about phoning Sheila directly but didn't have her number, and couldn't find one listed either for her, Clive or the bookshop. When Janet arrived home, she'd hardly got her coat off before Brennan was upon her.

'What did Sheila tell you about Clive?'

'Apart from Brigit, you mean?'

'Yes – you were looking up details of a prison record or something, weren't you?'

'You asked me to, I think – something Robert told you, the night you were attacked. That he'd been in prison.'

'Well, he hasn't – not according to the police.'

'No, well, she told me the other day that he'd been interviewed or arrested once, but never been sent down.'

'What for? What was it for?'

'A little girl on the same estate was murdered – he was hauled in for questioning . . .'

'Where? What estate?'

'I don't know. Taunton, I think she said.'

'*Taunton?*'

'Yes. Why the alarm?'

'Because I covered a story there once. Early eighties. A bloke had been banged up, forced to confess to a murder, of a child, on a new housing estate . . .'

Janet's face began to register a profound anguish as Brennan continued to trawl his memory.

'I got a begging letter from his lawyer. The police had fingered this bloke because he was a bit soft in the head. An easy target. I managed to prove that the local CID officer had forged most of the confession. So the guy was released while he was awaiting trial. That's all I remember,' Brennan concluded as he prowled the room.

Janet knew she'd fouled up. She should have taken notes. Shown them to Brennan. She took a deep breath.

'Sheila told me that she and Clive were driven off the estate. They started their new life in Frome . . . and changed their name to Parry.'

'From what?' Brennan snapped.

'Berry.'

Brennan clutched his palms to his face, and pulled the flesh on his cheeks downwards. All the colour had drained from his complexion.

'Fucking hell, Jan,' he said despairingly. 'Clive Berry. That's him. That's the bloke I got off.'

He pounded up the stairs to his office and virtually threw himself through the door. He began scrambling through his pile of cuttings albums, which were arranged in chronological order.

'What year did you start at the paper?' he shouted back to Janet.

'Nineteen eighty-three.'

'This was before I met you.'

He discarded three albums, grabbed at 1982 and 1981 and began to flick through them.

'Why didn't you tell me this?'

'You've hardly been here, Frank. Besides – I don't remember you asking.'

'It was summer, I remember now – because I went to watch Somerset play cricket one day at the Taunton ground.'

He flipped over several pages until he saw the dates change to June and July – and then suddenly there he was. Slimmer, no beard, short hair, no face tattoos, but just as tall – Clive Berry, on the steps of a courthouse, both thumbs up at the camera, celebrating the throwing-out of his case.

'Look.'

He thrust the cutting at Janet and brushed past her.

'What are you doing now?'

'Telling the police – I think Clive Berry murdered both Humphrey and Brigit.'

Janet ran after him.

'Can I phone Sheila first – make sure she's all right?'

'Hurry up. There was a pitched battle at the camp last night. A gang of security guards went up there to smack around the protesters, but they got badly beaten, carved up. Ambushed. This bloke Cernunnos is running amok.'

Janet pounded the buttons on the phone, while Brennan searched for his mobile.

'No answer.'

'Right – I'd better get over there.'

He pulled his coat on, and jammed the phone into his pocket.

'Call DI Blackwell at Frome – tell him all we've discussed. Clive's real name, that Taunton case, the incest, the lot.'

'But Sheila asked me—'

'This is no time for fucking secrets, Jan. I think the man's a killer.'

Chapter Fourteen

The taxi approached Frome from the northern side, and weaved its way into the complex of narrow eighteenth-century streets at the heart of which was Sheila Parry's bookshop. The cab-driver parked by a no-entry sign about two hundred yards short of the shop, and Brennan began to make his way down the hill, making a point of walking on the flagstones and not the already frosted cobbles. The line of charity and junk shops and empty premises was even more forlorn at this time of night. There was no sign of human movement, just the odd light from rooms above shops to suggest outposts of habitation. He crossed the street to avoid passing the doors of a brooding Baptist chapel, which threw an eerie Cubist shadow down the hill. Now he could see the frontage of the bookshop on its raised walkway. There were no lights in the shop window, and none upstairs either. He switched on his phone, getting the faintest of signals.

'Jan – I'm here. Doesn't look like she's in.'

'No. I've called at least three times and got no answer.'

'Did you speak to Blackwell?'

'Yes – he wants to see you.'

'I'll go round now. I'll leave the phone on so call me if you hear anything.'

'I will.'

'And Jan . . .'

'What?'

'Lock up tight, won't you?'

He pocketed the phone and walked across to the bookshop. He

stepped into the door-well and put his face to the glass. The counter was clear and the small till had its drawer open to show prospective thieves that there was nothing in it for them. Maybe it was an appeal to customers too, because the books on the shelves and those piled high on the floor looked like orphans. The door to the back room was half open, but it was impossible to see anything as the darkness was complete. Brennan backed away, taking one last look up at the windows of the flat above. Nothing.

He walked away, taking a route down a short passage lined with more sad shops and what seemed to be some sort of North African café, which like everything else around it was closed too. He was glad to emerge from this time tunnel on to the main hill into Frome, with its kebab takeaway and cider bar bustling with early evening trade.

Once at the police station he was ushered straight through to Blackwell's office, finding him sitting behind his desk in a dinner suit and black tie.

'There was no need to dress up for me, Detective Inspector,' he said, unable to resist the opportunity. 'What is it, masonic dinner?'

'Police welfare dinner and dance.'

'Oh well – maybe I should make a contribution.' He reached for his wallet.

'The best contribution *you* can make is to piss off out of my town, Brennan. I've had enough of you. You're just fannying about, aren't you? One minute one theory, one minute the next.'

'It's called investigation – perhaps that's why it's unfamiliar to you.'

'Look – I've checked Parry for a record, no sign. And I've checked Berry for a record, and, apart from the dropped charges at Taunton, nothing. You got him off, and it looks like you were right. So why don't you go home and sit on your bleeding laurels?'

'Any sign of Henderson yet?'

'Nobody's reported him missing.'

'Which probably means that Cooper and his squaddies are going to go back up there, fully tooled up, to make sure they win this time.'

'I'm paid to protect ordinary, tax-paying, law-abiding people. I'd sooner get a call-out for a cat stuck up in a tree than for something at a camp of smelly drop-outs. As for the other bunch – I've had a constable nearly die of boredom today protecting Mr Trilling.'

'I think Parry killed the kid Castleton – sacrificed him. Cut off his head. He's a psychopath. He believes he's the reincarnation of a Celtic god. Cernunnos.'

'You're barmy, Brennan.'

'I think he drowned his daughter too . . . another sacrifice.'

Blackwell frowned.

'His *daughter* – I don't remember Sheila Parry telling me about this.'

'That's because Sheila is his sister, but he fathered her child. She always pretended that the father had gone away to protect him. And herself.'

'So maybe when the daughter finds out this pillock's her dad, she tops herself. I know I would. Coroner should have brought in a verdict of justifiable suicide.'

Blackwell checked his watch and stood.

'I've got to go.'

'What about putting a guard on Sheila?'

'What for? If they're that close, he's not going to harm her, is he? Brother and lover – he must feel an awful lot for her.'

'You couldn't get less interested, could you?'

'If you'd been doing my job for the years I have, you'd reach the same conclusion, Brennan – white trash have no choice about their destinies. It's already been decided for them from the moment they're born. I'm more interested in stopping or catching the criminals who've made a *decision* to be that way. They're the ones that do the real damage in society.'

'What's this, the Darwinian detective? What are you going to tell that superior being Giles Castleton – that his son was killed by some lunatic you should have spotted months ago?'

'I'll show you out, before Sergeant Harris hears you shouting, Brennan. He's had a tough time from the coroner today thanks to you mouthing off.'

'That's only the start. Have a nice night,' Brennan said, letting himself out of the room before Blackwell could have the satisfaction of throwing him out.

'Will Dad be all right?' asked Lester suddenly.

'Yes, of course,' Janet lied. 'He's just gone to tell the police about this man they ought to interview.'

'But is he the one that believes in sacrifice?'

'Lester – you shouldn't believe everything you read in that book. It's about ancient rituals and beliefs – the same stuff's in the Bible and you don't necessarily believe that, do you?'

Lester shrugged.

'What if I do?'

'All right – so it doesn't mean that this man believes in human sacrifices.'

'But what if he does? It says in the book that the Celts used to do everything in threes – it was a symbolic number. That boy died, then the girl, so now—'

'Lester, will you please shut up and stop going on about it. You'll drive me up the wall. Your dad's working. Talking to the police, that's all. I can give him a ring on his phone any time if I'm worried.'

'But I know what he's like – he'll want to get the man before the police do. So he can have the story first for his paper.'

The telephone rang, saving Janet from the likelihood of whacking Lester round the chops for knowing too much.

'This'll be him now, telling me what time to put the dinner on.'

She answered the phone. Lester listened intently, trying to piece together the conversation at the other end of the line.

'Sheila. Where are you? Oh, right – Frank's not long been round there, you must have just missed him. How are you? Okay, I'm sure you are. Look, I'll give Frank a ring, shall I, tell him to pop in on you, make sure you're okay. You can come here for the night if you'd feel safer. Well, talk to him – see how you feel. I'll call him right now. He's only round the corner at the police station. 'Bye, love.'

Janet put the phone down and redialled immediately. She gave Lester a beady-eyed look as she dialled.

'Hello, love – Sheila Parry just phoned. She's back at the shop.

Would you mind popping in to see her? I've said she can come back if she feels she needs to. Let us know, right? How did it go with the police? Oh, sorry . . . might have guessed. See you.'

She hung up and walked back to Lester.

'There. Your dad's fine. The lady's all right. They'll be back here in half-an-hour.'

'Fuck it,' Brennan muttered to himself as he considered the prospect of going back down through the dank, narrow back streets of Frome to the bookshop. But he still found his legs taking him in that direction. He knew it was his greatest weakness, getting personally involved in the cases he worked on, allowing somebody to lean on his shoulder, occasionally allowing himself to exploit them by opening up to them. There were plenty of guys from the old days of Fleet Street, replicated in their hundreds now in the glass and razor-wire citadels of Wapping and Canary Wharf, who simply had no conscience about using everyone they ever met on a story, or stamping on them in a big way if they had the temerity to make demands. They always managed to keep their distance, even if they were shagging the witness in question. Disposable people – that's exactly how Sheila Parry would have been regarded. And right now, part of Brennan wished he could walk away from her.

As he trudged up the steps to the raised pavement, he could see that the lights in the flat above the shop were now on. He approached the door. A wedge of pale light came down the stairwell, illuminating the side wall of the back room where the old well stood. He rapped on the glass panel, waiting to see Sheila's shadow appear on the staircase, but as he knocked the door eased open. He pushed it with his finger and stepped in slowly.

'Sheila! It's Frank Brennan.'

There was no answer. He closed the door behind him and edged his way to the back room, feeling for a light-switch on the way in.

'Sheila!'

'Here,' a small, frightened voice said very close by. Brennan pushed the door back. Sheila was against the far wall, Cernunnos holding the blade of a dagger across her throat. Brennan's mind raced so much the room began to blur. Should he run? Should he shout? Should he fight? Instead he found himself calmly saying: 'Hello, Clive.'

The eyes flickered.

'Cernunnos. Horned God. King of the Woods.'

'Frank Brennan. The stupid bastard who got you out of a life sentence.'

Cernunnos broke into a sudden smile, as if a family album of a summer holiday had been opened up in front of him.

'I remember.'

'Good. But there's no need to look so surprised. This is more than coincidence, isn't it? Cernunnos. Me being back in your life.'

'I summoned you.'

'You could have written, or phoned. Rather than killing two kids to get to me. Oh, sorry – you don't call it killing, do you. It's sacrifice. Anyway, it's a strange way to say thank you to me, whatever your culture.'

'I did not need to thank you. You had another purpose.'

'Don't tell me. Public relations officer? Cernunnos, the Myth and the Reality – how to kill kids and stay out of jail.'

'You are my messenger. To the Romans. To tell them that their rape of the hills must stop. They listen to you. And you are not afraid to speak ill of them. To tell the world what plunderers they are.'

'Ah, but I'll only do that if *you* do something for me for a change. Let Sheila go. Please.'

Brennan looked at Sheila for the first time, seeing the genuine terror in her eyes. His calmness began to evaporate.

'Let her go, Cernunnos,' he repeated in his firmest tone. 'Let her go.'

Slowly, Cernunnos drew the blade away from Sheila's throat, swinging it round in Brennan's direction. Sheila visibly sagged, but his left arm was still across her chest, holding her against the wall.

'Let her come to me. You don't need her now.'

Cernunnos lowered his left arm a little, relaxing the pressure on Sheila.

'Good. Thank you.'

But then in one motion he swivelled and drove the dagger straight through Sheila's throat with such force that he pinned her to the wall. A great spurt of blood shot across the room and sprayed over the floor, as Sheila began to gurgle and twitch, life speeding out of her body. Brennan felt his arms and legs sag with shock, and then he summoned the strength to run, lurching out of the room into the shop. But as he stumbled towards the door, intent on diving through the glass panel, he tripped over one of the piles of books and sprawled on to the floor. He scrambled to his feet, but then felt Cernunnos's huge hand grab at the small of his back and begin to drag him away from the door.

'Help me! Help!' Brennan yelled suddenly, as a survival instinct began to kick in. But the old books and the grimy glass in the door and windows of the shop muffled his cries to a whisper, so if there had been anyone passing he couldn't have caught their attention.

'You stay with me,' growled Cernunnos, pulling him upright and bundling him into the back room. Mercifully, Sheila was dead now, and the fountain of blood from the ruptured jugular veins had subsided to a series of bubbling spurts. Despite the fatal collapse, she remained upright, suspended by the dagger which had been pounded through into the brickwork in the single blow. This made her look like a grotesque marionette whose strings had suddenly slackened.

'Stop this. Stop this killing,' Brennan panted weakly.

'She defamed me. The punishment for slandering a god is death, and banishment from the Otherwold.'

Cernunnos pushed Brennan into the space behind the door, and rammed him against the wall.

'I don't get this. You kill your daughter, the boy who could have been your son, the foetus that would have been your grandchild, your sister. This is not a god's doing, Cernunnos, but a devil's.'

Cernunnos showed no reaction but lifted the wooden cover off the well and reached inside it. He began to pull and Brennan saw the end of a rope in his huge hand. Cernunnos threaded the rope through both hands now, spooling the excess on to the floor.

Brennan could hear the sound of water running, and then from the well, looped on to the rope, came first the distorted, discoloured but still recognisable head of Humphrey Castleton, dripping water and a scented oil, followed by that of Henderson, whose death rictus smiled across at him. Brennan felt his breath give out on him. Darkness swirled around his brain. His eyes began to close and he pitched forward on to the blood-splattered floor.

This time, Cooper and his mates would make no mistake. They arrived stone-cold sober for one thing, and each carrying a shotgun for another. They also had torches, fire-lighters, petrol, knives, a sledgehammer and CS gas canisters. And this time, they wouldn't hang around. They'd be straight in through the front, on the run. They'd pull Hendo out if he was still captive, break every limb in every protester's body and then torch the camp to the ground.

Cooper parked the 4x4 Isuzu in the lane by the duck pond. He and his five colleagues got out and checked the time. In and out in fifteen minutes, just in case the local plods decided to interfere.

They trotted down the footpath, guns at the ready, and began to sing as they moved, marine-style, their old training-drill anthem:

Watch out cunts cos The Dukes are here,
To fuck your birds and drink your beer.
If you want a fight you can have that too,
'Cos we are the boys of Battalion Two,
Sound off!

They repeated the verse twice over as they crossed the bridge and mounted the hill at a steady pace. Once over the ramparts they 'swept and searched' the camp, bursting two-handed into each hut and tent for signs of Hendo or a member of the tribe, but apart from food waste and abandoned jars and pots, there was nothing. Even the bonfire was little more than a grey, smouldering pile of ash.

Cooper ordered his lads to burn the place to the ground, and they set about it with relish, spreading petrol and fire-lighters into the more substantial dwellings, and then kicking down the tents and throwing them on to the burning wood. Within five minutes the whole camp was ablaze and on its way back into history.

As a finale, Cooper and his men sprayed the fringes of the camp with shotgun pellets, congratulating themselves that anybody hiding there would be picking metal out of their arse for several weeks. But only as they kicked the ashes of the dying bonfire did the euphoria die, as first a human thigh-bone and then a hip joint became visible. As they crouched to disperse more of the ash with their boots and their knives, the remains of a human skeleton began to take shape.

'Jesus Christ, they killed Hendo,' Cooper said quietly, crossing himself.

'We don't know it was him, do we?' asked one of his mates, hoping for reassurance.

But Cooper's eye had been taken by something else, and he had begun raking the fire with his hunting knife, eventually lifting the object out with the tip. Though it had been dulled and distorted by the fire, he knew an army dog-tag when he saw it.

'Come on, time we let the police handle this one,' he said.

And they all backed away, no longer jubilant, but hunched and subdued by defeat.

Janet was puzzled. Brennan had made a point of saying he would leave the phone on, but now all she got was a robotic, microchip voice inviting her to leave a message. She tried Sheila's number again, but once more there was no answer. She counted back to the time of her call, calculated how long Brennan might need to talk to Sheila and to ferry her back to Bradford if necessary, and all she could come up with was the fact that he was running at least an hour late. She chastised herself for showing signs of being a silly woman, and decided that the rational decision would be to call the police if he still hadn't turned up in another half-hour. That would help soothe Lester's nerves too, which had not been quietened by his further incursions into the book on Celtic culture. She had been obliged to intervene and put the book away. All that guff about severing heads and keeping them, preserved in oils, for trophies was just the sort of thing that gave boys nightmares.

When Brennan woke, he felt for one moment that he might have entered an anteroom to hell itself. A complex web of piping ran above his head, set inside a bare-brick structure. To one side, three green-coloured generators hummed behind mesh cages. But in contrast to this technology he could see that his prone body was flanked by the two severed heads which he thought had been part of a nightmare, but were all too obviously not.

He then realised that moving around him, piling up kindling, was Cernunnos himself. He was now bare-chested, his torso a mass of bizarre tattoos of stags, fish, bears, snakes, rams and dogs – the creatures of the woods. He was also wearing a startling head-dress fashioned out of a pair of stag's antlers.

Brennan still felt groggy from his faint, and he half closed his eyes while he tried to work out what was going on. Lying doggo also gave him a chance to wait for a moment of weakness from Cernunnos. His nostrils began to twitch as he smelt a pungent odour, and then felt a cold sticky liquid dripping on to his bare chest where his shirt had been ripped open. He could stand it no longer. He sat up.

'Welcome to the feast of Imbolc, Brennan,' Cernunnos said, looking down on him. He had a pitcher in his hand from which he was pouring oil.

'Where am I?'

'I have found a most sacred place for our feast of purification.'

'Could I have some water, please?'

For the first time that Brennan could remember, Cernunnos laughed. But it wasn't a laugh of humour, more one of cruel superiority.

'I will give you plenty to drink, Brennan.'

He put his animal-furred foot on to Brennan's chest and pushed him back down.

'Is this how the Celts get their kicks, then? Slaughtering people? Cutting their heads off?'

'We worship the head, Brennan. That's why I have donated two to you for your journey.'

'Journey?'

'To the Otherworld.'

'I've got quite attached to this one, actually.'

'You will be welcomed there, Brennan. You are a good man. You have helped in the fight against the Romans. You deserve your place with the gods.'

'Look, Clive. You are living in late-twentieth century Britain. This isn't the past, just a fantasy that's taken you over. Killing people is wrong. Bad. A no-no.'

Brennan tried to keep the tone non-confrontational, but Cernunnos had picked up on the sarcasm.

'They summoned the past – the rapers of the hills. They woke ancient gods by disturbing the earth. Cernunnos was roused from his sleep. To take his revenge.'

'Why did you kill Lovernios? Lovernios was a good man too.'

'Lovernios lives with the gods. That is not death but everlasting life. He went willingly to sacrifice.'

'I saw the scratches on his arms. Whatever you'd doped him with had worn off by the time you came to behead him. He wanted to live, didn't he? To stay in this world. But you wouldn't let him.'

Cernunnos raised his boot again and this time kicked down on Brennan, knocking his head against the cold concrete floor. He kept his foot on the side of his head.

'You have been chosen, Brennan. You helped me once and now you will help me again. Sacrifice is an honour – even the Romans understand that, and the Christians. They have always said how noble it is. Is it not at the heart of Christian religion itself?'

'If it's that good why don't you volunteer for it?'

Cernunnos lifted his foot off Brennan's head and reached for the dagger tucked into his belt. Brennan rolled to one side and jacked himself up as quickly as he could, planting a flying kick into Cernunnos's celestial balls. The giant let out a roar of pain and anger and doubled up. Brennan grabbed the first thing to hand, a slice of wood, and whacked Cernunnos across the face. He lurched backwards. Brennan thought about another attack, but survival and escape were his prime considerations now. He ran round the other side of the generators. If it was an electricity sub-station, or something similar, it must have a door. At the far end of the wall, he saw it – a green metal door with a push-bar release. He threw himself at it and fell out into the freezing night air.

With his heart pounding, he ran, almost impervious to his surroundings, but gradually, as a pale yellow light filtered through the fog that had settled around the building, he realised he was in the quarry. A great smooth wall of rock loomed above him. To one side was a wide track of crushed earth, and a spread of cold green-coloured water. He was at the very base of the quarry, the pump-house, the run-off where Brigit had been ceremoniously drowned by her bastard of a father.

He ran on to the earth track, aware of the pains in his bare feet as they were cut and gouged by rocks, but he was alive and free, for the moment at least. He didn't want to look back, he just wanted to run, until he could see something, or somebody who could help him. On he went through the fog, his nightmare of before Christmas now a terrifying, living reality.

As long as he was going upwards, he felt safe, but every now and then, a bank of fog disorientated him, and he lost not only his sense of direction but also any sense of being higher or lower. He longed for the sanctuary of one of those huge trucks he had seen on his visit with Lovernios, he longed to be at home with Janet and Lester. The fog cleared again, and for the first time he saw the outline of the quarry's buildings and sheds above him. He ran on with renewed energy. He'd even welcome the presence of a Blue Chip Security man now, electric baton or not. Finally he was on the same level as the buildings, a complex of garages and conveyors and – what did they call it? – the crushing shed. He saw the admin building. There was a light on inside. He ran across to it and banged loudly on the locked door. But the light was only from a staff cloakroom. The nylon jackets and hard-hats of the workers were hanging abandoned on a rack.

He pushed away from the door, trying to remember the geography of the quarry as he had seen it that night, and again when he'd pretended to be meeting Lydia. There were two roads – one in, one out. The entrance was a long slope up to the gatehouse. The exit was across and to the left, past the railhead.

He scampered on, splashing through frozen puddles, his feet stung by the ice. To his right, the great stockpiles of roadstone stood like pyramids in the eerie light. He thought about calling out, but that would only alert Cernunnos to his position. He thought about hiding and waiting till morning, but he would surely freeze to death before then. His feet now slipped on a network of railway lines. A train was standing about two hundred yards to his left, its trucks loaded up. He could hear the hum of the diesel engine – there'd be a driver, a radio, sanctuary. He ran towards the train. But then it suddenly began to shudder into motion.

Brennan accelerated, running alongside the track. He drew level with the last truck which was moving at less than ten miles per hour, but it seemed like a hundred to his heaving lungs. He reached out and grabbed the hand-rail at the rear of the truck and pulled himself up on to the platform below the hopper. A great surge of relief washed through him. Now that he had stopped running he could feel that his body was coated with sweat. He almost felt like laughing, such was his euphoria. And then on the other side of the platform a tattooed arm appeared, and Cernunnos pulled himself up.

Brennan clambered up the metal ladder and leapt on to the pile of stones in the hopper, running across them as fast as he could, despite the stabbing pains in his feet. He turned. Cernunnos's antlered head appeared above the lip of the hopper. Brennan bent and picked up a handful of the 'scalpings' and flung them at him, but all he heard was their clang as they hit the far wall of the hopper. He turned and ran again. Reaching the end of the hopper, he pushed off from its edge and leapt forward into the next one.

The train had now left the quarry and had begun to run out down the single-track line that ran through the ravine and past Tedbury Camp. He turned and threw more rocks at Cernunnos in the hopper behind him. This time some of them hit, and he heard a yell of pain and anger. But Cernunnos advanced again. Brennan ran and jumped across into the next wagon, landing with a lurch that pitched him into the side wall of the hopper, banging his head. He was near to exhaustion now, but he staggered to his feet, and dragged his legs towards the end of the hopper. There, his energy was all but spent. He propped himself on the edge, trying to gulp in freezing air, but it was so cold it tightened his chest like a strait jacket. He saw Cernunnos clamber into the far end of the hopper and trudge towards him across the stones.

He resolved to throw himself off the moving train in the hope of finding shelter in the undergrowth alongside the track, but he didn't have the strength to get up. Cernunnos advanced on him then stopped to draw his dagger from his belt.

'You were meant to die in the fire which will bring back the water to fill the quarry,' he panted breathlessly. 'But now, I will cut your heart out.'

He took another step towards him and raised the dagger with both of his hands as if in a ritual. Brennan pulled on the side of the hopper, but his arms had not an ounce of strength left.

'*Salva me fons pietatis, salva me,*' he found himself whispering, on the verge of death, as fear welled up and triggered in him a schoolboy plea to whatever god might be listening. He waited for the blow, but then there was an almighty thump and instant darkness. Brennan saw Cernunnos, backlit by the night sky, topple and fall, his antlered head ripped off by the parapet of the tunnel through which the train was now running. He began to sob with relief, as the darkness of the tunnel smothered all light. He lay there for what seemed like hours, but soon he could see stars in the sky again. The train stopped for a signal at Westbury, and Brennan was able to climb down from the hopper. Shocking a station hand with his frightful appearance, he blurted out the bare details of his story, and begged for warmth and the chance to phone his wife.

By now Janet and Lester were at Frome police station, begging the duty sergeant to spare an officer to go round to the bookshop. But he was busy dealing with a handful of men who had reported finding the remains of a body on the hill-fort at Tedbury Camp. Janet overheard their conversation and for a few despairing moments believed that Brennan had been killed. But then the man called Cooper had brought relief by saying whose the body was.

When the beleaguered police eventually went round to the

bookshop and broke in to find Sheila Parry's body still pinned to the wall of the back room, they had no option but to summon Blackwell from his dinner and explain the mayhem that had taken place. Janet and Lester were taken to a side room and given tea, while they offered ideas on what had happened to Brennan, believing him to have been kidnapped by Clive Parry. Blackwell ordered a call-out of additional officers for a search, and requested the assistance of the Avon & Somerset police helicopter, with its powerful night-light and its heat-seeking infra-red camera. But then Brennan's call came through, and a patrol car was sent to Westbury, with Janet and Lester on board. When they were ushered into the room, seeing him battered but alive, the three of them formed a tangle of arms and bodies as they hugged each other, never wanting to let go again.

The unravelling of Clive Parry's trail of murderous fantasy took several weeks, with Brennan able to break the story first, not for Stuart Gill, who had failed to deliver the promised advance, but for the *Independent on Sunday*, who bought a 2,500-word feature, and a follow-up magazine article from him. The inquests into the deaths of Humphrey Castleton and Brigit Parry were reopened to great public interest, with verdicts of unlawful killing being returned. Clive Parry was forensically linked to both murders, and to the killing and cremation of Henderson, the security guard. Parry's own gruesome end was ironically dispatched into the record books as an 'accidental death'.

The fallout for Roadstone International and the protest movement against their quarry was considerable. Trilling was sacked, while Lydia Pearson was offered a directorship but declined it, taking up a job with a radical legal firm in London. Blue Chip Security, who were indicted in Brennan's story, were investigated by the Ministry of Defence Police and found to be in possession of stolen weapons. Their contract with Roadstone was cancelled without compensation. Major Nicholls stood down as chairman.

The protest groups held a silent vigil outside the gates for Humphrey and Brigit and a collective statement was issued to the effect that 'although there is widespread concern about the

STAN HEY

quarry's expansion, we urge all protests to be conducted in a peaceful and legitimate manner. A hole in the ground is not worth dying for.' A few weeks later, the Department of the Environment announced that the quarry's expansion plans had been put on hold, as the cuts in the government road programme made it fundamentally unnecessary.

Brennan was given a short course of counselling for the trauma he had suffered seeing the violent deaths of both Sheila and Clive Parry. And after a restorative three days doing his bollocks in at the Cheltenham National Hunt Festival, he found that any lingering nightmares had finally left him alone. He and Janet had a short break in Paris, via Eurostar, while Lester stayed with his grandparents in London. The trip was successful, not least in confirming Brennan's liking for tunnels.

Then, on Good Friday, while Lester was off at a church service, Brennan and Janet took coffee in their favourite window seat of the Dandy Lion. Brennan confessed that he had, at the last moment of desperation in his battle with Parry, called on God to save him.

'It's still there, then, is it?'

'I guess so. Maybe Lester was right – we need it just as much today as they did two thousand years ago.'

'You're not going to get it big, though, are you?' Janet asked him cautiously.

'No – be a bit hypocritical of me to do that. I wonder, though, if you can be spiritual without being religious?'

'Don't think I can answer that. It just leads to trouble as far as I can see. Clive Parry thought he was in touch with ancient gods and spirits, and look what it did for him. I think I prefer the rational world.'

'No room for imagination, then.'

'Depends on how it's used.'

Their conversation was interrupted by the sight of Christian worshippers marching up the hill of Market Street, led by the town's clergy. Behind them, five youths carried a wooden cross on their shoulders – one of them was Lester.

That same Easter afternoon, protesters of all persuasions gathered on a hill above a small market town on the Berkshire Downs to decry the imminent building of a by-pass around the town. Moving among the minstrels and the jesters, and the women in their woolly cardigans, and the Tory men whose land the road would consume, was a strange youth, dressed in animal skins with a crown of rams' horns on his head. He banged a drum under his arm for attention and invited the crowd to join him in a plea to the ancient Celtic gods of the hills and forests.

'This is our land, our earth!' he shouted, to general approval all round.